FRONT COUNTRY

FRONT COUNTRY

BY SARA ST. ANTOINE

chronicle books
san francisco

Library of Congress Cataloging-in-Publication Data available.

ISBN 978-1-7972-1563-1

Manufactured in India.

Design and illustrations by Jill Turney.
Typeset in Ashbury and True North.

10 9 8 7 6 5 4 3 2 1

Chronicle Books LLC
680 Second Street
San Francisco, California 94107

Chronicle Books—we see things differently.
Become part of our community at www.chroniclekids.com.

FOR ADELAIDE AND MARGOT

CHAPTER
1

Brooklyn spat the sunflower seed shell into her palm and flicked it into a paper bag without taking her eyes off the road. "You ever been to Montana before?"

"Only in my dreams," I told her. Through the windows, sprawling fields stretched out like rolls of corrugated cardboard under the biggest, bluest sky I'd ever seen.

"Good dreams?" Brooklyn asked.

"Totally."

"Cool."

Brooklyn was broad-shouldered but compact. She held the steering wheel like she was driving a tractor, not a nine-passenger van. Even in an airport waiting area full of outdoor enthusiasts, it had been obvious that she was my trip leader. A stretchy red headband cinched her cropped brown hair; black wraparound sunglasses hung on a cord around her neck. "TrackFinders" was stitched into the shoulder of her fleece jacket, and her hiking boots looked like she'd just done jumping jacks in a dust field.

I wanted to ask her if she'd grown up on a ranch or a farm, but so far, when I'd asked her about anything other than the logistics of our drive, she'd given me the same response. "We'll have time to talk about that at camp."

It seemed to me we had plenty of time to talk now, too, but I let it go. I was happy enough just to stare out the window and think. There was so much room out here and bushels of air—like maybe enough to inflate a flattened heart. I was glad the windows were open. The air rushed in, oven-dry and tinged with the smell of the coarse yellow grass. Montana's montañas hugged the wide horizon in a bumpy blue band.

We sped by ranches. American flags. Gas stations. I spotted a tennis court set at the end of an enormous open field whipping with dust. "That's random."

Brooklyn glanced my way. "You play, right?"

"Used to."

"Oh, right."

"How'd you know?"

She shot me a quick smile and reached for another sunflower seed. "We'll talk about it at camp."

I might have been more uneasy about the whole exchange except Brooklyn looked so absurdly reliable—like a cast-iron pot or a bowl of cornflakes in human form.

More flat fields scrolled past the window, but it was the mountains that had all my attention now. With every passing mile, they grew taller and new details emerged: folds, forests, shadows, dollops of white snow. I'd seen the Appalachians and climbed peaks in Vermont, but these were a whole different order of mountain—bigger and sharper, like the Earth had popped new molars.

"Wicked wildfire season last year," Brooklyn said, gesturing toward a gray slope with spindly black trees. "Whole summer was freakishly hot and dry. Super hazy."

My chest tightened with familiar dread. I fixed my gaze on the patches of white draped reassuringly over the highest ridges. At least there was still some snow.

The road began to ascend the first line of hills and we lost our view of the peaks behind them. My ears popped, though I couldn't tell if it was from the flight or the drive. When we finally pulled into a small dirt parking area, I climbed out of the van and took in a long draw of air. I was actually here. This far from home. This fast. The shock and wonder of it made me light-headed.

"I'm going to give you some food to carry in, if that's okay," Brooklyn said, pulling some bags from a cooler in the back of the van. "We get weekly resupplies, but this will give Kai a little extra security. He's my co-leader," she added, finally willing to share an actual data point.

I'd signed up for this trip almost the moment I knew it existed. Mom had said camping. Mountains. A month in the wilderness. Dad had reminded me of the great Outlands trip my cousin once took. What wasn't to love? TrackFinders was the organization's newest program, so there weren't any photos or testimonials posted for my trip yet. I figured it was straight-up backpacking with some animal tracking as an added bonus. And I'd created my own mental brochure: jelly bean–colored tents scattered across green mountain meadows, friendly teenagers in fleece jackets oohing and aahing over the local wildlife. It looked great in my imagination, but what did I know? I definitely hadn't expected to be driven alone to a dusty parking lot by just one tight-lipped counselor.

We loaded our packs and began the two-mile trek to base camp, as Brooklyn called it. Our hiking boots thumped on a hard-packed trail along a streambed before we climbed up into a dense evergreen forest that smelled like vanilla and butterscotch. I took in one hungry inhalation after another. If air was a food, this was definitely dessert.

Brooklyn didn't push the pace. She said my muscles and lungs needed time to adapt to the elevation, and she insisted on regular water breaks. It must have been late afternoon, Montana time, but my body was ready for dinnertime back in Massachusetts. Were Dad, Mom, and Vivian sitting around the table right now, missing me . . . or maybe enjoying their newfound peace? Reading my mind, or hearing my stomach, Brooklyn tossed me an energy bar and told me if we were lucky, they'd be prepping for an early dinner by the time we arrived.

"Are all the other kids here already?" I asked. When she didn't respond, I sighed. "I guess I'll meet them when we get to camp."

"Yep," Brooklyn said, without even looking back at me. She looked like a stolid pack mule. She looked like she never got tired.

We hiked on.

The scent of woodsmoke reached my nose just as a small figure appeared on the trail in front of us, holding his palms out like a traffic cop.

"Zombie or slime?"

"Er . . . ." I hesitated, not sure how to respond. Was this kid really old enough to be one of my tripmates?

The boy had close-cropped black hair and the tidy look of a kid on school picture day. He was dressed in green cargo pants and a gray *Star Wars* T-shirt that looked starched and almost bright against his brown arms.

"No tech talk, Elijah," Brooklyn said, grasping his shoulders and guiding him forward for several steps.

The boy spun around and leaned out to face me, hands cupped around his mouth. "If you have a phone, hide it!"

"Knock it off," Brooklyn said with a strained laugh.

Before I'd had time to process what he'd said, we reached the clearing. I stopped, confused.

This was *not* my imagined brochure.

Eight yellow-brown tents were lined up on the far side of the clearing, so low to the ground they looked like coffins. A fire burned weakly in the middle of a ring of rocks. Gray smoke and a feeling of lethargy—or even disappointment—hovered over the campsite. In the far woods, a youngish guy and four more teenage boys were collecting firewood, although the first guy seemed to be doing all the talking and most of the work. The boys shuffled along behind him at half speed. One sat under a tree, not moving at all.

5

Wasn't there supposed to be a friendly welcome when a new camper arrived? Where were the jelly bean tents? Where were the *girls*?

"The second to last one is yours," Brooklyn said, pointing toward the tents. "Next to mine. Go ahead and put your stuff away, get comfortable, take a breather if you need to. We'll call out when we're ready to circle up."

I glanced at Elijah, who returned my gaze with the look of a stray puppy—half lost, half expectant. "Got it," I said. But really, I didn't get it at all.

Fortunately, my tent looked less coffin-like up close. I dropped backward onto the nylon floor and yanked off my boots. My feet were hot. I peeled off my wool socks and wiggled my toes, wrinkly and pink from the day's exertions. Finally I pushed myself backward, all the way inside. I had a strong urge to lie down and chill out, but the ground was prickly under the nylon, and whoever had set up the tent hadn't noticed or cared that there was a chunk of rock underneath the floor. I inflated my camping pad, hopeful that would help.

I was shaking out my puffy purple sleeping bag when I heard a cough outside the tent.

"Knock, knock."

A tall kid with bleached-blond hair and dark eyes was standing outside. He was bad-boy handsome, and my first instinct, when he flashed me a smile, was that he looked like trouble.

"Name's Maddox," he said, offering a handshake. "It's a pleasure to have you with us."

Well, that was gentlemanly. A little tour-boat captain, maybe, but still gentlemanly.

"Thanks. I'm Ginny."

"We've been summoned to Circle Time," Maddox said, nodding across the clearing.

When I peeked over the top of the tent, I saw both counselors standing beside the campfire. The kids were gathered around them, hunched and listless as drugged herons.

"It doesn't seem too lively," I said.

"That's why they need *us*," he said, eyebrows flirty.

I stuffed my feet back into my boots and scuffed along behind Maddox. We took our places in the circle, and the second counselor beamed a welcome.

"So, wow. Here we are!" he said, clapping his hands. "I'm Kai. Welcome to TrackFinders."

I smiled back. This was more like it. Kai was a round-faced guy in his twenties with a quick smile and an obvious eagerness to connect. He wore a down vest over a flannel shirt, gray techie pants, and black trail shoes just trim enough that he wouldn't have looked out of place in a downtown coffee shop.

"Let's start with introductions. I'd like you each to tell us who you are and where you're from. And then share one thing you want everyone to know about you. Got it?"

"This is our first milestone," Brooklyn added, looking up from her clipboard. "We call it Community by the Campfire."

If eye-rolling had a sound, it would have been a somewhat noisy moment.

Kai turned to Elijah, the kid who'd greeted me on the trail. "Want to get us started?"

"Sure. I'm Elijah, and I'm from the Bay Area. San Francisco, I mean." He scratched his shoulder, then his head. "Last month I got Horde of Hoofbeats." He tried not to smile but it was obvious he expected us to be impressed.

I had no idea what he was talking about. The kid beside him snorted.

"Thanks, Elijah," Brooklyn said. She turned to the snorting boy, a tall, round-shouldered kid with pasty skin and a bad case of bed head. Elijah looked like he was barely out of elementary school, but this kid looked big enough to drive. "I guess you'd like to go next?"

The boy sniffed like maybe he had a cold or maybe he used his nose for communication. There was a dinosaur that did that— I'd seen it on a kids' cartoon. "I'm Dash. I'm from a suburb of Detroit you've probably never heard of."

"And one thing you want people to know about you?" Brooklyn asked.

"What? Um. I know. TrackFinders sucks."

"So, yeah," Kai said, clapping his hands again. "Love the honesty. But this is a good time to remind everyone about language." In quick succession he gave us about ten things to avoid bringing into our conversation, including any kind of swear words, put-downs, or aggrandizement of rule-breaking behaviors.

"What's aggrandizement?" Dash asked.

"Showing off," Brooklyn put in.

Showing off about breaking rules? I looked again at the faces around the campfire. What kind of *community* was this, exactly?

"So, Dash. Want to try again? Something about yourself?"

He stared blankly into the air. The pause grew awkwardly long.

"Or, if you..."

"No. I got one. I sleepwalk," he said finally. "No joke. Like, one time I woke up on my mattress—on the basement stairs. Totally drowning in drool." He snorted and scanned the group, checking for laughs.

"Something to keep an eye on," Brooklyn said, jotting something in her notes.

So Elijah was a tech-obsessed baby and Dash was a sloppy snorter with unreliable sleep habits. This was not a promising start. I peeked over at the trailhead, wishing so much that a pack of cheerful girls would come bursting into view. Or two. Even two would be a major improvement.

"You're up," Brooklyn said to Maddox, the tour-boat bad boy.

"Cool. Name's Maddox." He gave the group a confident chin nod. "I was born seventeen and a half minutes before my brother here," he said, gesturing toward Dash, "so you'll have to excuse him. It's a burden living under my shadow."

A few kids chuckled.

So they were twins. I could see the similarities now, but they hadn't been obvious. Everything about Maddox was clear and sharp—as if he'd been painted with a fine-tipped brush. A clean stroke of white-yellow for the hair. Two careful dots of brown for the eyes. A hard-edged line for the jaw. In Dash, it was as if too much water had been used on the portrait; all the same elements were there, but they'd gone loose and fuzzy. His hair was curlier, his face was whiter and wider, and his skin rippled with acne.

"We're from Grosse Pointe, by the way," Maddox said. "No shame in claiming it."

"No shame at all," Kai agreed. He nodded at the next boy, who was only an inch or two taller than me—reedlike and freckled, with watchful eyes. He had on an old wool plaid shirt, like something a grandfather would wear, over a black T-shirt and blue jeans.

The boy took his time responding. "I'm Greyson," he said finally. "I'm from a one-traffic-light town in Kansas." He glanced at the twins. "We don't have suburbs."

"Whut." Dash seemed to register a challenge.

"You got trailer parks?" Maddox asked, blinking like it was an innocent question.

"I think he just means it's really rural," Brooklyn said quickly, in case it wasn't friendly at all.

Greyson shrugged, leaving it to them to do the math. It was pretty clear he thought the whole exchange was stupid.

"And one thing about yourself?" Kai pressed.

Greyson looked at him calmly. "The male line of my family self-destructs by the age of twenty-eight," he said, like it was fact.

"That's a little freaky!" Elijah said.

Kai just looked rattled. He turned to the next kid. "Vidal?"

The last boy was wearing a loose camouflage hoodie and black track pants, but what was most noticeable about him was his hair. It was long in some places, shaved in others—like grass trimmed by a runaway lawnmower. He hugged his arms around his body, staring miserably at the ground.

"Can you introduce yourself?" Kai persisted.

Vidal whipped a stray lock of hair out of his face. His brown eyes were fringed with dark lashes. "I'm Vidal. I live on a base in Florida."

"Military?" Maddox asked, dropping his voice a notch.

"My parents, yeah." Vidal's voice was strained. His whole body was strained.

"And what's one thing you want us to know about you?" Kai asked.

A whirr of wings swept past our heads before he could reply, and we watched as a glossy black raven landed in a nearby tree, then bounced the length of the branch. It let out a loud squawk and Vidal looked at it with something like resentment.

"I hate nature," he said.

"Yeah, who doesn't?" Elijah asked.

"Um, *me*," I said, not taking my eyes off the raven. It turned its head and regarded the group with curious, keen eyes. The bird was smarter than all of us, and it knew it.

"Well, that's a perfect segue. Your turn," Kai said to me.

I redirected my attention to the meet and greet. "Hi, guuuuyyys," I said, drawing it out long enough for a laugh. "I'm Ginny. I'm from Lexington, Massachusetts. Birthplace of the Revolution and all that."

Maddox winked. The other boys just stared.

"So . . . ," I glanced again at the trailhead. "Is this everyone?"

"That's a question, Ginny," Kai said. "What do you want us to know about you?"

I wasn't sure I wanted them to know anything about me until I had a better sense of who these kids were and why they had signed up for a camp in the mountains if they didn't even like ravens.

"Let's just say that I'm pretty confused right now," I said.

"That's okay." Kai smiled. "Some say confusion is the seed of wisdom."

Dash snorted.

I gestured at the tents, the campfire, and our counselors' all-weather gear. "Didn't you guys know this was a wilderness adventure camp?"

"Try boot camp," Maddox returned, giving me a knowing look.

"Rehab," Dash added.

"Torture," Elijah put in, squirming like he'd felt an ant on his back.

Vidal shuddered, and Greyson just stared into the campfire, apparently pretending he wasn't even there.

I felt a wave of unease like the one that had hit me when I'd first reached the clearing. "What are you talking about?"

Kai made a T with his hands. "Time-out—this is not boot camp, or rehab."

"Or torture!" Brooklyn added with a tight laugh.

"Then what is it?" Greyson asked.

"It's a chance to explore the outdoors—and yourself—in some of the last best wilderness in North America."

Now Kai just sounded like a promotional video.

"We've found that the backcountry is a pretty great place to get away from your usual patterns," Brooklyn said. "Figure yourself out so you can be more functional in the front country again."

"Front country?" Elijah asked, slapping something on his arm.

"The real world," Brooklyn explained.

"Our plan is to get you back on track out here so you can reach your full potential in your day-to-day lives at home. That's why we're called TrackFinders." Kai looked ridiculously pleased with himself.

"Wait, what?" I asked. "I thought we were going to track wildlife."

"Well, we'll see some wildlife," Brooklyn said.

"But the main focus is you. And your path," Kai explained.

My heart sank. I didn't want to focus on me. I was sick of me.

"Being a teenager is tough," Kai continued. "Brooklyn and I get it. We were there not so long ago. And we know that if you let small struggles become big struggles, you can find yourself in serious trouble. So the whole idea of TrackFinders is to get in there while there's still time to . . ."

Vidal's eyes were wide and alarmed. "What? Fix us?"

"I wouldn't say 'fix,'" Kai told him. "We're going to help you learn things—about yourself, about your peers, about wilderness. But it's all going to be fun. I promise."

"It sounds like therapy," Maddox said.

"We're not therapists," Kai told him.

"We're trip leaders," Brooklyn said. "Track leaders."

"So this is mostly just a normal backpacking trip, then?"
I asked. I wanted to pin them down. I wanted to say "normal"
enough times to make it true.

Kai started to nod, but Brooklyn cleared her throat. "Well,
not exactly. We're more, you know, *intentional* than the typical
Outlands trip. We have daily goals and exercises. And expecta-
tions for your behavior," she told us. She gave Kai a meaningful
look. "And, well, I think it's fair to say you wouldn't be here if
your parents didn't think you could use some support."

Support?

The last bit of normal slipped away.

A weight fell over the group—it wasn't just me. Everyone's
eyes shifted suspiciously from face to face. I'm sure the boys were
wondering the same thing I was: *Why are* you *here? And you?
And you?*

But the biggest question for me was, *Why was* I?

CHAPTER
2

I suppose it all began on that day in February that felt like it could have been June. Zinzie and I pushed open the school doors into a shock of warm air. The sky was bright and blue with only a few clouds poufing along like lost sheep.

"Whoa—is this actual spring?" I asked her.

"Warm," Zinzie uttered, stopping in her tracks.

Zinzie had big black glasses and wore her hair in tight braids that used to end in beads until she decided she was too old to clatter. She closed her eyes and held her arms out in front of her—absorbing.

I nudged her forward. "Come on. Let's get closer to the sun."

We climbed up to the highest glinting spot on the metal bleachers, then sat down and took out our lunches. Mom had packed brownies. I felt the happy hum you get when you're sitting with your best friend on a picture-perfect afternoon with a guarantee of sizable chocolate.

I handed a brownie to Zinzie, then took a bite of mine. On the side of the teacher parking lot, some sixth graders were playing soccer with a dented milk carton that looked like it had been out there all winter. I was glad we wouldn't be near them when it exploded.

"A week ago, that whole lot was covered with crispy snow dregs," I told Zinzie. "Mini icebergs."

She pulled her sweatshirt over her head, leaned back, and stretched out her long legs. "Now it's island weather," she said with a blissed-out smile.

Maybe it was the chocolate speaking, but the whole day was starting to feel seriously above average. I unwrapped my sandwich, thinking. "You know how most Monday mornings the bus reeks of the basketball team?"

"Thanks for reminding me," Zinzie murmured, eyes closed.

"Well, this morning I get on and Amy Green is passing out cider and donuts. It smelled like cinnamon. Not stinky boy-pits. Cinnamon!"

"Shhh. Sleeping."

"Everything since then has been weirdly good," I told her anyway. "No homework in math. We got a movie in language arts because the Brontësaurus is having hip surgery. P.E. was outside, with Hula-Hoops—seriously the best gym utensil ever."

When Zinzie smiled, her dimples looked like semicolons.

"And Ms. Arocho is bringing her labradoodle to social studies. For National Random Acts of Kindness Day."

"That's a thing?" Zinzie asked. She propped herself up on her elbows and blinked into the light.

"Apparently."

"What are they trying to do—make us miss this place?"

We looked over at our school building. It was a prisonlike concrete slab that got sweat stains in the rain, but now that graduation was in sight it looked harmless. Almost cute.

"I wish I had Ms. Arocho," Zinzie sighed, taking a swig from her water bottle. "Last week Mr. McKnight called the American Revolution the greatest victory for freedom in the history of the world." She made a face. "I mean, slavery, anyone?" She set down the water bottle with an emphatic clank and finally started in on her food. "High school will be better, right?"

"I hope so." We'd started making our ninth-grade course selections the week before; now high school was all my parents wanted to talk about. Even my little sister, Vivian, had opinions, and she was only a fifth grader. "Dad says I'm going to have to be on my best game."

"Tennis game?"

"Everything game."

Zinzie looked offended. "When are you not on your best everything game, Ginny Shepard? I mean, we're co-valedictorians!"

"Potentially."

"Definitely." Zinzie has a way of catching you in her spotlight gaze and drawing you in—like a human lighthouse. "How's your average?"

"Still 98.7." She knew I'd know. Our school had an online platform where kids checked their grades regularly—or, in our case, *daily*—for every incremental change.

"Excelente. But let's do the Spanish extra-credit project this weekend anyway, okay?"

It wasn't really a question. We always did the extra-credit projects.

I balled up my wax paper and stuffed it in my lunch box. "Yeah, Dad made me apply to summer school, actually. Some pre-college STEM program at Columbia. In New York City. He says it's a good thing to have on my high school record—because colleges love girl scientists."

Zinzie paused, spoon in midair. "Do they?"

"You know my dad's never wrong, Zinz. I mean, according to him."

I expected a laugh, but Zinzie just nodded, filing it away.

"So, no more camp for me, I guess." I sighed. My Vermont summer camp had old wooden canoes and campfire pancakes and a wide, moody lake. I thought about our resident raccoon, who cleaned under the picnic tables like a whiskered vacuum. "Do you think Dyson will miss me?"

But Zinzie wasn't listening. "Look, Ginny. Your boyfriend's ditching school."

A trio of boys slipped out the school door, hooting with laughter. The tallest one was Nico Malone, a boy I'd kissed once in seventh grade, somewhat regrettably.

"I can't believe I used to think he was cute," I said, shaking my head.

"You have a crush on a delinquent," Zinzie teased.

"Had." I kicked her shoe. "Finish your soup. It's almost time for the bell."

She took a few last spoonfuls, but her eyes were still on the boys. "I wonder why they even bother showing up."

I stood, lunchbox in hand. "I guess you can't be a dropout if you've never dropped by."

"Ha. Good one." She capped her thermos and gave it a quick twist. "We should put that in our acceptance speech."

>·< ♥ >·< ♥ >·< ♥ >·< ♥ >·<

I was still feeling the solar glow from lunchtime when I took my seat in science. Mr. Stelling fussed over his computer until a giant image of a pika appeared on the whiteboard.

"Awww," I said, gushing more loudly than I'd meant to. Pikas could do that to a person.

Have you ever heard of a pika? It's a mountain mammal so cute it could star in its own K-pop video. Think of a cross between a baby bunny and a really excellent teddy bear. Pikas are small enough to fit in the palm of your hand, round as pom-poms and covered in velvety fur. Long whiskers stick out from their muzzles and little ears pop up from their heads like scraps of felt. When they sense a threat, they crane their necks forward and *eeeeeeeep* out an alarm call.

But pikas aren't just cute. They have grit. Maybe they look like something you'd find on a toy shelf, but they can survive an entire Rocky Mountain winter without even thinking of hibernation. Which is more than a grizzly bear can say.

"Ginny, that's your thing, right?" asked my lab partner, Charlotte, sliding into the seat beside me. She dropped her elbows on our table and raked her fingers through her pink hair, no longer even looking at the screen.

"Hey—you remembered," I said, genuinely touched.

"Mica, right?" she said.

Well, almost remembered. "It's a pika," I told her. "Mica's a rock."

Charlotte and I had been in the same third-grade class when I'd written a report about pikas for our mammal unit. I'd even made one out of clay for our final presentation. A lot of people thought it was a potato, but that hadn't dampened my enthusiasm; I'd been obsessed with pikas ever since, and still had the blobby clay one on my bookshelf to show for it.

Mr. Stelling dimmed the lights and my favorite animal loomed like a genuine movie star.

"Single cutest thing the world has ever produced. Admit it," I said to Charlotte.

She peered at the screen through her curtain of hair.

"Like if you had a global contest, there'd be some major competition heading into the Final Four." I was kind of jabbering, but I wasn't about to stop now. "Maybe you'd end up with lion cubs, red pandas, golden retriever puppies, and pikas. But pikas would still win, wouldn't they?"

Charlotte was frowning. "That new chorus teacher just told me I look like a My Little Pony." She flattened her hair with her hands and slumped down in her seat.

"Where is everyone?" Mr. Stelling asked, scanning the half-empty room.

"Cleaning the cafeteria," someone snickered.

Charlotte mouthed "food fight" and gave me a knowing look.

"We'll just get started then." Mr. Stelling had permanent frown lines and a narrow mustache that twitched when he was unhappy—like now. "This is an American pika. P-I-K-A, *PIE-ka*," he added for emphasis. "A diminutive member of the rabbit family. You may be wondering why I have placed its portrait in front of your wan and impassive faces this afternoon."

He looked around. A few kids shifted in their seats. Well, if no one else was going to say it:

"Because they're perfect," I said.

Mr. Stelling scratched his eyebrow. "Is anyone aware that summers have been getting drier and hotter?"

"Beach time!" Athena Vry sang under her breath, snapping her fingers.

But Mr. Stelling's tone did not convey sunshine and ice cream cones.

"In the Mountain West, rising temperatures and increased drought have proved a lethal combination for our little lago-morph."

"Mr. Stelling, could you speak English?" someone asked.

"Hot plus dry equals bad," he said, with a condescending edge. "Extinction looms."

"Wait—for pikas?" I asked. They'd left this out of my third-grade picture books.

"Yes, for pikas. And soon," he told me. "Very soon."

"Bummer for you," Charlotte murmured.

People like to shock teenagers. That's a fact. It gives them a smug sense of power. Which is the only reason I could come up with for why Mr. Stelling actually seemed to be enjoying himself.

I wanted to smack him.

"Some people say pikas are the canaries in the coal mine," Mr. Stelling went on, sounding like he was reading his lines straight off the National Geographic website, "giving us our first taste of how a rapidly changing climate will alter the future for all species."

"'Taste'?" Athena asked. "People actually eat those things?"

Someone threw a plastic spork at her head, and the class exploded with cackles.

I was still processing Mr. Stelling's pronouncements when the door opened and our local class clowns stumbled in, their hair wet and their shirts splotched with condiment tie-dye.

"Sorry, Stelling. We were, uh, assisting the custodians," said Noah, clearly lying.

"Look, it's Pikachu!" said Ari, pointing at the screen.

"Pika," Mr. Stelling corrected.

"PEE-ka-choo!" Ari persisted. "You're mispronouncing it."

"Dude, stop sneezing," Noah told him.

"Take a seat," Mr. Stelling snapped. "We're trying to learn something here."

"Gotta catch 'em all, right?" Noah joked, and Ari chimed in with the Pokémon theme. Were these guys really headed to high school in a few months?

A red flush crept up Mr. Stelling's neck.

"This is not a cartoon," he said, smacking the whiteboard with his hand.

"It's a photo," someone volunteered.

"Beams of light, actually."

"*The pika is a genuine living thing*," Mr. Stelling continued, trying to regain control of the class, "that has been able to survive on Earth for tens of thousands of years. Until now." He glared like he held us all responsible.

"Easy now, Stelling."

Someone imitated a dog growl.

I hated seeing anyone suffer, even a sarcastic middle-aged teacher with hyperactive facial hair. The color was rising up above his ears. I shot a look at the delinquents. Everyone needed to shut up or the guy was going to have a heart attack. Besides, he was talking about my pikas. I actually wanted to hear what he had to say.

Mr. Stelling crumpled his lecture notes and tossed them across the room. "Let's forget the script, shall we?"

For the first time that afternoon, he had everyone's attention. He unbuttoned his cuffs and rolled up his sleeves like he was going to hit someone. A muscle in his jaw twitched and he gave us a piercing look.

"Here's the take-home message of today's lecture in five simple words. Ready?" He held a fist in the air and popped up his fingers, one by one. "The. World. Is. On. Fire." He kept his hand up, like evidence. "Your world. On fire. Things are going to start dying—everywhere—faster than you ever thought possible."

Someone laughed, of course.

Mr. Stelling let his hand fall. "Maybe you don't care about pikas. Fine. But they will soon have plenty of company. Penguins. Monarchs. Tigers. Whales. Coral reefs—well, they're practically dead already. Koalas—half cooked."

My stomach lurched. Coral and koalas were halfway dead?

Mr. Stelling nodded, like he'd read my mind. "We're expecting a die-off unlike anything humans have ever seen before. And it's not like we're going to be living large ourselves. Think about what we've seen just this year—wildfires, floods, record droughts. Did you think these were momentary blips? That everything else was fine? Because everything is not fine, people. Those were previews of the horror show that is your future."

Something shifted in the classroom. It felt like Mr. Stelling was lowering a dark umbrella over our heads. No teacher had ever talked about climate stuff like it was *this* bad. I waited for the usual reassuring words about technology, global cooperation, hope.

"Earth is a rapidly sinking ship," he said instead.

"They can fix it, though, right?" someone asked.

"Remind me, who's 'they'?" he asked, like it was a genuine question.

When no one answered, he continued. "We've been pumping heat-trapping gases into the atmosphere for decades. It's too late to retrieve them. They're out there now like another virus, of the very worst kind. You can pretend they're not—a popular, if hazardous, option. Or you can start preparing, now, for *colossal global disruption.*"

It was the knockout punch—mentioning the virus, reminding us how fast the world could turn upside down. The room went silent.

Reeling, I put my forehead in my hands and closed my eyes. I would never forget how people had talked about Covid in the beginning. *It's only happening over there. Stop being so hysterical. It won't get that bad. It's a hoax.* It was actually a lot like what people said about climate warnings, wasn't it? No one truly believed the worst forecasts. And no one was going to do anything differently if they couldn't see it with their own eyes.

But that *was* hazardous. Mr. Stelling was right. If the pandemic had taught me anything, it was that just because you didn't like the awful predictions, that didn't make them wrong.

A massive die-off. A sinking ship. This was really happening. Like, now. No wonder my hands were shaking.

"Questions? Comments?" Mr. Stelling asked the room.

The whole class sat perfectly motionless and perfectly quiet. Everyone was feeling as stricken as I was—I was sure of it.

Then someone broke the silence with a massive fart.

The class erupted in raucous laughter. "You can say that again," someone snickered.

Wait, seriously? They could still laugh? After all this?

Mr. Stelling shook his head and reached for his remote. For the rest of class, he toggled between sweet pictures of wildlife and some of the ugliest photos of climate devastation I'd ever seen. The whole presentation was like a taunt. *I dare you to love this,* he seemed to say as he filled our view with another watchful pika, innocent and unknowing. A baby orangutan with hair like a troll doll, nuzzling its mom. A spotted snow leopard resting on a rocky ledge, and an emperor penguin balancing a single white egg on top of his feet. Of course I loved them. How could I not? Then *click,* the burning trees. Mudslides. Cracked earth. Reminder after reminder of the destruction and chaos that would take them all away from me.

I'd never known a heart could get broken over and over like that, in the space between two class bells.

I wanted to tell Mr. Stelling, *Enough—please stop,* but I couldn't speak. If we were about to lose this much, this fast, I didn't know what to think. Or how to breathe.

I glanced around me to see if anyone else was feeling even a teensy bit obliterated, but it was hard to tell. The room felt strangely remote and, come to think of it, a little flimsy. Wood, linoleum, denim, polar fleece—none of it felt completely solid. Or maybe I was the one who was floating, with no more density than the images on the screen. I gripped the table hard and was almost reassured when it hurt my fingers.

"We'll be studying global climate change inside and out for the next few weeks," Mr. Stelling said, finally switching off his machine and turning on the lights. His face had returned to its normal color, but now he looked exhausted. "So. Right. In other news, whoever put their retainer in my coffee should come see me after class."

"Gross," Charlotte said as she stood up to leave.

"I can think of worse things." I stared at the blank board.

On the walls of the room were maps and science charts, the whiteboard filled with scrawled reminders about homework. Posters announced possible themes for the eighth-grade dance. It was all perfectly typical middle school stuff. Right now it looked strange and pointless, though. What were we thinking? The ship was plunging into the abyss and we were arguing about Disco Daze versus Crazy '80s?

I pushed my way through the crowded hallway. I had one hundred and twenty seconds of passing time to locate the only human I could count on to make me feel better. When I didn't find her, I briefly considered going to see the nurse. Then I got to Ms. Arocho's doorway. And saw Taffy.

Thank goodness for Random Acts of Kindness Day. A minute later I had my arms wrapped around the labradoodle's shoulders and my face smooshed into her soft woolly neck.

"I think she likes you," Ms. Arocho said.

"She has no choice," I said without lifting my head.

I ignored the other kids who were giving Taffy a quick pat. Eventually they peeled away and I was the only one left, stuck to the dog like static cling.

"Ginny, are you ready to take your seat?"

The dog's fur smelled of grass and wind. Her heartbeat was a steady tap, helping my own to fall into line. I shook my head.

Ms. Arocho squatted down and spoke quietly. "What if you scooched over next to my desk and let Taffy lie in your lap so at least you can see the board?"

I nodded, so surprised by her understanding that I had to blink back tears.

I slid across the linoleum and let Taffy settle in my lap. She was not a small dog. She was heavy and warm, and her hot breath gave off a scent of old ham. She was just what I needed, though: an anchor to the classroom so steady and smelly I couldn't forget she was there. When the bell rang, I planted a kiss on her forehead and told her I would pay her back soon, in bacon. And then I slipped away before Ms. Arocho had a chance to ask me any questions.

Outside on the tennis courts, it was pushing eighty degrees. I went through all the usual motions—stretching, drills, warm-ups—thinking the exercise would make me feel better. Then, halfway through practice, my teammate Ella Montgomery fainted. Coach said she'd worn too much clothing and hadn't stayed hydrated. But I knew the real reason: It wasn't supposed to be seventy-six degrees in Massachusetts in the middle of winter. Mr. Stelling was right. We were rocketing into the death zone.

"Ginny? You okay?" Coach called.

"I'm a little woozy, too," I said, just to get away.

⇥⇤ ❧ ⇥⇤ ❧ ⇥⇤ ❧ ⇥⇤ ❧ ⇥⇤

My parents were out late at an after-work dinner. The moment I heard their key in the door, I hurried to the kitchen and blurted out everything Mr. Stelling had told us, not even waiting for them to get settled.

"Sounds like someone was having a bad day," Dad said distractedly, frowning at his phone.

"Um, yeah."

"He means Mr. Stelling," Mom said, catching my look.

"Oh. Well, I don't think it was just a bad day," I told them.

"Any time I read an article about climate change, I basically want to scream," Mom said, shaking off her coat. "I get why this upset you, Ginny. But gosh, I still think he could have framed things a lot more hopefully."

"Hopefully?" I asked. "How?"

Dad slipped his phone into his sport coat. "He was exaggerating, Ginny," he said in the clipped, confident voice he uses in the courtroom. "We are not on a sinking ship. We are on a very solid planet that has survived meteors, earthquakes, DDT, ozone holes, and several inept federal administrations. This climate situation is a doozy. But we'll find a way to handle it, too."

"It's amazing what engineers figure out," Mom added, like that would actually console me.

Vivian was sitting on a stool eating tortilla chips straight out of the bag. "Ruby Palermo says you can get energy from a jellyfish," she informed us.

"See?" Mom said. "And my computer store knows when my ink cartridges are getting low without my doing anything. I'm still figuring out how that works!"

How had we gone from global extinction to ink cartridges?

"I feel like you guys aren't really listening to me."

"We are, Ginny," Mom said, plugging her phone into a charger. "But if you ask me, Mr. Stelling wasn't *thinking*. His job is to teach—sensitively and responsibly—not scare the living daylights out of you."

Dad loosened his tie. "You ever wonder what makes a person decide to teach middle school?"

"Oh my god—you're actually going to get snarky now." I couldn't believe it.

"It's usually not a searing intellect," he said, tapping the side of his head. "Just saying."

"Can I use someone's computer to work on my history project?" Vivian asked, hopping off the barstool.

"Sure, sweetheart," Mom said, pecking her on the top of her head. "How was *your* day? Better than Ginny's, I hope."

I hesitated, caught between wanting so much more from them and doubting I could stand to be around them for another minute.

My phone was lying on a side table next to a spiky potted cactus. I hoisted my backpack onto my shoulder, pocketed the phone, and then, on impulse, scooped the cactus under my arm.

"Ginny?" Mom asked as I started for the door.

Dad and Vivian just stared.

"What?" I said defensively.

"Cactus?" Vivian said, eyebrows scrunched.

I shrugged. "I need a friend."

I held my fingers over the computer keys. The internet sometimes felt like one of those escape rooms we went to for parties: Even if you entered freely, even happily, you always had the uncomfortable feeling you might actually get trapped for good. But I needed to know if Mr. Stelling really was exaggerating as much as my parents said. I tapped in *pika extinction*. Dozens of sites popped up—legit ones for the kinds of organizations my parents had been supporting for years. I typed in *glaciers shrinking. Seas rising. Wildfires. Drought. Species loss.* By the time I saw the starving polar bear, I was feeling shaky again.

Then I thought it might be a good idea to see what NASA had to say because, heck, if anyone can get you out of a jam, it's a rocket scientist. But the only thing that was different was the tone. In fact, it seemed like every time scientists had made a climate model predicting what would happen next, they'd had to revise it—not because the bad things weren't happening, but because they were happening so much faster than they'd expected.

I felt even worse than I had at the end of science class. We were on the verge of catastrophic planetary collapse, and everyone was humming along like it was just another beautiful day in the neighborhood. I didn't get it.

Mom poked her head in the door, sporting earbuds from a late work call. Mom's good that way: She may spend ten hours a day trying to save asylum-seekers from the death squad, but somehow she still manages to keep a part of her brain constantly focused on Vivian, Dad, and me. Dad says it's her superpower.

"You feeling better now, Gin-gin?" she asked.

She caught sight of the cactus propped up beside me on the bed and frowned.

"You're the one who said no to a kitten," I pointed out.

She picked up my jeans from the floor, smoothed them out, and folded them over my desk chair. I handed her the cactus, and she set it on my bedside table.

"I'm sorry about today. I hate seeing you get upset," she told me.

"I'll be okay." I didn't like seeing her get upset, either.

"I know you will." She took away my laptop. "A good sleep does wonders."

"Thanks. Love you."

"Love you, too. Sleep well."

I turned out the light and dropped my head on my pillow. I could hear the white-noise machine whooshing in Vivian's room next door. The sounds of buzzers and voices rose from the living room, where Dad was watching a basketball game. Glasses clinked in the kitchen. The rest of my family was going on with life as usual. Vivian was probably even asleep.

My heart was bumping up against the top of my chest, but Mom was right. I'd feel better tomorrow. I tried to think about the good parts of the day. The donuts. The Hula-Hoops. Sitting with Zinzie under the warm sun.

The creepy-warm sun.

When I turned on my fairy lights, the pika on my bookshelf lit up like a shrine.

CHAPTER
3

Maybe for everyone else the days still felt ordinary. Alarm clocks, breakfast cereals, earbuds. Slouching through school and practice on the playing fields and maybe even a little late-night homework while the Earth did its hokey pokey and turned itself around. Frogs stirring under the mud. A coyote dodging cars on Route 2. Maybe these seemed like the kinds of days we'd always had here in Lexington, give or take a few wardrobe changes, or the kinds we'd always have. But they weren't. I knew that now. And once you knew a thing like that, it was hard for anything to feel right again.

Tennis was the first thing to fall.

➤◄ ❧ ➤◄ ❧ ➤◄ ❧ ➤◄ ❧ ➤◄

"So imagine there are these two ants," I said to Ella Montgomery at our next practice.

"Ants?" She wrinkled her nose.

"And the first ant is using its antenna to hit a crumb to the second ant."

"Okaaay." Ella glanced nervously over at Coach, but he wasn't paying attention.

"For the next two hours, that's all they do. Hit crumbs back and forth. Meanwhile, a ginormous storm is coming toward them. But they're so busy swinging at crumbs that they don't even notice. Their world is about to be destroyed and they don't even bother to look up."

"Huh," Ella said.

"Think how bad that would be."

"You'd better start serving or Coach L is going to yell at you."

I made my way back to the baseline, launched a ball in the air, and whacked it hard. It was a good one. Ella couldn't even get close.

"That would be pathetic, right?" I called to Ella.

"What?"

"The ants! Hitting crumbs while disaster loomed." Even saying it made my heart skip a beat.

"I guess?"

Ella had the curiosity of a pea.

My next serve went straight into the net. Ditto for the one after that.

"What's up, Shepard? You woozy again?" Coach Lowry asked, ambling over from the next court.

"She's thinking about ants," Ella said, like it was a violation.

Coach eyed the cracks in the court. "They're never going to resurface this thing."

"It's not ants. It's tennis," I told him.

"It is?" Ella asked.

"Remind me why we play this game, Coach," I said.

The corner of his eye twitched. "Say that again?"

This was the guy who wore his warm-ups every day of the year. Who once said the sweetest sound in the world was the *pop-piff* of opening a new can of balls. If anyone could answer, it was him. I tried again.

"I mean, in the great scheme of things . . . why does tennis *matter*?" I asked.

Coach shifted on his feet and stole a glance at Ella. "Because it's fun. It keeps us healthy. What's not to love?"

I shrugged. "I'm just not feeling it these days. I might need to take a break."

"From *tennis*?" Ella turned pink, and for a moment I thought she might faint again. "But Monday's our first match!"

Coach eyed me steadily. "No worries, Shepard. We can make some adjustments." That's what good coaches do. Look you in the eye and make everything seem as simple as proper foot placement and the right grip. "Why don't you take the rest of the afternoon off? Chill out. Watch some shows. We can touch base on Sunday and see how you're doing."

"Really?"

He nodded.

"Don't worry about the match, Ella," he added with a wink. "I know our Ginny. She'll be there."

"Okay, so, see you," I said as I turned to go.

But they were already setting up for a volley. Coach sent Ella a ball and she raced after it—like it was the best crumb in the world.

➤·◄ ❦ ➤·◄ ❦ ➤·◄ ❦ ➤·◄ ❦ ➤·◄

"Short practice?" Zinzie asked, coming out the front of the building with a bunch of girls from orchestra. She held the door open with her back so I wouldn't have to buzz the office.

"Coach sent me home. To work on my attitude."

"Wow. That's serious." She gave me an appraising look and squeezed my hand. "I know. Come home with me. I'll make you one of those tropical smoothies you love so much, and we can do the Spanish thing. You know, the extra credit?" she added when I looked confused.

"Oh. Sure."

"Max Lee claims he's up to a 99.4. He might be lying, but still. We can't let up. Not now."

I knew how she felt. Sometimes being undefeated in tennis and having the highest GPA in your grade felt like being on a tightrope: You either had to stay perfect all the way to the end, or you went down—fast and hard.

"And we can work on our social studies speeches while we're at it," she added with a gusty nod. Zinzie was going to run the world someday.

That is, if there still was a world someday.

"What?" she said, eyebrows crinkling behind her glasses.

"What *what*?"

She pointed to my eyes. "You just got that look. The griefy one."

"What? No. I was just thinking about *you*."

I looked across the schoolyard, trying to erase whatever expression she'd seen. The grass under the flagpole was still flattened and yellow from the winter's snow. The tree branches overhead were uneven and contorted where they'd been clipped away from the power lines. A gray squirrel had its nose in a trash barrel, tail up like a ragged flag. For some reason the whole place felt a little beat-up, compromised . . . temporary. Even the biggest trees looked like they were just waiting to be shoved offstage and put out of their misery.

"You're still upset about the pikas, aren't you?" Zinzie said, not missing a trick.

"What? Oh, I guess. I don't know. But I should probably go talk to Mr. Stelling," I said finally. "My parents thought it might help."

"I'll come with you," she volunteered, swinging her violin case around and following me inside.

Mr. Stelling was at his desk, grading papers with quick strokes of a red pencil. I hovered next to the door.

"You got this," Zinzie said with a gentle nudge.

"I hate him," I whispered. "Or I'm terrified of him. I forget which."

"Put a chicken on him."

It was a trick Dad had come up with in his pitching days. If he found himself getting rattled by an intimidating batter, he'd imagine a rubber chicken on the guy's head. Or on his bat. Or in his pants. Whatever it took to make himself laugh and relax. Zinzie thought it was genius.

"*Bawk, bawk, bawk,*" she whispered.

Up close, Mr. Stelling looked like one of the guys on Mount Rushmore, all stern, stony angles. "Yes?" he asked, looking up.

It was hard to imagine a chicken staying put on such a sharp nose.

"Is it really as bad as you said, or were you just trying to mess with our weak little teenage brains?" I tried to sound casual, but my knees were shaking.

"What?"

"My parents say you were exaggerating about the climate stuff on Monday. Were you?"

His mustache twitched. "I was perhaps excessively blunt. But it was only because no one was listening. You people seem to think this is just a big joke."

"*I* don't."

"Well . . . ," he said dismissively.

"You basically made it sound like the end of the world. Do you really think everything's going to die?"

Mr. Stelling looked out the window, and for a moment something like real sorrow passed over his eyes. Then he turned back to me and resumed his Mount Rushmore impression. "We've killed off smallpox. We've invented driverless cars. Human ingenuity may save us yet again."

"Okay, but who's 'us'? Are you including the polar bears, the sea turtles, the sugar maples, the pikas . . . ?" I stopped for air. "I don't want it to just be humans and mosquitoes."

"I'm sure it won't be just humans and mosquitoes." He turned back to his grading.

It took me a moment to realize that was the best he could do.

➤·◄ ❦ ➤·◄ ❦ ➤·◄ ❦ ➤·◄ ❦ ➤·◄

I sent Coach Lowry a text on Sunday afternoon letting him know I was going to sit out Monday's match. When he tried calling me back, I didn't answer. There was nothing to talk about. The team would be fine. Ella would take my place at number-one singles, and one of the hotshot sixth graders would move up to varsity. I'd probably made everybody's day.

➤·◄ ❦ ➤·◄ ❦ ➤·◄ ❦ ➤·◄ ❦ ➤·◄

"What are you doing home?" Dad asked when he and Vivian came in on Monday and found me sprawled on the couch with my laptop on my chest.

"I decided not to play today." I tapped a few keys. "Actually, I'm thinking of quitting the team."

"What? Jesus, Ginny," Dad said, throwing down his grocery bags. "You can't. Shepards don't quit—you know that. You're their number-one player. And you made a commitment."

Vivian was taking off her soccer cleats. "I'd kill Maddy Epstein if she quit," she said with a decisive shake of her ponytail.

"She wouldn't be very helpful dead," I pointed out.

Vivian cracked a smile. "Okay, fair."

I swung my laptop around to show them a photo. "Do you know how many koalas have been treated for burns this year?" I spared Vivian the death toll. The bandaged koala was bad enough. "And I was just reading how manatees are—"

"Talk to me, Gin." Dad sat down on a chair opposite from me. "I'm missing something."

It was nice of him to give me an opening. I shot Vivian a look and she left the room.

"I don't want to be a quitter, Dad," I said, closing my laptop. "But I just can't get worked up about hitting a ball over a net at a time like this. The world is burning up. Right? Like seriously totally teetering on the edge of disaster. And I'm supposed to care about a stupid middle school tennis trophy?"

"No. Only the big gold one," he said with a wink.

"It's all junk. Metal alloy over plastic or whatever. Think about *that* environmental footprint."

Dad's hairline shifted. "Probably some truth to that." Our basement was full of his college baseball hardware; he should know.

"But you're losing your perspective, kiddo," he went on. "Right now, you're at the top of your game, cruising along on the road to success. Flying, actually. You're like a Formula One driver at the front of the pack. This is no time to hit the brakes."

"Race car driver? Me? You've been watching way too much ESPN, Dad."

"No, listen up—it's a good metaphor. You can't overthink things, Ginny. You just need to focus on your next mark and pick the best path to get there. Drivers call it following the racing line. You pick your mark, and . . . *zoom!*"

He looked at me expectantly.

"Zoom," I repeated.

Vivian came into the room, holding a stack of mail.

"You eye the next mark, and *zoom!* Then the next one. *Z—*"

"I get the idea, Dad," I interrupted. "And then?"

"You win!" he said, like it was the most obvious and perfect result.

"I win," I repeated flatly.

"You get the glory!"

"I get the glory." I sounded like a robot.

Vivian giggled and came to stand near me.

"You're rich. Famous. Happy!" Dad said.

Vivian took my hand and we spoke in robot unison. "Rich. Fa-mous. Hap-py." She jerked her arms and swiveled her torso like it was on a metal bolt, and we dissolved into giggles.

Dad shook his head, but he seemed relieved to see us laughing. "The point is, now's not the time to throw away all your successes, Ginny—everything you've worked so hard to achieve. Just focus on getting good grades and honing your athletic potential so you can go to the best college possible and figure out how you want to contribute—to climate work or whatever's got your attention then. That's the way we've set things up."

I couldn't believe how earnest and certain he sounded.

"But the world...," I began.

"The world will be there waiting for you when you graduate. Trust me."

I held his gaze and tried not to let my expression change. The thing is, I didn't trust Dad—not the way I used to. He should have figured that out by now.

Vivian handed me a large white envelope. The return address was in New York City.

"What's that, Ginny?" Dad asked as I slid it behind a sofa cushion.

"Nothing."

"It's from Columbia University," Vivian volunteered.

"The summer program? Open it up. What's it say?" he asked, starting to empty a bag of groceries onto the counter.

After flashing Vivian the evil eye, I opened the envelope and pulled out a colorful brochure and a letter. "'We are delighted to inform you that your application has been *blah-blah-blah*.'"

I stopped reading and tossed it onto the coffee table.

"Ginny," Dad said, looking displeased.

Vivian picked up the brochure. "This looks cool."

"Great. You go."

I closed my eyes and thought about the summer—the world rising to a boil and creatures everywhere scrabbling to maintain a foothold. Pawhold. Winghold. It was just so wrong. Last week I'd felt shaky, but now I just felt mad. Who, I wondered, was responsible for this mess, and how could I make them pay?

I felt warm breath on my face and opened my eyes to see Vivian peering at me.

"You look scary."

"That's because I'm experiencing cosmic rage."

"Ruby Palermo's mom says if we could bottle teenage anger we wouldn't need nuclear power plants."

I stared into her freckled face. "Ruby Palermo's mom should shut up and pick on someone her own age." She really should, actually. It was her mom—all our parents and their parents and their parents—who had let this happen.

Vivian straightened up. "Dad! Ginny's being mean."

"That's because she didn't get her exercise today. Right, Gin-gin?"

"Wake me up when you guys are normal," I said, rolling onto my side and pressing my whole body into the back of the couch.

The racing line. It was a strange image for Dad to use when cars were not exactly on my list of favorite things right now. But I understood the idea. Keep it simple. Focus on the next mark in the path, check it off, then move on to the next one. It was probably a sensible strategy if you were still in the race. But what if you'd already spun off the course?

Or, okay, what if you did somehow manage to stay on the racecourse, hit every mark, and cross the finish line first? What difference would it make if everyone you knew and loved was still miles behind you, or—worse yet—stranded and suffering in some roadside ditch?

When I rolled back over, Dad was folding up grocery bags. He crumpled a piece of wax paper into a little ball and shot it in a perfect arc across the room. It landed in the trash can.

"Yes!" he said, throwing his hands in the air with a triumphant, goofy grin.

It usually made me laugh when Dad acted like a kid, but this time it just made me feel really far away.

CHAPTER
4

Spring continued with a fanfare of forsythia and daffodils, three more seventy-five-degree days, a random May snowfall, and a whole bunch of dents in my once-perfect academic record.

"Did Harriet Tubman have Velcro?" I asked Zinzie, watching her attach a strip to the black dress she was making for her social studies presentation.

"You should be making your own outfit instead of criticizing mine," Zinzie said, peering at me over her glasses.

"I'm pretty sure Sonia Sotomayor and my mom wear the exact same clothes. I'll borrow."

"Your mom has a black robe?"

I shrugged. I didn't even know what I was doing celebrating Sonia Sotomayor. Mom had floated her name months ago when I'd needed a person for our Valiant Leaders project, and I'd taken her at her word that I'd find her story amazing. And I'm sure I would—once I started the research.

I scrolled through my phone. "Did you see there's going to be another climate walkout next month?"

Zinzie pressed the Velcro down hard with her hands and stayed there like a human iron. "No one does those anymore."

No one. "Well, that's obviously not true."

"You know what I mean, Ginny." She leaned harder onto the Velcro, as if being more forceful would make it stick better. "This is a terrible time of year to miss school, if you ask me. Not that you'd ask me."

Zinzie hated that I was no longer a contender for valedictorian. But now she stopped pressing and gave me one of her trademark looks. "Can I ask you something?"

"Anything." I put down my phone.

"Do you ever think this is actually about your grandparents?"

My parents had asked me the same question and I'd gotten mad. But it sounded different coming from Zinzie. She'd been there with me, right by my side, in that awful time after they died. We walked all over Lexington. For hours. For weeks. She saw me stunned and she saw me crying. No wonder she'd gotten to know the griefy look in my eyes so well. We were already wearing masks by then; that was all anyone could see.

"It's like you got triggered or something," she added.

I shook my head. "I do miss them," I told her. "Like crazy. But I'm really, actually upset about other things now."

"Freaked out," she said.

"Okay. Freaked out."

"About, like, elephants. Coral."

She wasn't teasing me. She genuinely didn't understand.

I stared at a spot over her head. Sometimes you could have great big feelings that just didn't fit into words. Zinzie wrote prizewinning poems; maybe she could do it. But me?

"Elephants are these huge walking miracles, right?" I said, trying. "Big-eared gray giants with incredible memories and those crazy trunks they use to throw and slurp and even, like, snorkel. But they're going to be wiped off the face of the planet. And it's all our fault."

She waited.

"They're completely powerless, Zinz. And corals—they make rainbow-colored *worlds* under the water. But we're boiling them away, too. And there's nothing they can do about it. They can't speak … or even move!"

Didn't she see how unfair this was?

"We broke the planet and now all these plants and animals are going to suffer."

She scrunched her mouth up to one side, thinking. "I get being worried about that stuff, Gin. But people will suffer too, you know."

She thought I didn't care about people? I tried not to sound exasperated.

"I know, Zinzie. I worry about humans, too. A lot," I told her. I made a face. "Though some of us are just jerks."

Zinzie nodded. I meant the ones who didn't even seem to care about how much they were messing things up, but she seemed to be on to another train of thought. "Did you see your boyfriend got suspended?" she asked, picking up her dress and smoothing it top to bottom.

"Yeah, yeah," I said, ready to be done with that joke, but glad we were joking again.

➤-◄ ❤ ➤-◄ ❤ ➤-◄ ❤ ➤-◄ ❤ ➤-◄

My parents developed odd ways of interacting with me, like my kind of angst could be batted away like a fly or blown off with a blast of good cheer. Mom pointed out all the good news stories in the paper about solar gardens and electric cars. And whenever Dad saw me doing my homework, he did a little steering motion in the air. "*Zoom zoom!*" Sometimes I controlled my annoyance enough to manage a weak smile.

I tried to find positive things to say, too, even when my insides felt achy and heavy.

"I have an idea," I said at dinner one night. "It might sound a little out-there at first. But give me a chance, okay? Ms. Arocho says an open mind is a beautiful mind."

Vivian glanced at Mom and Dad, like she was on their side now instead of mine. I wondered if she had any idea how lonely it made me feel.

"What is it, Ginny?" Mom asked with a strained voice.

"I think we should take a year off. Close up the house and bike all around America. We can talk to people about climate stuff and see the rest of the country while we're at it. Wouldn't that be startling and amazing and useful?"

No one was chewing.

"You know that song 'America the Beautiful'?" I continued. "For spacious skies. Amber waves of grain. Purple mountain majesties. Fruited plain. We have all these great national treasures. And I've never seen any of them. I've never seen the deer and the antelope play."

"That's another song," Vivian said.

"We need to break out," I went on. "See the oceans and the national parks and the wildlife while we still can. I actually think the Rocky Mountains might be the landscape of my soul—and I've never even been there."

"Landscape of your soul?" Dad asked, stealing a glance at my plate.

"The place where you feel most connected. When I look at pictures of those mountains, I just want to be in them."

Dad made a face like he'd swallowed a bone and nodded at my plate. "What—are you a vegetarian now, too?"

I glanced down at my heavily ketchuped hamburger bun. "So I don't want to eat cow. Is that a problem?"

"You can't just eat bread," Vivian said. "You need protein." She made a fist and squeezed her bicep, looking psyched.

"Ginny, is this about summer school?" Mom put in.

They weren't even trying. "It's about everything!" I sat back in my chair and folded my arms. "Including that stupid summer school. As if *that* matters. Why aren't you giving my idea even three seconds of serious consideration?"

Dad put down his knife and ran his hand over his face. "Ginny, this stuff is crazy-making. We're not giving up our house and our jobs to go on a bike tour of America. I don't even own a bike. You're going to go to Columbia summer school. And come to think of it, it's time to go back to tennis, too. Tomorrow. Seems to me this time off has been a big mistake."

I shook my head. "No, it hasn't."

"Ginny," Mom said.

"You can't make me go back to tennis," I insisted.

Dad clenched his jaw. "I can make you do whatever I want. I'm your dad." He glanced at Mom. "You're our kid."

"You're acting like you own me," I said.

"Nobody owns you. You're a short-term rental," Mom said, trying for a lighter tone. "But we do want to make sure we pass you on in tip-top condition."

Vivian giggled, making everything worse.

"We're your lifeline," Dad went on. "We provide you with a house, food, clothes, education, medical care, emotional support, and free Wi-Fi. And as long as we do, you need to live by our rules."

"Wow, really generous," I said, getting up so fast my chair fell backward.

"Ginny, sit back down!" Mom said, finally running out of patience.

"I have to go to the bathroom," I lied. I lifted the chair back to its place. "But for the record, you guys have a very strange definition of emotional support."

➤◄ ❦ ➤◄ ❦ ➤◄ ❦ ➤◄ ❦ ➤◄

The social studies presentations were scheduled for the first week of June. Everyone had an assigned slot during one class period to recite, perform, sing, or otherwise share the central story of their Valiant Leader. The rest of us were supposed to ask questions and fill out feedback sheets that would end up counting for thirty percent of our assignment grades. It was grueling and stressful preparing our own material, and even sort of exhausting to sit and take in so much information from our classmates. Still, on the day of Zinzie's presentation, I got special permission from my gym teacher to go to her social studies class. Hers was the one presentation I actually wanted to hear. Her mom was there, along with a few other parents and even Mr. M-Z, our principal. Needless to say, Zinzie knocked it out of the park.

"You were amazing," I told her at the end of the day. "Confident. And so pretty. Your Velcro didn't show at all! I almost teared up at the end."

"Thanks, Gin." She'd put her hoop earrings back in, but she still looked like she'd stepped out of another century. "It was nice of you to come. I didn't know we could do that. I didn't even ask if—"

"I think even Mr. McKnight learned something," I said quickly. "Talk about an achievement!"

She smiled and let out a long exhale. "One more day."

"Actually, I'm done," I told her. "Tomorrow's the walkout. I'll be in Boston."

"Really? Did you get permission?"

"From the supreme authority: Mother Nature."

"Very funny. But thirty percent of your grade is giving feedback, Ginny." She scratched her head, calculating. "Actually, I guess this would just be one-fifth of the thirty percent. But still, that brings you down to an eighty, tops, in that...."

"My grade will be fine, Zinzie." Had I ever been this obsessive about fractions of percentages? "Anyway, congrats again. Your mom must be so proud."

I turned to go.

"You're not worried about missing some really good presentations?" Zinzie called, sounding weirdly desperate.

I shook my head and waved goodbye. Of course not. This was eighth grade. How good could any of them be, especially compared to hers?

Besides, one of tomorrow's presentations was supposed to be mine.

I walked out after first period so my parents wouldn't get bombarded with text notifications from school and worry I'd been kidnapped or hit by a car on the way in. They were still getting used to my new routine of walking to school instead of taking the bus. I ducked into the side stairwell and hurried down the concrete steps and out through the big metal doors, heart racing. When I heard a noise behind me, I turned around fast, convinced it was Mr. M-Z. But it was just one of Nico Malone's fellow delinquents, skipping class again. He grinned and gave me a nod, like he knew exactly what I was up to. I ignored him and moved on.

Once I'd made it off school grounds, my trip felt easier. Mom and I had traveled to Boston on public transportation plenty of times. I took the city bus to the edge of Cambridge, then hopped on the T to Park Street, emerging to a view of the golden dome of the State House.

A crowd of protestors filled the street—so many more than I'd expected. Who were these people? A lot of them looked like people who would have family responsibilities, important jobs. Did they call in sick? Or just open the door and walk away, like I had?

"Nice sign," a woman said. She was wearing a purple fleece and Birkenstocks. A long white braid curled over her shoulder.

"Thanks. I know it's kind of small, but..."

I'd drawn it that morning on the back of a big cereal box. The letters were crowded and uneven:

I WANT TO BELIEVE IN MY FUTURE.

She smiled. "It's a big message."

I settled beside a group of students who looked closer to my age. High school kids, maybe, about twelve in all. They were gathered around the base of a large statue, holding signs that were only slightly less preschool-looking than mine.

When everyone started chanting, I lifted my sign and yelled, too.

Shouting felt weirdly good.

"Did you guys skip school to come here?" I asked one of the teenagers during a break in the noise.

She shook her head. "We just finished finals at school. In Vermont. This is how we're starting summer vacation."

"Wow. That's commitment," I said.

"I know, right?" said the girl next to her. She spread her arms out dramatically wide. "We could be at the beach!"

"Instead we're hanging with Mary, making sure the world doesn't fry," a boy beside her joked.

"Mary's your teacher?" I asked.

The boy shook his head and pointed at the statue above us. "Mary Dyer. Some Quaker lady. She got hanged for her beliefs."

"Oh. Ouch," I said.

"We did come with a teacher, though," the girl said. "Ms. Kelly. Tomorrow she's taking us to Maine to go campaigning door-to-door."

As if on cue, a woman with curly red hair emerged from the back of the group. "Okay, crew. Time to eat. This way." She backed away with her hands up, flapping her fingers toward herself like a flight attendant.

The girl eyed me, almost apologetically. "You want to, I don't know, share our picnic blanket?"

I did. I wanted to hang out with them all day, if not all month. But they'd be leaving for Maine in a couple of hours. It wouldn't last.

"Thanks," I told her. "But I should stay here with Mary. She looks a little, you know…"

"Persecuted?" the boy put in.

"I was going to say lonely. But yeah. That, too."

They gathered up their backpacks and signs and water bottles, then waved goodbye.

After an hour, my arms were tired. I took a water break, then wandered through the crowd, checking out the signs and the people who were holding them. I wanted to know everyone's story—the chatty old people, the moms with strollers, the purple-haired kids with confrontational T-shirts. What would they normally be doing right now? What made them come here? Did they have any answers? Did they believe in their future? I might have summoned the nerve to start talking to someone, but too much time had passed already. I needed to leave soon or my parents would beat me home.

A couple of college students had set up a booth at the edge of the Boston Common, giving temporary tattoos to raise money for their climate-action group. Before I descended into the T station again, I put down a ten-dollar bill and took a seat in a folding chair.

"Do you have any pikas?" I asked a boy with nose piercings and long black hair.

"Pikes?" he asked.

"Pikas," I repeated. "Pikes are fish."

"She's talking about those alpine mammals," the girl beside him said, elbowing him in the arm. "Sorry, we don't," she said to me. "But it's a good suggestion. Maybe next time."

The boy riffled through the tattoos. "How 'bout a polar bear?"

"Sure."

He opened an alcohol wipe and rubbed down a spot on my arm. "It's cool seeing kids your age being political."

"I'm not, really. Political, I mean. I just don't want a world where everything's . . . you know . . . *dead*."

"Yeah, well, these days that's political," he said. He pressed the tattoo against my arm. "You can take the sticky part off in an hour. It'll look light at first, but it darkens pretty fast."

"Cool."

When I stood up, the girl handed me a yellow postcard. "Our next meeting's in Cambridge in a few weeks. You should come."

I looked down at the postcard. They had a meeting in June and a group hike in July. A small, warm feeling spread across my chest. Maybe they could be my people.

I smiled. "Thanks." I waved the card and gestured at my arm. "For both."

The T was crowded and the bus from Cambridge took forever. By the time I reached my house I was sweaty and exhausted, ready for a glass of water and a flop on the couch. I tucked my sign under my arm and was just reaching for my keys when the door swung open and they were all standing before me. Dad. Mom. Vivian. My whole loving family. But their expressions weren't loving at all.

"Where have you been?" Mom asked, her voice high and tight.

Dad's eyes were boring into me but he didn't open his mouth.

"You missed your presentation," Vivian said.

"Ms. Arocho called you?" I asked, surprised.

"She didn't have to. We were there," Mom said.

"It was supposed to be a surprise," Vivan added. She was wearing a sundress and her special sandals.

I swallowed back guilt. "I'm so sorry."

I'd never let my family down like this. Not even close. Part of me wanted to start all over again, do everything differently, make them happy and proud. But the protest at the State House had been so good. I wanted them to know that, too.

"I went to the climate thing!" I said, hoping they'd understand. I held up my sign. "See?"

"What's that on your arm?" Dad asked instead.

"God, Ginny, please tell me that's not a tattoo," Mom said.

I'd peeled off the sticky backing on the subway ride home. The polar bear was standing on an ice floe, which seemed especially apt. "It's temporary," I told my parents. "Though I kind of wish it wasn't."

Dad squeezed his eyes like his head was throbbing. "Go to your room, Ginny Shepard. Actually, first go to the bathroom and wash that goddamn thing off your skin and then go to your room. We have a lot of talking to do."

I nodded and slunk inside.

In the bathroom, I rubbed soap on a washcloth, but I couldn't bring myself to use it on my arm. I didn't want to erase the polar bear. Maybe they'd forget about it. I washed my face instead. Back in my room, I checked my phone for the first time since morning. There were the texts from my parents, from Vivian. Zinzie had written about five times, too.

> People say your parents were here.
>
> Are you okay?
>
> Ginny?
>
> Where are you now?
>
> Should I tell them where you went?

There was even an email from Ms. Arocho, asking me to come meet with her before school on Monday morning. I sighed. I looked at my polar bear tattoo and thought about the protest. The woman with the white hair. The kids from Vermont. How could going there have been so wrong when it felt so right?

➤·◄ ❧ ➤·◄ ❧ ➤·◄ ❧ ➤·◄ ❧ ➤·◄

My parents took away my allowance and doubled up my chores and supervised my homework for the rest of the weekend to ensure that I didn't risk failing eighth grade, even though I told them a hundred times that it was mathematically impossible. I dreaded going back to school and facing Ms. Arocho. But strangely enough, she was the one person who didn't freak out, even when I admitted that I'd never quite finished my presentation. She listened to me talk about climate change and pikas and the walkout and seemed to understand that Justice Sotomayor, extraordinary as she was, just wasn't the person I wanted to spend time with right now. In class that afternoon, she gave me a slip of paper with three names written on it. *Rachel Carson. Jane Goodall. Wangari Maathai.*

"Here," she said. "Read about these women and write a letter to one of them—a long letter about everything you're thinking and feeling right now. They're not all alive anymore," she added with a rueful smile, "but that doesn't mean they won't hear you."

"Okay," I told her. "I will."

Mom and Dad stayed on red alert. They challenged me on everything. Yelled at the slightest slight. They looked at me like I was a complete alien and never seemed to completely trust me, no matter what I said or did. Vivian wasn't much better.

"You used to be nice, you know," she pointed out.

Was I not nice?

"I'm upset, Vivian. That doesn't make me *mean.*"

"Whatever."

Her face had a quality to it I couldn't quite give a name to—a softness, an unknowing, that was not quite ignorance and not quite innocence, but something in between. I worried about her future. She used to say she wanted seven kids. What kind of world would be left for *them*?

"Anyway," she said before stalking off, "if Mom and Dad disown you, I get Nana's necklace."

"And you say *I'm* not nice?" I shouted at her back.

My parents signed me up for after-school tutoring, which really made no sense since I didn't need academic help; I just needed someone to explain the point of a scoring rubric when it was the world that was at risk of failing. After a few weeks of tense dinners and slammed doors, Mom finally told me she wanted me to talk to a therapist, or at least my school counselor.

"I'm not mad at you, Ginny. I'm worried. You just haven't seemed yourself in a long time."

"I'm okay, Mom. I'm . . . you know . . . confused. But I'm not depressed."

"I knew we should have found you someone to talk to last year," she said, almost to herself.

"Mom, stop. This has nothing to do with Nana and Grandpa, if that's what you mean. I'm just paying attention to what's happening. Right now."

When Dad came in, I flat-out begged them to give me a break. If they were still concerned about me in the fall, we could rethink the therapy.

"What's going to happen between now and the fall to make anything different?" Mom demanded.

I opened my mouth to speak, then closed it again.

"Let me guess. You don't think it should be summer school," Dad said.

"Obviously. I just don't see the point of it."

"The point of it?" he fumed. "The point is giving you every advantage here, Ginny. For college. For your future!"

"My *future*?" I looked at him in disbelief. "But there might not be any future. *That's* the whole point." It was like they hadn't heard a word I'd said all spring. I crossed my arms across my chest and rubbed the faded tattoo. "You don't understand anything. Especially me."

Saying it made me want to cry; so did the look on their faces. I couldn't believe I had so little control over my life.

I felt like coral.

"You can send me to summer school if you have to," I said, resigned. "Whatever. Just don't think you're going to change me."

Mom sighed. She looked tense and bewildered, but to be honest, the love was still there. Is that a thing? Loving something even when you don't understand it? I held her gaze, feeling the promise of something shifting.

She and Dad exchanged glances.

"Well, I did find another possibility. It's an outdoor program in the Rockies," she said.

"The Rocky Mountains?" I asked, taken back.

She nodded. "Camping for a month in Montana and . . . well, exploring. With a group of fourteen- and fifteen-year-olds. Is that something you'd like to do?"

"We can change plans this late?" It wasn't like her to pivot on the family schedule.

"Seems like we can."

"And it's just camping? No tests? No college credit?"

"Nope," Dad said, looking a little unhappy. "It's with that Outlands outfit your cousin did a trip with a few years back. But you'd have to carry a pack and sleep in a tent for four weeks . . ."

I was already pulling up the Outlands website on my phone. "I'm up for that," I told him.

The photos on the home page were enough to tell me this was a major improvement over the summer school option. These kids weren't stuck in computer labs and tiny dorm rooms; they were crossing sunlit streams, standing on mountaintops, smiling like they meant it. A catalog of trip descriptions filled six pages. The Montana one they'd picked for me had three symbols: a boot for hiking, an *I* for intermediate, and a paw print symbol indicating that it was part of their new TrackFinders program. You were supposed to call for more information.

"Did you call?" I asked Mom.

She nodded. "I had a long conversation with the Outlands director himself. And I came away from it very impressed."

I handed her my phone. "Sign me up. Please. I want to go."

"You don't need more time to think about it?" Dad asked.

A chemistry lab or the landscape of my soul? What was there to think about? "Quick. Before it fills up."

My parents looked guilty, like they were throwing away my future college prospects, but I wasn't concerned.

"Don't worry," I said. "This could be just what I need."

"Maybe it is," Mom said sadly. "Maybe it is."

➤◄ ❧ ➤◄ ❧ ➤◄ ❧ ➤◄ ❧ ➤◄

When Zinzie officially made valedictorian, I bought her a cactus and took it over to her house.

"It's called cristata," I said, holding it out to her.

"It looks like a brain," she said uncertainly, peering at the mass of tubular green shapes.

"People call it brain cactus, too. It's a tribute to your genius."

"Hard work more than genius," she said, adjusting her glasses. "But thanks." She set the cactus on the edge of her stoop and we sat down, knees touching. "I saw you talking to Ms. Arocho in the hall. Did you write that letter she wanted you to?"

I nodded. "I'm not a dropout, Zinz. Promise."

She looked relieved. "I wonder what's going to happen to your spot at Columbia summer school," she said, sounding wistful.

"I'd give it to you if I could. I seriously would. But my parents probably asked for a refund and now someone from the waitlist can go to stinky New York in my place."

"New York smells sweet next to the peanut vendors."

My best friend was a beautiful human who wanted my life more than I did. I gave her an apologetic smile. "I feel like a brat."

"Nah. You're just you. Good you." She tugged on my braid. "So, Montana. You're really going to eat and sleep outside for a whole month?"

"Yep."

She made a face. "You should take my sit-upon."

I laughed. They were something we'd made in Brownies in second grade—little mats to keep our bottoms dry when we sat on the ground. "That's okay. I'll tough it out."

"I wouldn't last a day," she said, shaking her head. "What'll you even *do* out there?"

I shrugged. "Hike. Think. Track mountain lions. I may even get to see a pika. Just in time to say goodbye."

"That sounds sad."

I nodded. Zinzie looked sad, too.

"Maybe we can get scholarships and go to Columbia summer school together next year," I said.

"Maybe." She shifted her knees and gave me a smile, but it was so small her dimples were only commas.

➤·◄ ❦ ➤·◄ ❦ ➤·◄ ❦ ➤·◄ ❦ ➤·◄

On the last day of June, my family took me to the airport in Boston and checked me in for a morning flight to Bozeman. I was wearing pants and a T-shirt, and hiking boots over wool socks. I checked my backpack—one of those big ones people wear for trekking up mountains, stuffed with a sleeping bag, a raincoat, a down jacket, a wool hat, toiletries, and several changes of clothes—and carried a fleece jacket and a small daypack for the flight. Vivian watched me with wide, wondering eyes. Mom and Dad looked massively agitated.

"It's only four weeks," I said, trying not to laugh.

"You know us," Mom said, running her hand through her hair and pulling it back behind her head. It looked like she'd forgotten to brush it. "You have your ticket? Your watch? Your ID?"

"Oh," Dad said, reaching into the pocket of his jacket. "I got you mint Lifesavers. In case they're serving nachos."

Dad knew how much I hate stuffy airplane air, especially when it smells like microwaved cheese.

"Thanks," I said, hugging them each in turn.

After I passed through security, I turned back and looked through the glass. The three of them were still standing huddled by the door. They lifted their hands and gave one last wave. They looked small. Sad. In that moment, I couldn't remember why I'd ever found them so annoying.

CHAPTER
5

I stared into the campfire, my mind racing. It had to be a mistake. That's what I told myself. A simple mistake. And if it was a mistake, it could be fixed—like in fifth grade, when the computer had accidentally assigned me to the class for prekindergarten. I'd gone straight to the principal's office and made things right, and I could do the same thing here with Brooklyn and Kai. For the moment they were too busy figuring out dinner to give me their attention. But I could wait.

After introductions, things only got worse. Dinner was overcooked ramen and freeze-dried green beans with the texture of hair bristles.

"Dudes. Seriously? Let's order pizza," Dash said, flinging his entire cup into the firepit. It was a Sierra cup, made for camping, sturdy and metal with a long handle for easy holding. He looked around expectantly.

"Don't be an idiot, bro," Maddox said, swiping the cup out of the fire and setting it on a rock. Good thing it was sturdy.

"What? Somebody delivered *him*." Dash pointed to Vidal.

"A scary hombre on a horse," Vidal said. He flicked a piece of ash off his sweatshirt, then stuffed his hands back into his pockets. "I don't think he does pizza."

"You came here on a horse?" I asked.

"Dude refused to walk," Dash said, looking impressed.

Elijah had finished his food fast and was now sitting with his head on his knees. "There's nothing to *dooooo*."

Dash sprinkled pine needles on the back of Elijah's head, then looked up to make sure we were watching and flashed us a clownish grin.

Greyson scraped his spoon against the metal bottom of his Sierra cup, eating up every morsel, not saying a word.

When everyone had made their ramen disappear one way or another, we circled up for s'mores and some more rules. First came the technology rules, which were simple: You couldn't have any. You weren't even supposed to talk about technology, which was why Elijah was such a mess. The kid clearly had a serious screen habit. Halfway through dessert I swore I caught him texting on his graham cracker.

Second came the proximity rules. If you left camp without telling someone where you were going, then for the next twenty-four hours you had to shout your name every time you went out of view again. Even if you were just going to the bathroom.

"You're joking, right?" Greyson asked. He spoke half as much as everyone else, but with twice as much anger.

"Where *are* the bathrooms anyway?" Dash asked, squinting into the woods.

Kai smiled and spread his arms wide. "The world is your bathroom!"

"Huh?" Elijah asked, putting down his graham cracker.

"No bathrooms in the wilderness, guys," Brooklyn said, checking something off her clipboard. "But we'll show you how to keep things pristine under the trees. And private." She looked around. "In fact, let's say that the woods behind me will be designated for the girls and the woods on the other side of your tents will be for the boys. Sound good?"

"Sounds like 1850," Vidal muttered under his breath.

Dash's prankish smile was gone. "This whole camp is a pile of—"

"Dash!" Brooklyn said, cutting him off.

"You know, now's probably a good time to review our code of conduct," Kai said, crossing his arms across his body. "Listen up. We start camp with trust. We trust you. We want you to trust each other. Happy. Good." He nodded my way. "Like a totally ordinary backpacking trip."

"But if someone breaks a rule," Brooklyn said, "the trust gets broken and things get harder. There will be consequences to fit the infractions."

"Will you have to send us home?" Elijah asked. He caught my eye. "At home I have a heated toilet seat."

Kai shook his head. "You don't want to go home. I promise."

But Elijah didn't look so sure.

These poor kids. TrackFinders was sounding more and more like a doomed reality TV show. I half-expected to see a camera crew in the woods, capturing the whole scene.

"Now," Brooklyn said, "last big topic before we call it a night is bears."

The boys looked up fast.

"You better be talking gummy," Elijah said.

"Grizzly," she told him, shaking her head. "And black bears."

Wild bears, in other words. The best kind.

"We're hiking right through their habitat," Kai said. "So that means we have to follow bear-safety protocol. No messing around."

Everyone was looking out into the darkening woods. Potty jokes and boy talk had temporarily made the clearing feel like a middle school locker room, but the truth was, this was wilderness. A great bumpy swath of Montana wilderness. And even if it was being scorched to the breaking point, it still had predators in it now. Toothy ones.

Elijah pointed into the shadows. "I just saw something."

Vidal shrank into his sweatshirt.

"Trees, dude," Maddox said with a smile.

"No, something moved," Elijah insisted.

"Where?" Dash asked, shifting closer to see where Elijah was looking.

Brooklyn checked her watch and pressed on. "The number-one rule is that we can't have any food in our tents. None."

"Dash. Elijah. What did she just say?" Kai asked.

The boys turned back. "Uh..."

"No food in our tents," Greyson said wearily.

"Right," Kai said. "We can't even have scented products—like soap, toothpaste, or lotion."

"He's already a scented product," Maddox said, punching Dash's arm.

Dash glared back.

"We can't brush our teeth for a month?" Vidal asked.

"You can definitely brush your teeth. You *have* to brush your teeth," Kai said. "You just need to store your toothpaste and everything else in the bear-proof packs. We've got some special fencing that we put around them, too."

I ran a quick inventory of the toiletries I'd left in my tent, not to mention Dad's pack of mints. I was about to ask if I should run back to get them now, when Brooklyn caught my eye.

"Don't worry. I went through your stuff already. It's all in one bag in here," she said, toeing the pack.

"You went through my stuff?!" I asked.

Elijah leaned in toward me. "I think you need to update your privacy settings."

"Elijah, no tech talk," Brooklyn said, giving him a look.

"It was a joke!" he whined.

"We're going to be really strict about this, guys," Kai said. "After every meal, all the food, containers, and utensils will be packed and stowed inside the electric fence. Ignoring these procedures could make a bear curious."

"And you don't want a curious bear," Brooklyn said. "Trust me."

There was a moment of collective silence as everyone took in her warning. Then Dash leapt at Vidal with his fingers arched like claws.

"*RAHRRRR!*"

Startled, Vidal dropped his s'more. He picked it up fast, but it was too late. A layer of black dirt and ash coated two sides. "Jerk," he said, flinging it at Dash's face.

The s'more struck Dash's cheek, then landed near my feet.

"Whoa, there. No one gets to assault my brother except me." Maddox scooped up what was left of the trashed s'more and flattened it on Vidal's head. "Take it back."

"Hey!" Vidal cried, shrinking out of Maddox's reach.

"That's enough, you two," Kai said, ushering the twins off to the side. "Let's go get more firewood."

Vidal glared at their backs. When he lifted the s'more away from his head, strands of marshmallow stayed glued to his hair. "The bears will go straight for my brain," he said miserably.

"Let's try rubbing alcohol," Brooklyn said, gesturing for him to follow.

Vidal walked behind her on tiptoe, as if that would keep bears off his track.

Elijah held his s'more stick at an angle to the ground and stomped it hard.

"It's not the stick's fault if you charred your marshmallows," I told him.

"Twenty-five. Twenty-six. Twenty-seven," Elijah said with every stomp. "This thing must be made of titanium."

"Either that or you ripped it off a live tree," Greyson pointed out.

"What do you mean?"

"Elijah, come help," Brooklyn called.

"Twenty-nine. Thirty. Whatever." He dropped the stick with annoyance and followed her.

Greyson and I were the only ones left. He'd spent the whole evening holding his stick over the campfire, torching one marshmallow after another like emergency flares. He never ate a thing. Still, his silence made him far and away the best candidate for friendship here. The hazel eyes didn't hurt, either.

"This is the part in the movie when we hear screams from the woods and realize we're the only ones left," I told him, climbing up on a log and taking a panoramic peer. "Spooky, right?"

He looked up, expressionless.

"Either we get the demented psychopath who just escaped from federal prison. Or he gets us." I paused. "What'll it be?"

I thought it was a fair opening, but Greyson seemed unmoved.

"How do you know *I'm* not the demented psychopath?" he asked me.

It didn't seem like he expected an answer, but I wasn't ready for the conversation to end.

"Just a hunch?" I suggested.

Greyson stood and dumped out his water bottle onto the remains of our campfire. The embers hissed and smoked.

"You seem more at home out here than the other guys," I told him, stepping off the log.

He capped his bottle, shook his head. "I'm not at home anywhere."

He kicked over the biggest log, either to finish off the fire or because he was mad—I couldn't tell which. Either way, it was clear he was done talking. He lingered till the last of the smoke was gone, then walked away.

It was time to talk to the counselors.

I found Kai and Brooklyn in a clearing through the trees, putting away the food.

"Hey. I hope I'm not bothering you guys. . . ."

"What do you need, Ginny?" Brooklyn asked, pressing the air out of a nylon food sack and closing it tight.

By her tone, it was clear she wasn't interested in small talk. I got straight to the point.

"I think there's been a mistake."

"Mistake?" Kai asked. He took the sack from Brooklyn and tucked it into a large collapsible pack that looked waterproof and, I guessed, critter-proof, too.

"Me being here. I don't think my parents knew what kind of program this was when they signed me up. I mean, I know you said it's not therapy, but it's a little like therapy, right? And the other kids might need all these rules, but I—"

"It wasn't a mistake, Ginny," Brooklyn said, cutting me off.

"They definitely knew," Kai added with an uncomfortable smile.

It felt like a slap in the face. For ten awkward seconds, I stood there, not saying anything, afraid that if I did, I might start crying. Did my parents seriously think I belonged with kids like *these*?

If Kai and Brooklyn could tell how stunned I was, they didn't let on.

"Go to bed, Ginny," Brooklyn said, picking up another nylon sack. "You've had a big day."

Confused and stung, I stumbled through my bedtime preparations, then fled to my tent. I wanted to fall asleep fast so I could escape this whole scene. With any luck, I'd wake up someplace else—like back on the airplane and on my way to the kind of camp I'd actually enjoy. I burrowed into my sleeping bag, but it smelled like home and that just made me feel worse. What were my parents thinking? They'd told me they'd hold off on any kind of counseling until the fall, and then they'd turned around and done this. Without telling. Pretending it was a favor, even.

It was a total betrayal.

I curled into an angry ball, thinking I might never forgive them. Then another thought came to mind, even worse than the first.

Maybe I was actually in worse shape than I knew.

Sleep didn't come fast, and my reality just got worse. The boys traded jabs, crude jokes, and burps; Brooklyn and Kai asked them to be quiet and, when that didn't work, moved on to warnings and then consequences. I wondered if the whole month would be like this—an unbearable combination of bathroom humor and petty rules. I kind of hated everything that had happened since I'd reached the clearing. In fact, no offense, TrackFinders—but it wasn't even that pretty here.

A feeling of dread pressed upon my chest. I couldn't last four weeks here. No way.

I knew what I needed to do. I needed to find a way to reach my parents, reason with them, flat-out beg them to let me out if they didn't automatically say yes. Maybe there was room for me on one of those regular Outlands trips like my cousin had taken. If not, I could offer to go to Columbia summer school after all, if they'd let me back in. Heck, I'd play tennis. I'd start in on my college applications, four years ahead of schedule. But not this. This was going to make me a crazy person.

I rolled over in my sleeping bag and reached for my pack. Brooklyn hadn't specifically mentioned my phone. Was there a chance she'd missed it? I dug into the front pouch, feeling with my fingers because I couldn't see a thing. It wasn't there. I reached for my jacket and felt inside every pocket. Not there, either. Finally, I dumped everything out and turned on my flashlight for a full inspection. But of course the phone wasn't there. It would have been the first thing she would take. And it wasn't likely I could have gotten any reception this deep into the backcountry anyway.

I groaned and rolled over onto my back. The sleeping pad wasn't thick enough to keep that chunk of rock from pressing into my spine. I began to fidget, rolling this way and that, lifting my feet and stretching the bottom of my sleeping bag into the air like a giant inchworm looking for a new twig. I bumped the top of the tent. It didn't even matter that the rest of the group had finally settled down; I'd never fall asleep in a nylon doghouse—not in this mood, anyway.

I had to get out. Unzipping my tent as quietly as possible, I leaned my head out and peered around. It was hard to see anything, but once I stepped into my boots and climbed out all the way into the darkness, it was immediate relief—like splashing into a lake on a hot, sticky day. I grabbed my down jacket and crossed to one of the logs by the firepit. The smell of wood smoke lingered, but the forest smells were making their claim again. Piney. Earthy. Crisp. I tilted my head back to take in the stars, popping out in glittery patches whenever the clouds drifted apart.

Around me, the woods formed a dark, impenetrable margin. Kai and Brooklyn had talked about the grizzlies, but there was so much more out here than bears. Bobcats. Martens. Elk. Lynx. Wolves. Twelve kinds of owls. What was the chance that one of those animals was hiding in the shadows, watching me?

"Is anyone home?" I called quietly, hopefully.

I stared into the darkness. If I saw even one wild animal, this day would be worth the carbon I'd burned to get here.

The whine of a zipper broke the silence and a tall figure emerged from one of the tents. It was Dash or Maddox—I couldn't tell which. I stayed stock-still as he shone his flashlight around the clearing and then walked in the direction of the trail opening. The good news for me was that he wouldn't see me now.

Flashlights don't actually help you see better in the dark; they help you see one spot better, and everything around that worse. I'd learned that at camp—my normal, happy Vermont camp.

The boy sniffed—it was Dash, apparently. He'd said he was a sleepwalker, but right now his steps were deliberate, like someone fully awake. When he reached the opening onto the trail, he hesitated for just a moment and then headed down it.

This wasn't sleepwalking; this was running away.

Maybe I should have given a shout and alerted Kai and Brooklyn, but I didn't think it was my job. If Dash wanted to dash, why should I get in the way? A few seconds later I heard a twig snap farther down the trail. He was seriously doing this.

Adios, I thought.

It wasn't a bad idea, actually—running. A couple of miles, flat or downhill, without a pack. I could cover that in under a half hour. I tried to remember how far it had been from the last gas station to the parking area. Or maybe I didn't need a gas station. Maybe I just needed a house. If I knocked on someone's door and claimed I'd escaped abductors, anyone would let me in. All I needed was to buy enough time to call my parents.

Or Zinzie. What if I just called Zinzie? That girl could deliver anything you asked for, on time and in perfect condition. Maybe she could even deliver me.

I could wait another half hour until Dash was well ahead, and then make a run for it. I could be that bold.

My eyes had adjusted to the darkness, but I still couldn't see anything in the woods except the vertical strokes of trees. My ears strained for any sound. I sniffed the piney air again and enjoyed the feeling of cold molecules drifting around inside my nostrils. It was the opposite of school, where I'd always worked so hard to block out the sensory input: gym stink, cafeteria noise, the sight of soggy trash decomposing under the bleachers.

Then from the valley below came a sound I'd heard only once before: the yipping and howling of coyotes. They sounded like puppies, crazed and unquenchable. I felt a stir of recognition. The stars, the air, and the coyote chorus. This part of therapy camp didn't feel so wrong.

A louder yelp followed the yipping. I crossed the clearing and listened. Footsteps pounded up the trail, and I barely had time to step out of the way before a body burst into the clearing and went sprawling across the grass. Four words in strict violation of TrackFinders' code of conduct emerged into the night air.

"Hey, Dash," I said quietly. "Back so soon?"

He flicked the flashlight into my face, then turned it off. "There are effing wolves out here," he muttered under his breath.

I could hear bodies turning over inside the tents. The whine of another zipper—surely it was Brooklyn or Kai, here to police us.

"What are you going to tell them?" he whispered in the dark.

I didn't much like Dash, especially now that he'd wrecked my chances for an escape of my own. But I was no snitch.

"That I saw some beautiful stars," I told him.

A flashlight went on by the tents.

"Good one," he said, like we were in this together. But being lumped together with these guys was exactly what I wanted to avoid.

CHAPTER 6

Maddox stood over the remains of last night's campfire, pitching twigs into the ashes. He was dressed in a blue zip-up soccer jacket and Adidas slides. As far as I could tell, he was the only camper awake.

"Well, well," he said, smiling as I approached. "Sounds like something interesting went down last night."

"Not that interesting," I told him. I took a seat on a damp log opposite him.

Brooklyn strode over with an armful of nylon food sacks, sparing me any more comments.

The official story was that I'd been out getting fresh air and Dash had been sleepwalking. One truth, one lie. But in the end, it didn't seem to matter what we said. We both got the same penalty: For the next five nights, they were taking away our boots.

"It's for your own safety," Brooklyn had insisted.

"Until I step on a snake," Dash had told her, shuffling back to his tent.

Kai came out of the woods carrying a large pot of water. He nodded at Maddox and me, then leaned toward the tents. "Rise and shine, team—it's a beautiful day! I want to see those bright, chipper faces of yours!"

One by one, the boys crawled out of the tents, moving in a collective stupor. I wondered if they'd slept at all. They dragged themselves over to the firepit, looking as bright and chipper as a heap of dirty laundry—which they sort of were. As far as I could tell, no one had bothered changing clothes. Vidal had put up his hood and pulled himself all the way inside his sweatshirt. He tested the top of a log with his finger, then drew it back into his sleeve and stayed standing.

"You need a sit-upon," I told him, thinking of Zinzie.

His expression was so dark it looked toxic. "A what?"

"Never mind," I said quickly.

"Ginny and my bro tried to run away last night," Maddox informed the other boys when the counselors were out of earshot.

Only Elijah reacted, wide-eyed and maybe even envious.

Maddox chuckled. "And I'd always thought you were scared of the dark, Dashy."

He was, actually. But I wasn't going to tell.

"Shut up," Dash scowled, his face puffy and pale.

I ate my breakfast of raisins and granola in silence, washing it down with some kind of orange powdered drink that was supposed to count for juice. Being here this morning felt just as strange and dislocating as it had yesterday afternoon, but without the added feeling of excitement or potential. The trees around me were unfamiliar, but they weren't really any prettier than the ones I could see back home at Walden Pond. The boys were strangers I wasn't sure I ever needed to know.

I stretched out my legs and glanced up at the oval of sky. Kai was wrong: It wasn't even a beautiful day; it was a nondescript gray day. I needed better company to make this work. I wanted Zinzie here, desperately. Or at least within phone reach. I could text her every fresh insult and she'd respond with immediate sympathy. I could play up the cluelessness of the boys and know I was making her laugh. The worst parts of TrackFinders would become the best parts because they'd give me such good material.

But I had no Zinzie and no phone. It was just me, the boys, two overeager counselors, and another overscheduled day.

>·< ᙛ >·< ᙛ >·< ᙛ >·< ᙛ >·<

"Our milestone for today is called Bonding at Base Camp," Brooklyn announced after morning chores.

Maddox coughed into his sleeve.

She glanced at her clipboard. "To start, we want everyone to go back to your tents and come back here with a bandanna."

"A banana?" Dash asked.

"Bandanna. It was on the packing list," Brooklyn said.

"They're in there, bro. Come on," Maddox said, pushing him toward the tents.

"I thought those were snot-rags," Dash said.

I was back at the campfire ring with my green bandanna five minutes later, but most of the boys lingered so long in their tents, it was pretty obvious they'd tried to go back to sleep. Kai and Brooklyn shook them out of their sleeping bags, then organized us into teams of two.

I was paired up with Vidal, who was still retracted inside his giant hoodie. The kid looked like a hermit crab—a miserable hermit crab with a camouflage shell.

"Either one of you know your knots?" Kai asked us.

"A few," I said.

The hermit crab wouldn't say.

Kai demonstrated a square knot just to be sure. Then he told us to practice tying our bandannas together. Vidal went first. When it was my turn, I knotted two corners together and lifted the double-long fabric like a flag.

"Our bandannas just Bonded at Base Camp,'" I told Kai. "Did we reach our milestone?"

"Not so fast," he said, plucking the bandannas from my hand. He knelt on the ground and tied two of our ankles. Together.

"Wait, what?" Vidal said, straining against the hold.

"Relax, buddy. She doesn't bite."

But I could feel Vidal's discomfort through my anklebone. The other boys looked on, repulsed.

"No way," Maddox said, gesturing at Elijah. "You can't tie us together. Dude doesn't even come up to my butt."

"Maddox, you'll be doing Elijah's dishes after lunch," Brooklyn said as she checked their knot and then tied up their ankles. She moved on to Dash and Greyson.

"Is this a three-legged race?" Elijah asked when she was done.

"Close," Kai said.

"Today's milestone consists of three activities that you and your partner will do together. Very together," Brooklyn explained. "The winner of each one gets a prize."

"Money?" Maddox asked, like he wouldn't stoop for anything less.

"My friend," Kai said, feigning dismay, "what value does money have in the wilderness?"

"We could pay you to let us leave," Maddox joked.

The other boys laughed, but Kai pretended not to hear.

"For the first task, we want you and your partner to go to your tents, take out all your gear, and put it neatly on your sleeping pad," Brooklyn told us. "And I mean *neatly*. Then look for me. I'll point you in the direction of a path through the woods." She reached into her jacket pocket and pulled out strands of yellow plastic tape. "I've made a trail with this flagging tape. Follow it through the trees. Kai will be waiting for you at the end."

"With our prize?" Dash asked.

"No, *our* prize," Maddox said, giving Elijah a confident look.

Talk of competition had wakened up the boys, but it sounded like fake excitement to me. Worse than a tennis match. Was this camp going to be just as much of a waste of time as that? I glanced at Vidal, who seemed equally unmoved.

"One more thing," Kai said. "No talking allowed. You have to do this entire first task without saying a word. No directions. No questions. Move in silent awareness of your partner."

"Got that?" Brooklyn said. "No talking."

"No talking," Dash repeated.

"That was talking," Elijah pointed out.

"So was that," Dash said.

Greyson turned his head away from Dash like he was willing a one-mile separation.

"And that."

Maddox pretended to lose his balance and gave Elijah a hard check in the shoulder, which finally shut them up.

"Okay, ready?" Kai asked. "On your mark. Get set. Go!"

I gave a tentative lift to my outside leg. I thought Vidal saw, but it was hard to tell with the hood. When I took a step forward, he stayed put, pinning our shared leg to the ground. I lost my balance and pitched forward, pulling him down with me.

Good thing I didn't care about winning. The other boys hadn't gone far, but at least they were vertical.

We staggered up to standing. This would be so much easier if we could make eye contact. I tugged on Vidal's hood, hoping he'd let it drop, but he shrank away from me fast, shaking his head. The crab needed his shell. So again I lifted my outside leg, holding it out as far forward as I could and even shaking it a couple of times to get his attention. Then I lost my balance again, and down we went.

It was a relief to see that Maddox and Elijah had fallen too, muttering swear words under their breath. But they hopped back up and kept going, and Greyson and Dash were already closing in on the tents. Meanwhile, Vidal sat on the ground, methodically wiping the dirt from his palms. It took another two minutes for us to finally get up and moving.

We were a terrible team. I couldn't see Vidal's face, he couldn't see my feet, and he didn't seem to pick up on my directional nudges. By the time we reached the tents, the other boys were starting toward the woods. We hauled the gear out of my tent, then crashed to our knees in front of his. The kid wouldn't even open his own tent, so I finally had to do it myself.

There were two odd things about Vidal's stuff. First, every-thing but the sleeping bag and pad was still inside his backpack, like he hadn't even touched it since he arrived. Weirder still, all three pieces of visible gear still had price tags attached. I wanted to ask why—I really might have asked—but rules were rules. Also, we needed to get going or we would still be chasing down the yellow flags at sunset.

With Brooklyn's help, we found our way to the start of the trail through the woods. I took to whistling every time I spotted a yellow flag on a branch, but I still had to drag Vidal to get to it. I couldn't figure out why he was so resistant. Was he tired? Did he hate stupid races? Did he hate *me*? There was no way to know.

Finally I glimpsed a small stream below us, with the four other boys and Kai standing in a cluster beside it. We stumbled down the slope, and they watched our arrival with a mix of smiles and scowls.

"You lose," Dash said, as if we needed to be told.

"And we won," Maddox said.

"Like a day ago," Elijah added. Today he was wearing a black T-shirt with the computer "loading" symbol on it. I was surprised the counselors hadn't taken it away.

Kai gave us an encouraging smile. "Great job. All of you. This isn't easy stuff. And yes, Elijah, you and Maddox have earned . . ." He reached into his daypack and pulled out a bag of apples.

"Fruit?" Elijah said.

"Premium organic, straight from Washington. I'll hold on to them for now," Kai said, ignoring Elijah's tone.

To our relief, he let us untie the bandannas. That was the good news. I shook off my sore ankle and wandered over to the stream for some personal space while Kai explained our next task. This time we had to follow the trail back up the hill to the clearing where our food was stored. Once there, we'd circle a tree—he'd tell us which one—and then return to him.

It sounded like a simple race. Then came the bad news: One person in each team had to wear the bandanna as a blindfold.

Vidal's hood shook a big no.

"I'll do it," I said, when Kai came near.

I wasn't worried about walking blind—it wasn't so different from walking around outside in the dark—especially with a partner playing the part of guide dog. My problem was I had a guide *crab*.

"On your mark, get set, go!" Kai called again.

Right away I heard Dash shouting commands to Greyson. Elijah's cries—"Ouch!" "Put me down!"—made me think Maddox was basically carrying him. But Vidal said little, and not much of it was helpful.

"Go there," he said quietly, to start me off.

"There where?" I asked, holding up my palms. "I can't see anything, remember?"

"Watch the mud," he said another time, as if I cared what happened to my boots.

At one point he tried tugging me by my shirtsleeve, which wasn't exactly effective. I bumped into branches. I tripped over a root and went sprawling.

"Why didn't you warn me?" I asked, rubbing my knee.

"There was a bee," he said, as if that explained everything.

The only upside to stumbling around in the pitch black was catching sounds I'd missed before. The *chirr* of a bird. A wood-pecker hammering in the distance. Something skittering in the leaves. More bees. I wouldn't have heard any of it if the other teams had been close, but once again, they'd left us in the dust.

When I finally heard voices again, I knew we'd reached the clearing. Kai told Vidal which tree to take me to and said my job was to find my way around the trunk and get to know the tree better before coming back.

I didn't mind meeting a tree. We'd already lost the race, so there was no need to rush. I ran my hands over the bark, tracing the deep grooves with my fingertips. I leaned in close and inhaled. The tree smelled like a holiday wreath. I stretched my hands up the trunk as far as I could, then continued my circuit. A slender branch bumped my face. I ran my hand down its length, feeling soft feathery needles, and shook it when I reached the end. "Nice to meet you, Big Bird."

Vidal made a funny noise, like a quick exhale out the nose. He probably thought I was a dork, but I didn't care.

"Big Bird is my *fwend*," I said, wrapping my arms around its trunk.

This time, Vidal let out a quiet laugh.

"What's so funny?"

"You sound like Lola," he said.

"Lola?"

"My baby sister. She lives for that show."

Baby sister. It was the only cute thing anyone had said since camp had started. I held on to it like a life raft.

"How old is she?" I asked.

"Two."

"I bet she's adorable."

Vidal didn't answer. Damn the blindfold; I could deal with his silence if I could see his expression.

"She's perfect," he said finally.

It felt like the sun had just come out from behind the clouds.

Vidal guided me back to Kai, who spun me around five times, then told all of us with blindfolds to take them off.

"Well, Maddox and Elijah won the footrace again, but there's a bonus task that decides who gets the prize. I want the three of you who were blindfolded to go back and find your tree. Without your partner."

"Seriously?" Elijah said. "Don't all trees feel the same?"

"Idiot," Maddox said under his breath.

Greyson was already angling into the woods like he might never come back. I started forward, too. I could do this.

There were so many trunks, so many limbs. I could rule out the small trees, the ones with leaves, the ones with forked trunks, and the ones with even, smooth bark. I was looking for a big tree with grooved bark and soft needles. Wider than my hug, but not by a lot. The first conifer that looked promising had very high branches. The others I saw were far back in the woods. I didn't think Vidal had needed to steer me around a lot of trees. I looked around the clearing again, all the trees blurring into one.

Then I noticed a tall, stout conifer with a single trailing branch. As soon as I saw it, I knew it was mine. I ran over and threw my arms around the trunk just to be sure. "Big Bird!" I said, when it felt right.

I looked over at Vidal. He smiled and put up a thumb.

"Most people call it a Douglas fir," Kai said. "But Big Bird works for me."

Greyson found his tree, too, and since he and Dash had beaten us to the clearing, they won the round. This time the prize was four packages of cinnamon-spiced instant oatmeal.

"Whoo-whee," Dash said sarcastically.

"I think you'll be glad for it later," Kai said, slipping it back in his pack.

It was time for the third task. Triple the fun, Kai said. We had to find our own way back to the campsite, have our ankles tied together again, *and* have one person blindfolded again—whoever hadn't done it before.

"Brooklyn will be standing on the far side of the clearing by your tents. Whoever reaches her first gets the final prize. And this one is especially sweet," he hinted.

For reasons I couldn't explain, my sweet tooth and my competitive spirit kicked in at the exact same moment. I glanced at Vidal. Could he do this?

"You'll need to take care of each other out there, though," Kai continued as he tied Dash's bandanna. "Don't let your teammate get hurt."

I looked at the crowded trees, the fallen logs—obstacles everywhere. I looked at Maddox and Greyson, sizing them up, too. These guys were just as competitive as I was, and possibly faster.

But there was one thing I was willing to do that they weren't. I eyed Vidal again. He was back to frowning, but he'd smiled about Big Bird. So maybe there was hope. Maybe he was more shy than defiant.

"Vidal, do you trust me?" I asked quietly.

He didn't answer.

"I just think we can do this a whole lot easier if I"—I freed my inside arm and lifted it above my head—"do"—I extended it out over his shoulder—"this." I put my arm around his outer arm and

94

held it tight. I could feel his ropy arm muscles tense, but he didn't try to wriggle away.

"I'll steer you where I go, so you know it's safe. I'll tell you when exactly you need to lift your feet. And, Vidal?"

"What?"

"We're going to win."

"Ready?" Kai asked.

"Outside leg is one, inside leg is two," I said.

Vidal didn't say anything.

"Start on one," I added.

"Set?"

Vidal nodded.

"GO!"

We took off into the trees. Greyson and Elijah were aiming straight for the most obvious opening—probably the path Kai had taken before us. Taking a chance, I veered left into the unknown. "One, two. One, two," I said, as we covered the first few yards. It was tricky to keep ourselves in sync, but so far we were managing.

"Big log," I said, holding Vidal tight. "Inner leg up on two. Two!"

We stepped up onto the log with our shared leg, then wobbled.

"One!" I said, and we threw down our outside legs and went on.

It helped not having to give Vidal a verbal command for every turn. I guided his body right and left like he was my partner for a bizarre forest dance. To his credit, he got it—so much better than I would have in his place. When we came to a low branch, I put my hand on his head and he let me press it down. When we hit a depression in the ground and started to stumble, I pulled him back and he responded with a quick skip like he'd been planning it all along.

We were getting close to base camp. I could see Brooklyn standing across the clearing with a red bandanna in the air. I also saw something moving in my peripheral vision, farther down the line of trees. Boys.

"One, two! One, two!" I said, counting faster as we hit open ground.

I couldn't tell if Vidal was still giving it his all.

"Lo-LA! Lo-LA!" I chanted fast as I recognized Dash and Greyson breaking out of the trees.

Vidal burst forward like a jackrabbit, springy and strong, so fast his hood blew back from his head. We leapt with the last three Lolas and I snatched up Brooklyn's bandanna seconds ahead of the other boys.

"We did it!" I shouted triumphantly.

Vidal whipped off the blindfold and leaned forward, breathing hard, his whole face out in the brightening air.

The other boys had stopped running the moment we claimed the bandanna. They yanked off their blindfolds and ankle binds and approached us, looking tired and cross.

"You probably cheated," Dash said.

But Elijah was focused on something behind me.

"Hey, someone killed our tents," he said.

I turned around. He was right. Our tents were lying flattened on the ground, the stakes and poles in neat piles beside them.

"I did," Brooklyn said, sounding proud. "After lunch you get to put them back up again. For practice. You don't want to be learning how when we arrive at a new campsite. It might be dark. Or raining."

Her plan didn't exactly improve the general mood.

When Brooklyn turned away, Dash came closer and gave Vidal a hard flick to the head. "Dude, you need a new barber."

In a flash, Vidal had his hood back up, head down.

"Prize time," Kai sang out cheerfully as he approached us across the clearing. He pulled a plastic bag filled with individually wrapped caramels out of his pack. "Told you this one was sweet."

"Wow, that's a lot of caramels," I said.

"And we got *apples*?" Elijah said. He shook his head at Maddox. "We got ripped off."

"Elijah, let's keep the comments positive," Brooklyn warned him.

It did seem a bit unfair, though. We got caramels. They got apples and cinnamon oats.

Or wait... was this some sort of test?

"Do you guys have any extra foil?" I asked the counselors.

"Sure," Kai said. "Why do you ask?"

I whispered in Vidal's ear, and he nodded.

"We were thinking," I said, trying very hard not to sound sarcastic, "maybe we could put our prizes together and end up with the best prize of all. Caramel apples?"

"Oooh," Kai said gleefully, confirming my hunches. "Sure sounds like bonding to me!"

The scent of caramel and cinnamon filled the air as we sat around the firepit after dinner. Brooklyn asked if anyone wanted to share an observation about the day's milestone.

No one said anything at first.

"My ankle hurts," Elijah finally offered.

Not even sticky caramel could keep that boy's mouth shut.

"Sorry to hear that, buddy," Kai said. "I'll take a look at it later. Anyone else? I saw some great cooperation during the morning races. Did you feel like you and your partners found a rhythm?"

Kai was like a teacher fishing for an over-obvious answer. Didn't he know no one ever took that kind of bait?

"I noticed some of you working together on setting up the tents," Brooklyn added. "Anyone have anything to say about teamwork?"

This time not even Elijah spoke. We *had* helped each other a bit with the tents, but mostly because it was the quickest way to put an end to the grumbling.

"Well, we saw good stuff today," Kai said when none of us answered. "But you all seem beat. Why don't you get ready to turn in?"

The boys nodded and got away fast.

I stood up slowly. I'd made it through my first full day of TrackFinders. Three-legged races and caramel apples had kept me distracted during the daylight hours, but now that the trees were sinking into their inky shades again, I could feel my angsty feelings return. I looked longingly at the trail.

"Ginny. Dash. Don't forget to bring us your boots before you turn in," Brooklyn said.

With a sigh, I sat back down and started in on my laces. I felt a hand on my head and looked up to see Maddox giving me a knowing grin.

"Someone needs to stay here with all the bad boys," he said, squeezing my beanie. "Right where she belongs."

CHAPTER
7

In the morning after breakfast, Brooklyn pulled out her trusty clipboard and read the description of our next milestone. After Bonding at Basecamp, I could have used an adventure—maybe Wading in a Waterfall or Peeking at Peaks. Instead, she handed out pencils and spiral notebooks and told us our third milestone was Journaling the Journey. She didn't even mean our current journey through the wilderness. She meant our own life journeys so far. We had to write down our birthdays, describe our first memories, and draw portraits of ourselves—as babies. How were we supposed to know what we looked like as babies? I doubted even Picasso could have pulled that one off.

"I still don't get all the milestone stuff," Elijah said, staring at his pencil like it was a piece of prehistoric flint.

"Our milestones are our daily goals," Brooklyn explained. "Markers in our path. All you need to do is focus on the day's milestone, and then the next, and then the next. And before you know it, you'll be back on track."

The whole thing sounded almost exactly like Dad's racing line. No wonder I hated it so much.

The following morning, our milestone was Honoring Home. First we made a floor plan of our house. Then we colored our favorite spaces. I felt more tied down than I had with a bandanna around my ankle. Instead of trekking through miles of wilderness, I was stuck on a log drawing pictures of my sock drawer. This was useless.

In the afternoons, we practiced more camp chores—filtering our water, working the gas cookstoves, learning about the bear-proof fencing that went around our food packs. The fencing was surprisingly lightweight, with electrified strings between the poles that you turned on and off with a switch. Kai asked Greyson to help take it down and set it back up again so we could see how it was done.

"This really works?" Maddox asked.

"Yep." Kai held his hand between the strings. "If a bear tries sticking its nose or a paw through here, it'll bump a string and get a wicked jolt. Not enough to hurt it, but enough to send it running."

"Sick," Dash said with an appreciative laugh.

I shook my head. I understood the point of the fencing, of course, but it still sounded mean.

Elijah pointed at the protected packs inside the ring of fencing. "I want to sleep in there tonight."

"Yeah, yeah," Brooklyn said with half a smile.

There were moments when no one was arguing and the sun was shining when the whole scene at camp felt better, and livelier, too. A pair of chipmunks zigged and zagged around our woodpile like it was playground equipment. Gray jays supervised our meals, hopping across the ground and cocking their heads, inquisitive and alert. Kai said some people called them camp robbers, a name we understood after a jay made off with a piece of Vidal's pita. Vidal said again how much he hated nature. But for me, the jays were the best part of the day.

Evenings brought more clipboard time and more complaints. Brooklyn and Kai asked us to share from our journals like this was kindergarten show-and-tell. Anyone who refused to share lost more privileges—dessert, free time—and earned more chores, like hauling water and splitting wood. Maybe there was a point to all these rules, but from what I could see, they just wrecked everyone's mood.

"I'm getting a blister," Elijah complained, setting down a small ax and holding out his thumb.

"Wish I could help you, my friend," Kai told him. "But you made this bed and now you have to lie in it."

"Lying in bed would be fine," Elijah muttered. "It's the chopping I hate."

Then, just when it felt like we were never going to do anything more interesting than pump water from a stream, Brooklyn and Kai announced milestone five: Tough on the Trail. And just like that, we were finally moving on.

We packed up camp after breakfast and heaved on our back-packs, now weighted with the tents and other gear. We looked like top-heavy turtles who might suddenly tumble backward and find ourselves pinned. Vidal's backpack may have been brand-new, but it fit him awkwardly and he kept tugging on the straps, trying to make it right. Greyson's was an old canvas pack with thin, unpadded straps, but he didn't seem to care at all. When we were all more or less vertical, we formed a ragged line and headed onto the trail. This was it. We were on our way, and there was no getting out of this now.

Though, actually, it wasn't at all clear how far we'd ever get.

Now that we'd had time to adjust to the altitude, Kai and Brooklyn set a relentless pace. There were planned food and water breaks, but mostly we stopped out of necessity because someone was whining. Or needing blister triage. Or just sitting down, refusing to move.

"My parents are going to sue you if I die," Elijah panted after the first hour, leaning on a tree.

I was a little worried about him, but Brooklyn just stood near, encouraging him to have some water and one of her energy bars until he was ready to continue.

Years of tennis gave me a boost, but that didn't mean I felt none of the pain. My pack pulled on my shoulders and, even with good padding, the hip belt chafed my skin till it was raw. I expected to enjoy the views, at least, but the landscape was strangely monotonous, the trail descending into a stream valley that was wetter and denser with undergrowth than the woods where we'd started. For the rest of the day, it felt like we were circling at that one low elevation instead of advancing to the best parts of the mountain. Down here along the streambeds, the mosquitoes cruised at neck level, eyeing any exposed skin and moving in for the attack as soon we let our guard—or rather, our hands—down. A big afternoon shower rolled through, leaving us briefly refreshed but then seriously soggy.

The effort of hiking kept talking to a minimum. It even kept the thinking to a minimum—for me, anyway. I found myself listening to my breath or staring at the trail with a strange kind of blankness. *Mud. Root. Stream. Rock. Mud. Rock. Rock.* My only job was to watch my step, keep moving, and not topple over. In some ways, the mindlessness was a relief.

I didn't understand why the counselors were suddenly working us so hard, though. Were they trying to get us warmed up for bigger ascents? Were they trying to break us? One thing was for sure: They wouldn't need to take away anyone's boots that night. Who would try to run away after a day of hiking like this?

As the day wore on, Dash and Maddox grew increasingly winded, making me think their lungs had some experience with firsthand fumes. Elijah looked close to collapse. When he caught his breath during water breaks, he used it to inform anyone who would listen that he had never done anything so miserable in his entire life. Greyson moved quietly, steadily. He may have been tired, but he gave off an air of stoic resolve bordering on total apathy. Vidal peered out from his hoodie, eyeing everything like it was a potential threat.

"You okay?" I asked him after following him for a long stretch.

He slapped his cheek.

"The mosquitoes are always worse after rain," I said.

Still no answer.

I missed the friendly Vidal who'd laughed about his baby sister.

"Do you think Lola would like being out here?" I asked.

As soon as the words were out of my mouth, I regretted them. Vidal whipped his head around. "Please leave me alone."

"Sure, sorry," I said quickly, wishing I'd kept my mouth shut. The last time we'd talked about Lola it had come out naturally, and it had started with him. You couldn't force these things.

Vidal was still walking on his tiptoes, like before. If he thought being quiet was a good way to avoid bear trouble, though, he had it all wrong. The last thing you wanted, as Brooklyn reminded us, was a surprise encounter. Better to talk, clap, shake some bear bells, and raise a ruckus. If bears heard us coming, they'd be smart enough to huff out of there as fast as possible.

Fortunately for Vidal, Kai kept the volume high enough to scare off wildlife for miles. The guy talked constantly. As we soon learned, he was a New Yorker—half Korean, half Italian—who had never set foot on a hiking trail until he went to college in Maine. After an hour of his nonstop monologues, I began to wonder if his favorite thing about the great outdoors wasn't the beauty and tranquility but the fact that he could hear his own voice without any background noise. He wasn't bad company, but it would have been nice to catch a birdcall once in a while.

"Anyone here ever gone kayaking?" He was munching on trail mix and hiking at a good clip while we tried to keep up. "I took this geology class one time where we studied coastal rocks from sea kayaks. Cool, right?" And off he went naming seventeen different kinds of rocks and minerals found along the Atlantic Coast. Describing his favorite clam shack. Telling us a very long story about studying Eastern philosophy with a ninety-year-old professor who still took daily ocean swims, even in the middle of winter.

"Where's the mute button?" Elijah whispered.

I held back a laugh. Sometimes Elijah said it just right.

But I appreciated Kai's monologue more when he started telling us about the wildflowers sprouting up beside us on the trail. Showy asters were purple with yellow centers, but not as purple as the sticky geraniums, prettier than their name. Yarrow was tall, with tiny white flowers and fernlike leaves. Harebells looked like clusters of tiny lavender bonnets bent in prayer. Goldenrod glowed like there was sunshine packed in its petals. Paintbrush, vertical and bristled, looked ready to mark the world with deep red brushstrokes.

For the remainder of the hike, my inner chant changed. *Paintbrush, aster, harebell, yarrow. Aster. Yarrow. Geranium.* Mindlessness had never been so colorful.

Our new campsite was in an even smaller clearing than the first. I set up my tent on an even patch of grass, avoiding all rocks. We cooked the usual half edible dinner, then clamored around the food pack for our dessert portions—a couple of vanilla wafers and a small chocolate bar. The way we were hiking, it felt like we'd never be able to eat enough to feel full. The boys gobbled everything down fast. I savored my bites slowly and shared the crumbs with a line of ants that popped up like a flash mob on the edge of my log.

Maddox sat down beside me and held out a closed hand. "A little reward for all your hard work," he said, dropping a chocolate bar into my palm.

It felt sweet—the soft thud of chocolate, the sense of being looked after. But I couldn't take a guy's dessert. I pushed the bar back toward him. "It's yours."

"Keep it," he insisted. "I got double."

"How?"

"Connections." He winked.

Kai and Vidal were heading off with the food packs, and the other boys were occupied with the usual stuff: fighting, sulking. Brooklyn was nowhere to be seen. Maybe no one cared.

"Thanks. I owe you."

As I took the chocolate, I caught Greyson watching us. He raised his eyebrows, like he'd caught us doing something wrong, but it was too late for second-guessing.

Maddox smiled. When I was finished eating, he took back the wrapper, letting his fingers trail against mine.

"So," he said. "You got a boyfriend back in Lexington, Ginny?"

"Nope. And no girlfriend, either."

He squinted. "There something you need to tell me?"

"I'm just saying, don't assume. It makes you sound parenty."

Something flashed in and out of his eyes, meteor-fast. He turned his attention to Dash and Elijah, sword-fighting with camp forks. "My brother is such a hamster."

"You're twins, Maddox. You might want to rethink that."

He pushed his fingers back through his bleached hair. "My theory? My parents just say we're twins to boost his self-esteem. I think they found him in a dumpster. I mean, look at him."

Dash's trail pants were hanging so low I could see the top of his red underwear. His T-shirt had dirt marks and chocolate stains, and I was pretty sure a horsefly was caught in his hair. I looked back at Maddox, hair still combed and neat, soccer shirt pulled tight over his broad shoulders. It really wasn't fair.

"You could help him, you know," I said.

"It's all I do," he told me.

Brooklyn and Kai gathered the group for another get-to-know-you game and another lecture about nighttime rules and bears. Not surprisingly, bathroom breaks were exceptionally speedy.

Before bed, they gave us each some paper and told us to write a letter home to our parents. I stared at the blank sheet of paper under my flashlight for a full five minutes, pen in hand. I wondered if anyone else was even trying; I could have sworn I heard weeping. Finally I got started.

Dear Mom and Dad,

I stopped. Emotions crackled inside of me, just looking at the words. I had too much to say, too much to shout. I switched to a new sheet of paper.

Dear Zinzie,

This one wasn't easy either. Writing a letter was different from texting; I couldn't imagine telling her where I'd ended up. She'd be appalled. I decided some things were best left unsaid.

Hi! I'm here now. Montana. Wow. We've been hiking like maniacs and living on a steady drip of trail mix and s'mores. No wildlife sightings to report yet except for a wizard-worthy raven, a bunch of chipmunks, and a lot of hungry jays. The other kids are—well, let's say interesting. I'm not seeing much in the way of friend potential, but you never know. If a fairy gave me a wish, I would definitely wish for her to poof you here. But then, of course, you'd take one look at the woods and the bathroom situation and tell your fairy to poof you straight back to civilization. So maybe we should save those wishes for invisibility. Or earrings? Hope you're liking summer so far. Counting the days till I can see you again.

I signed my name. Then I really did count the days. Twenty-five. Right now, twenty-five felt like way too many.

CHAPTER
8

The next day brought more brutal hiking. More monotonous scenery. More mutinous boys. Our milestone for the day was Silent Spring.

"Every time we call out those two words, we want you to spend the next ten minutes in silence," Kai had told us before we started off. "Listen to your breath. Pay attention to your thoughts. Be in the now."

The boys looked at him with such stunned disbelief that I accidentally laughed out loud.

"Is something funny, Ginny?" Brooklyn asked as she rubbed a daub of sunscreen onto her nose.

"What? No. Not at all."

Maddox grinned. He was just like the kids at school who loved it when the good kids slipped up.

"Let's go," Brooklyn said, slipping the sunscreen back into her pack.

Maddox sidled up beside me after a few yards. "Dude's a total airhead, right?"

"Silent Spring!" Kai announced before I had to answer.

Elijah was the first to have a meltdown. We were half-walking, half-bushwhacking down a narrow trail, when a branch smacked him in the face. He threw off his pack and just started screaming. "I hate this! I hate this!"

"Easy there, buddy," Kai said.

"Don't tell me what to do," Elijah snapped, wrapping his arms around his body. He sat down on the trail, rocking ever so slightly. "I hate hiking. I hate all this green stuff."

"Plants?" I asked.

"This is real life, my friend," Kai said, "in all its green, leafy glory."

"Well, I hate real life," Elijah muttered.

"Can we go?" Maddox asked.

"We'll just take a little break here till Elijah's ready," Brooklyn said calmly.

"That'll be never," Elijah said furiously.

The other boys rolled their eyes, looking impatient.

Elijah finally started walking again, but he still seemed shaky. He was mumbling to himself, swatting at flies, and kicking rocks like they were enemies.

"Tell me a place you'd rather be right now," I said, when the next call for silence was over.

"Anywhere."

"First choice?"

"My room."

"Just sitting there?"

"Gaming, duh."

He seemed to be kicking and swatting less, so I kept at it. Vivian had always done better with distraction than direct sympathy, so I had practice.

"If you think about it, TrackFinders is kind of like a giant video game," I told him.

He shot me a look. "Are you high?"

"No, really. Like, we're the players, advancing through levels," I persisted. "Right? So what's your player's name?"

He kept his eyes on the trail. "Misery."

"Nope, not going to cut it. It has to sound more like a superhero."

"Super Misery, then."

I stopped trying. Vivian would have perked up by now; this kid was a lost cause.

"I'd pay someone ten thousand dollars to take me to a beach resort," Maddox said from behind me.

"I'd pay someone ten thousand dollars for a Coke," Dash added.

"Make it a Red Bull," Maddox said.

"That stuff is so gross," I told him.

"Oh?" Maddox said. "So what's your diet of choice, Ginny from Lexington?"

"Healthy and varied," I said reflexively, primed by years of nutrition talk with coaches, health teachers, parents. I froze in my tracks. "Whoa. I think my mom just hacked my brain."

The boys were already snickering.

"You don't like junk food at all?" Maddox asked.

An image came immediately to mind: Nana's pantry, unchanged since the 1960s, with its painted pink cabinets and round aluminum knobs. Every time we came for a visit, she'd have a shelf stocked for me and Vivian with boxes of treats Mom and Dad would never buy.

"I like Pop-Tarts," I told the boys. "Frosted brown sugar cinnamon Pop-Tarts. Yum."

Mom called them sugar cubes, which was a little weird when they were basically pillowed rectangles. Vivian and I didn't care what shape they were, though; we thought they were the best junky treat of all time.

Dash and Maddox had gone silent. When I turned to look, they were eyeballing each other and grinning. Dash's face was red.

"What?" I asked. "No, actually, I don't want to know." "Pop-Tart" was probably Grosse Pointe slang for something that would ruin the taste of them forever.

The boys laughed and went back to their high-priced escape fantasies. I was half-listening, half-tuning them out, when Elijah suddenly spoke up again. "So what's *your* player's name?"

I smiled. Maybe not such a lost cause after all. "Pikagirl," I told him instantly.

"Spell it."

"P-I-K-A-G-I-R-L. Why? You going to make me a cape?"

"I just don't think it sounds like a superhero."

"It is to me. Every time Pikagirl saves an animal from the deadly... er... death fire, she earns..." I hesitated. I didn't know video-game language. At all.

"Yummy cake? Extra lives? Power-ups?" Elijah suggested.

"No tech talk, you two," Brooklyn said, hiking past us.

Elijah's shoulders stiffened and he kicked a rock so hard it flew up and hit Vidal in the back of his leg.

"Ow!" Vidal shrieked. He pulled up his track pants and rubbed the spot, glaring at Elijah. "This is my most important leg!"

"Wow, sorry," Elijah said. "Next time I'll aim for second-most."

"Silent Spring!" Kai called again.

On we hiked, with pretty much everyone silently fuming. It was hard to imagine how days like this were going to prepare anyone to function better in the so-called front country.

At lunchtime, Brooklyn explained that our trail lunch was always going to be the same thing—six rye crisp crackers, cheese, peanut butter, jam, raisins, and chocolate—so we'd better get used to it. She put Greyson in charge of distributing our rations. He started with the rye crackers and doled them out like a blackjack dealer, silent and swift.

"We should set up a game later," Maddox said, eyes shiny. He'd seen the cardplayer, too.

When Greyson finished cutting slabs of cheddar cheese, I slid my cracker toward him. "Hit me," I said.

Greyson tossed a piece of cheese on top of the cracker.

"You're a pro," I told him.

"I got no choice," he said, not even looking up.

I didn't try to talk with him again, but I found myself keeping him in my peripheral vision for the rest of the meal. There was something weighty about Greyson—on the inside, I mean. Like his core was a heavy metal, or maybe a deep, dark pond.

It made me curious. I liked deep ponds. Sometimes you could find interesting things down in the murk.

After lunch, Brooklyn and Kai announced a Silent Spring siesta, leaned back against their packs, and closed their eyes. It was the first time I'd seen either of them pause. One by one, the rest of us followed suit, at least in the leaning. I couldn't keep my eyes closed for long, afraid I might miss something important if I did. Out on the trail, we were never this quiet, even during our Silent Springs. There were too many footfalls and sneezes and sighs and jingling bear bells echoing into the trees, announcing our presence at every turn. Maybe in the silence of our siesta, though, one of those legendary Montana animals would finally meander into view.

All around us loomed pine trees with trunks as straight and smooth as flagpoles. The branches started halfway up, long and strong and full of dense green needles. An owl might be dozing in a spot like that. A porcupine, even.

"Dudes—don't move," Dash said under his breath.

He was looking up at the same tree I was, eyes wide.

"This is a Silent Spring, Dash," Kai murmured.

"That tree. It's freakin' infested," he said anyway.

I looked back at the branches, trying to figure out what I'd missed.

"Wasp nests, right?" he asked.

"Shoot!" Vidal said, scrambling to his feet.

"Hundreds of them," Dash went on.

Elijah scooched back, crab-style, straight over his pack.

"Where?" I asked. The branches looked empty and unremarkable except, perhaps, for a slightly higher than normal concentration of…

"Pine cones, Dash," Brooklyn said. "Those are just pine cones."

"But they're all clumped and nasty, like giant alien warts. Tell me that's okay."

"Earth to Dash," Maddox said. "Time for your meds."

"Actually, it's not a bad observation," Kai said. "That's a lodgepole pine you're looking at. Trees like that often make extra cones when they're stressed."

"I'm stressed," Vidal murmured, biting his thumbnail.

I squinted at the pine cones. "Trees get stressed, too?"

Kai might have explained more, but Brooklyn said if we couldn't handle a Silent Spring siesta, we should just move on.

"Besides, this will give us more time for chores at our next site."

The boys groaned.

"It's all your fault," Maddox said, shoving his brother in the back in what was becoming a trademark move.

"Come on, team," Kai said. "Grit. Resolve. Power. You got this."

"I got nothing," Elijah grumbled, stumbling as he heaved on his pack.

We trudged forward. The sun was high and warm, but the trees pooled their shadows on the ground, keeping us cool. I walked behind Greyson, staring at the back of his flannel shirt, taking in the muted colors and spotting a bite-size hole at the hem.

"Let me guess," I said to him. "You have a small dog or a very feisty cat."

He gave me a questioning look over his shoulder. I was pretty sure the only impression I'd made on Greyson so far was that I talked too much. But I wasn't going to stop now.

"Or very large moths?" I gestured at his shirt. "Your shirt has—"

I never finished my sentence.

In the time it took to walk ten steps, the shade had evaporated. We'd left the cover of the forest and arrived at an open slope, exposed and hot. Blackened trunks filled the hillside, some nearly whole, but ugly as scorched skeletons; some burned to half their height. Logs covered the ground like pickup sticks. Even the new green growth sprouting up between the logs wasn't enough to change the atmosphere.

It felt like death. No one spoke. Maybe everyone felt it.

"Wildfire blazed through at the end of last summer," Brooklyn told the group. "We had to evacuate two of our programs."

"Where to—the city?" Elijah asked, sounding envious.

But all I could think about was the flames, tearing through the trees. And what was it like for the animals? Did they have time to get away?

On the edge of the trail was another tall lodgepole pine, trunk charred but with intact needles growing from its upper branches, like maybe it was still half alive. I put my arms around the trunk like I'd done with Big Bird, and leaned my forehead against the scratchy bark. It smelled like yesterday's toast. I felt achy and a little sick. Before last summer, people had hiked through here and seen trees that looked healthy, whole, secure. Maybe they'd taken pictures of this very trunk, or walked right past without even paying attention because everything looked so reassuringly right. But I'd arrived too late for that. I'd been *born* too late—too late to have anything be normal. Too late to be oblivious to what it all meant.

"Yo, Ginny—you good?" Maddox asked.

"I think she has a nosebleed," Vidal said.

"You need my snot-rag?" Dash asked.

I lifted my head away, shook my head. "No, thanks. I'm okay."

But of course I didn't feel okay at all.

The line started moving, but it took us almost half an hour of solid hiking to get past the burn. Even when we reached the shade of healthy woods again, I couldn't stop thinking about the wildfires. What if these trees were next? Would another girl come through here in five or ten years and find them blackened and toppled, too?

Maybe I'd had it all wrong. Maybe I wasn't seeing the mountainside more scorched than it had ever been before; maybe I was seeing it as intact and pine-perfect as it would ever be again.

I felt gutted. This was just the kind of thing Mr. Stelling had warned us about. It wasn't our scary future. It was our scary now.

I angled to the front of the group and stayed quiet.

Kai was leading the line at his usual clip. When he turned and saw me, he pounced. A fresh conversational victim.

"You ever scuba dived, Ginny? Hang glided?" he asked.

"Nope." Did he not notice I was having a moment?

"Explored any caves?" he asked, all eagerness.

"Just my uncle's man cave," I told him, hoping that would shut him up.

"Ha, that's funny," he said. "You two close?"

He really couldn't take a hint. "Isn't it time for another Silent Spring?" I asked.

When Kai turned around, he looked confused, maybe even hurt. "Wait, why?"

I felt bad. Just because I'd been thrown back into my personal abyss didn't mean I had to drag everyone else down with me.

I tried again. "What's it's like—a real cave, I mean?" I asked him. "You ever see bats?"

Kai brightened. "All the time. Spelunking's awesome!"

"Dude!" Dash exclaimed from behind me with a whoop of excitement.

We wheeled around, expecting to see something amazing. Or at least Dash's version of amazing, which, come to think of it, might not be anything I wanted to see. To my surprise, though, he was pointing at Kai—practically hopping even though his face was sweaty with exertion.

"He swore! Kai swore!" Dash said. "That's a warning, right, Brooklyn? Ha!"

"No, I didn't," Kai said, confused.

Dash nodded with delight. "I heard you. You said something was, well, you know, '*mmm*-ing awesome'!"

Kai and I stared at him wonderingly, replaying our conversation.

"I said 'spelunking's awesome,'" Kai said.

"Spe-lunk-ing," I repeated. "Going into caves."

Elijah giggled. "You thought that was swearing?"

"What?" Dash looked around nervously. "I thought he . . ."

"Shut up and stop embarrassing our DNA," Maddox said, shoving him hard as he passed.

Elijah giggled some more. Brooklyn told Maddox he was going to have to wash out the cooking pot after dinner.

"Onward, people," she said, tucking away her map. "Looks like another half mile to our next campsite, and it'll be a climb."

➤⋅◄ ❥ ➤⋅◄ ❥ ➤⋅◄ ❥ ➤⋅◄ ❥ ➤⋅◄

That night I was asleep in my tent when I became aware of a soft thump against the nylon. Then another. Pine cones? Four more thumps followed—like a whole shower of pine cones. Was this another thing trees did when they were stressed? When the next thump landed against the front of the tent, I unzipped the door. The white-blond hair of Maddox caught the glow of my flashlight. He held his finger to his lips and ducked inside.

"This is a one-person tent," I whispered, squeezing over to avoid contact. "*My* one-person tent."

He shrugged and hunched down beside me on the sleeping bag. "We can go outside if you want."

"It's against camp rules, remember?" Then again, maybe this was against the rules, too. I racked my brains, trying to remember.

"I brought you a surprise."

He dropped something on my lap. A rectangular packet, silver and shiny. I touched it with my fingers.

"You've got to be kidding me."

"Frosted brown sugar cinnamon, no less," he said, delighted.

My mouth watered. The shiny iced top. The floury edges you ate first and fast so you could savor the gooey sweet cinnamon on the inside. I'd missed them more than I'd realized. But how on earth did he find Pop-Tarts in the middle of the Montana wilderness?

I looked up. "Who are you—El Chapo?"

"Pretty much." He chuckled. "I could escape from this prison any time."

"No, seriously. Where did these come from?"

"Dash had them hidden in a secret pocket. For emergencies. But I traded for them, fair and square. So eat."

"I can't. Not in my tent. Bears—remember?"

"There aren't any bears, Ginny. They just say that to scare the rug rats."

"No, they don't. There really are bears, Maddox."

"Aww—you scared? Don't worry. I'll protect you."

"I'm not scared. Just respectful. Which you should be too, by the way."

"I can handle a grizzly."

"An eight-hundred-pound predator? You're funny."

"So tell me, Ginny," he said, changing the subject. "You've had five days here. Who's your favorite?" Without waiting for me to answer, he started to tear open the Pop-Tart wrapper, right there in my lap.

I yanked it away. "Don't."

He smiled like he'd just been teasing and lay down on my sleeping bag, hands behind his head. "I'm guessing it's not my slow bro. Or the anxious military dude."

"Vidal. His name's Vidal and he's not in the military."

"You sure do talk a lot to that Black kid from San Fran. Maybe him?"

"Are you seriously unwilling to use their names?" I asked.

"Okay, now I'm thinking it's Mr. Kansas. Kinda white trash, if you ask me, but you're probably into that. The sexy, brooding farm-boy thing." He gave a little laugh, like he expected me to join in.

As if. There was only so much tolerance that Pop-Tarts could buy. "Maddox, go." I kicked his feet and pointed toward the door.

"Aw, don't be mean. I was totally joking. Those dudes are cool. Vidal, Elijah, Greyson. Is that better? Couldn't love them more."

Before I could respond, a voice came from the next tent.

"Ginny? Is that you?"

It was Brooklyn. Maddox and I froze.

"Yes, sorry." I wondered what she'd heard. "I think I was having a bad dream." It wasn't so wrong. "Can I go out for a bathroom break?"

"Make it speedy."

I unzipped the door and shoved Maddox through, throwing the packet of Pop-Tarts at him as he stumbled out.

"I'll be saving these," he said, the silver foil shiny even in the dark.

I whipped the tent zipper back up fast. They weren't even tempting anymore.

CHAPTER
9

Our hardest trail came a couple days later: a rocky path so steep and so relentless that we had to stop every ten steps to get more air. We never could have done it on the first day out. But by now all our blisters were smothered in moleskin, and I was pretty sure everyone was conditioned to shutting up and walking, no matter how hard it felt.

Still, that didn't keep us from straining, wheezing, and groaning for the whole first hour. Brooklyn passed around Jolly Ranchers, but that just turned into an extended joke about who was the biggest sucker. I scratched at my mosquito bites and tried to ignore the growing stench of sweaty boys as we crawled up the steep slope. Showers. We all really, really needed showers.

We trudged through another long hour.

And then I felt it—a breeze through the trees. It gave me hope: Mosquitoes hate breezes. Twenty minutes later, the trees started to look different—more spread out, with open spaces underneath. The air and the ground felt drier. A pair of goldfinches traced an invisible path from one tree to another. The clearings grew broader, sunlit and strewn with a rotating exhibit of wild-flowers, until open meadows were the norm and trees the patchy punctuation.

After another half hour, we emerged from a cluster of ever-greens into, well, heaven.

In front of us was a tiny lake like a melted bead of turquoise surrounded by coarse grass. Large white boulders were scat-tered around like oversize marshmallows. Clumps of orange flowers nodded encouragingly in the breeze. Beyond the lake rose rounded green slopes and steep granite cliffs, and beyond them loomed an actual snow-covered peak. I wanted to pause and take a picture. I wanted to stay forever.

Oh please, I thought. *Please don't tell us to keep moving.*

"You guys can go set up your tents over there," Brooklyn said, pointing to a flat area partway around the lake.

"Omigod, I love you," I told her.

"Seriously?" Elijah asked, gaping.

"Sucks for you, bro," Dash said to his twin.

Maddox flipped him the bird without either counselor noticing.

But I just kept my attention on the clearing. I chose a flat spot beside a bed of tiny purple flowers and set up my tent fast. Then I crawled inside, stripped to my sports bra, and pulled on a pair of running shorts. When I emerged, Brooklyn was shaking out her tent stakes.

"It's okay to go in, right?" I asked her, pointing toward the lake.

"If you can stand it. Stick close to shore, though. The numbing comes on fast."

"Does it have a name?" I asked.

"Map says Trapper Lake."

"Gross," I said. "Trappers trap things."

"Yes, they do."

That was the best she could come up with? Brooklyn never stopped working and organizing enough for friendly banter.

A cloud was passing in front of the sun. Now the lake looked more sapphire than turquoise, but the shape hadn't changed, of course. "I'm going to call it Bead Lake, if you don't mind."

"Works for me," she said.

"Can I set up my tent next to you two?" Vidal asked, dragging his backpack behind him.

"Actually, I'd prefer it if you picked a spot down by Kai," Brooklyn said. "Girls over here, boys over there. I think it's a better arrangement."

Did she know about Maddox's midnight visit? Her expression gave nothing away. I shrugged at Vidal, who made a weary pivot.

The frigid lake water was a shock but not an unwelcome one. I walked in a few steps and then dipped down and up for a high-speed bath. My feet were already aching from the cold, but I wasn't going to miss my chance for clean. I leaned my head over and dropped my hair back into the water, letting it spread out like silky seaweed. By the time I lifted my head back up, I had spectators.

"Is it warm?" Maddox asked. Instead of waiting for my answer, he pulled off his shirt and ran past me into the water, stumbling just as he registered the cold. He stood up fast, yelling a very forbidden word, then splashed wildly back out.

The other boys laughed. I was already on the rocky shore, rubbing my skin with my too-small camp towel.

"Yeah, you try it," Maddox said, shoving Dash into the water. Before Elijah could scramble away, Maddox grabbed him around the torso and tossed him in behind Dash. The boys yelled and staggered out, hardly wet at all.

Meanwhile, Greyson had stripped to his shorts and walked in without flinching, like he could stay there all day.

I made my way over to a flat, sunny boulder. For the next minute, the boys and their teasing calls disappeared as I lay against the warm rock surface, seeing nothing but the orange glow of my eyelids, feeling every tingling pore in my skin, feeling transformed.

"Hey, what's up with Vidal?" Maddox asked.

So much for my moment of bliss. I sat up and blinked in the light. Vidal had entered the water on the opposite side of the lake. It wasn't too far, but Kai and Brooklyn didn't like it.

"Hey, Vidal, we need you to stick with the rest of us," Brooklyn called as Kai started walking briskly along the shoreline.

Not hearing them, or choosing to ignore them, Vidal swam straight out to the middle of the lake. All the other boys were on the shore by now, in various stages of dress, shivering from the icy water. What was Vidal thinking?

"Friend, that's not safe," Kai called. "The cold can catch up to you all of a sudden and you'll have trouble swimming back."

But now Vidal was just staring at us, treading water.

"Vidal!" Brooklyn called. "NOW!"

"Dude's a freaking narwhal," Maddox said.

"Maybe his parents are Navy SEALs," Dash said.

"Vidal. Narwhal. That rhymes, actually," Elijah said, teeth chattering.

None of us could take our eyes off Vidal. He could hear us; we were sure he could. But he showed no signs of caring about anything we said. He held his chin just above the water and stared out at us with a look that was determined, stubborn, and, I realized, sad.

Kai began jogging back toward us again, then paused. There was no way to get closer to Vidal now. He was in the exact center of the lake. Was he trying to test himself? Prove himself? Or something worse?

"He's going down," Greyson said quietly.

Greyson was right. Vidal's chin dropped into the water, then his mouth. A few seconds after his nose went under, he came suddenly alive, thrashing and fighting. But his limbs weren't moving fast enough. It was like watching a movie scene suddenly shift into slow motion.

Greyson made a half start toward the water, but Brooklyn pushed past him. "I got this," she said severely. She waded in fast and then swam freestyle to where Vidal was bobbing and grabbing clumsily at the water. Somehow she found a way to get her arm around his neck, then swam him back to shallow water with determined one-armed strokes. Kai helped her haul him the last few feet to shore.

We stared, stunned.

"Come on," Kai called to us. "Help me get him dry!"

Jolted into action, we grabbed towels and sweatshirts and smothered Vidal from all sides. We could make him warm—I was pretty sure we could make him warm—but somehow it didn't feel like it would be enough to make things right.

➤◄ ❧ ➤◄ ❧ ➤◄ ❧ ➤◄ ❧ ➤◄

In a strange way, Vidal's emergency gave us our first moment of group bonding, even if we didn't fully understand what had happened. After we rubbed him down, we helped him get into dry clothes and gave him two cups of hot cocoa. He didn't move for a long time, just sat there in a ball, apologizing again and again until Maddox told him if he said the word "sorry" one more time, he was going to throw him back in.

"What were you doing, anyway?" Dash asked him when the counselors went off to consult about dinner.

"Yeah. Like, *trying* to drown?" Elijah asked.

"Leave him alone," Greyson said to them so sternly that they actually did.

We could tell Kai and Brooklyn were concerned about Vidal, too; I overheard them telling him he needed to stay within sight of one or the other of them for at least the next several days. It was for his own good, they promised. But Vidal looked more miserable than ever.

➤◄ ❦ ➤◄ ❦ ➤◄ ❦ ➤◄ ❦ ➤◄

"So, this is a big day," Kai said when we were sitting around the campfire a few hours later.

"Because nobody stinks?"

"You will always stink."

"Your mama stinks."

"My mama could whip your rear-end zone with her hands tied behind her back."

I dug into my rice and beans. It was becoming a familiar chorus, the boy talk. Like the drone of voice-changed mosquitoes but with even less purpose.

"Listen up," Brooklyn said, getting us back to business. "The plan is to stay camped here for a week."

A feeling came over me like when Mom fluttered up my bedsheet and let it settle back on my body, cool and just right. Brooklyn couldn't have said anything to make me happier, except, perhaps, to tell me that a new kid named Zinzie was arriving after dinner—and bringing ice cream.

"We're proud of you for making it this far as a team," Brooklyn said. "Now it's time for a different kind of work."

"Yes!" Elijah said, pumping a fist in the air. "No more milestones!"

"Actually, we're moving on to the bigger ones," she said, tapping her clipboard. "Our next milestone is called Talking Truth. It'll take six nights."

Kai explained that we were each going to take turns speaking about our lives back home and what we thought brought us to TrackFinders.

"A scary guy on a horse," Vidal said quietly, stuffing his hands into his sweatshirt pocket.

Everyone laughed because it was funny but also because we were relieved he was ready to crack jokes, relieved he was here to be able to crack jokes.

Kai looked around the group with his usual encouraging smile. "So. Talking Truth. Who's brave enough to go first. Elijah?"

"Why do you always ask me first?" he said.

"'Cause you're the shortest." Maddox grinned.

"And the ugliest," Dash added.

"Shut up," Elijah said, mouth full of food.

"Dash, Maddox, you're on trash duty tonight," Kai said.

"I'll go," I said, to put an end to it. "What do you want to know, exactly?"

"Why don't you tell the group a little bit about your life in Lexington—school, activities, friends—basic stuff," Kai suggested.

"Well, I have a lawyer mom and a lawyer dad," I began. "My little sister, Vivian, she'll probably be one, too." I didn't know what else to say. "It's not for me, though, the law. Despite my name."

"Aren't you named for Ginny Weasley?" Elijah asked.

I shook my head. "That's what everyone thinks. But it comes from Ginsburg, believe it or not. As in Ruth Bader, the Supreme Court justice. Mom loved her."

The boys cringed.

"At least they didn't call me Ginzy. My best friend is Zinzie. We would have sounded like a pair of circus poodles."

Kai smiled. "So tell us what kinds of things you do with yourself, how you spend your time."

"Really? It's not very interesting."

"Come on, you must have done something bad," Maddox said with a half smile.

"Why else would you be here?" Dash added.

"I don't know. I've been sort of a scholar-athlete type most of my life. You know—tennis. Honor roll. Kind of a nerd, really."

"Really," Maddox repeated, giving me a quick once-over, like he'd missed something the first time.

"Snore," Dash added.

Kai and Brooklyn gave me long stares. And waited.

"What?"

"You still play tennis?" Brooklyn asked with that breakfast-cereal matter-of-factness.

Of course. This was something we'd talked about on the van ride in. I shook my head.

"And did you make honor roll this spring?" Kai asked.

He knew. I could tell he knew. I tried not to get defensive.

"Okay, so sure. I quit tennis this spring. And my grades took a little tumble. And I started to wonder what the point of it all was—a perfect GPA and glowing college applications, that kind of thing. So what?"

Elijah coughed.

"So basically I'm here because I got my first B."

"Well, maybe you can explain what set you off," Kai said, nudging me along.

"Sure." It wasn't fun to sit in the hot seat, but I wasn't going to lie. "I just got upset about what's happening to the..." I lifted my hand to the space around us. "To everything. I mean, the Earth is burning up. Pretty much everything is going to die. Drown. Burn. Starve."

Elijah's mouth was hanging open.

"You're fun," Greyson said, but for the first time since we'd arrived, there was an actual flicker of interest in his eyes.

"Tree hugger. 'Wah—they're killing all the baby polar bears.' You really believe that BS?" Dash asked.

"Dash, that's two days on trash," Kai told him.

"Yeah," I said, "actually, I do. Do you know how many glaciers have melted? How many billions of birds we've lost? How many bees? The world's on fire, you guys. We're in a massive death spiral."

"Fake news," Maddox deadpanned.

I couldn't tell if he meant it or not, but I wasn't going to let it go unanswered. "Oh, I see. You guys know better than thousands of trained scientists with decades of experience. Is that it?"

"Chill, Ginny. I was just yanking your chain," Maddox laughed, which only rankled me more. He glanced at Dash, who nodded like a bobblehead.

I turned to Kai and Brooklyn. "If my parents think I need to be in therapy camp because I'm upset about what's happening to the world, well, then they're the ones who should be here with these losers."

The fire popped. Elijah glowered.

"That's a warning, Ginny," Kai said.

"What?"

"You called us losers," Greyson said. He looked amused.

I'd never had a warning in my life. I crossed my arms across my chest. Of course I shouldn't have said "losers," but if I explained that I'd meant just Dash and Maddox, it wouldn't exactly help my case.

"I'm sor—"

"You seem a little angry, actually," Maddox said.

"Must be that time of the month," Elijah volunteered.

"Dude," Vidal said to him. "Not cool."

"Elijah, that was uncalled for," Kai agreed. "I need an apology and you're sweeping up the campsite tomorrow."

"Do bears smell it?" Dash asked Maddox. "Is she going to be a friggin' bear magnet?"

Maddox punched him in the arm, but it didn't make me feel any better.

"I hate this!" I said, standing up. I turned to Brooklyn. "This is our big milestone? Heckled by the … by the …"

"Handsome dudes?" Maddox suggested.

I had the weirdest impulse to spit on him. What was it with this place? It wasn't making me more functional; it was making me an actual delinquent.

"All right," Brooklyn said, standing up. "Looks like we may need to take a pause here."

"Oh, great. You're just going to let it go," I said incredulously.

She shook her head and pointed at an impressive band of dark clouds advancing swiftly toward us. Lightning zigzagged out of the midnight tarp.

"Let's clean up fast so you can be in your tents when the storm hits. If it passes quickly, we may have time to get back to the circle. But if not, you can use the extra time to finish your letters home. There's been a lot to, um, reflect on today."

"You can say that again," Maddox said, eyeing me across the campfire.

Fifteen minutes later I lay in my tent, listening to the raindrops batter the nylon. A squad of spindly insects had sought shelter between the rainfly and the top panel of my tent—thin black forms silhouetted against the mesh. I pressed my finger against the panel and a couple of them lifted and hovered, as if reluctant to depart.

I pulled out a sheet of paper.

Dear Mom and Dad,
How could you think this was okay? At first I was sure it was
a mistake, that two people who loved me wouldn't actually,
on purpose, do something this cruel. You said this was a backpacking trip, not a stupid quasi-therapy camp with ridiculous

milestones and a million rules. You lied to me! And you didn't even think it was a problem for me to be the only girl here??

Dad, you always say we're only as good as the company we keep, right? So if I come home as angry and messed up as a bunch of dysfunctional teenage boys, it's all your fault. And if I don't make it out at all, well, that's on you, too.

Ginny

I poked another insect and it fluttered up for just a second before returning to the nylon.

"Love the loyalty, guys," I told them.

Around here, you could forget the meaning of the word.

CHAPTER 10

We left our campsite just before dawn the next morning with nothing on our backs but featherweight daypacks. After days of hauling my loaded backpack, I felt like I was flying–flying through a bright, wide landscape that was set on lifting my spirits. Wildflowers sprang up in the green valleys in rolling patches of purples, whites, reds, and yellows. The sun climbed a cloudless blue sky. The trail ribboned over and around the slope before us, turfy and irresistible.

I pulled off my fleece and tied it around my waist. "Have you done much of this before–hiking, I mean?" I asked Elijah as we climbed. His leg muscles looked a little, well, underutilized.

He turned and gave me a look.

"Want me to carry something for you?"

He shook his head. "Don't try to act nice," he told me. "I know you hate us." He stalked off.

"Wait–I don't hate you," I called after him. "I don't even know you!"

When I turned my head, I saw that Greyson had witnessed the exchange.

"Looks like you just lost a friend," he said.

"Yeah, well, don't worry about me," I sighed. "A posse of mosquitoes moved into my tent last night, and we're really starting to bond. So I'm good."

Another flicker in the hazel orbs. "You're kind of funny."

I gave a half shake of my head. "Actually, I'm kind of sad."

The rest of the group had decided to stop for trail breakfast on a slope covered with a jumble of gray rocks. The smaller ones made grinding noises as we hiked on top of them; the medium ones held our weight like stepping-stones; the largest ones were big enough to climb up and sit on.

Kai handed out granola bars and I settled down on a boulder-for-one. I didn't mean to be antisocial, but it was nice to just focus on the scene before me. The broad field below us was filled with puffy white stalks that looked like exploding Q-tips, downy batons. If I turned my head at just the right angle, I could believe I was alone out here. Me, the jumbly rocks, the meadow ear swabs, the blue sky, and—

"Oops," Dash said, striking my head as he took off his backpack. "My bad. You know us losers . . ."

But I didn't even register the hit. Because just in that moment, I caught sight of something peering at me from a nearby rock. A tufted brown form sitting perfectly still. Potato-shaped. Ears like two scraps of felt.

"Oh," I said, my heart swelling like a silly balloon.

It was a pika.

Here.

Now.

With me.

I had been thinking and dreaming about pikas for so long that this one's presence felt like a minor miracle. The pika was round and fabulous and oh-so-alive. The sun caught the tips of its fur, highlighting the golden fluffiness.

"Hello, you," I said quietly. "I'm so, so happy to see you."

The pika stared. Its nose quivered. It really did have a teddy-bear mouth.

My eyes felt watery, as if I'd tasted my first sugar. I didn't move, hardly daring to breathe.

Several minutes passed before I even remembered all the terrible stuff I knew about the pika's future. This little bundle of life. Did it have any idea?

There must be a proper way to commiserate with the world's most climatologically challenged animal, but I didn't have the first idea of what it was. Should I say some sort of pledge or prayer? An incantation, even? I needed a handbook full of guidance and rituals.

Or maybe the rituals were mine to create.

"I'm so sorry, little guy. About everything we've done wrong."

The pika held still. There was thinking going on inside that furry head—I knew there was. I just wished I had a way to under-stand it.

"You really are insanely cute," I said, giving up on the rituals. "But you probably hear that a lot."

If the pika had squeaked out a response, I think I would have been less surprised than I was by the object that came flying over my head, striking the boulder just inches below its perch. The pika scrambled away and a rock clattered down the hill.

I wheeled around and saw Dash and Maddox standing right behind me, casually eating their granola bars.

"Did one of you just throw that?" I asked.

"Throw what?" Maddox asked, shaking a second bar into his palm.

"A rock."

"Rock? Sure!" Dash said with a sloppy grin. He swiped a stone off the ground and tossed it over my head, all in one motion.

"Stop! You'll hit it!" A wave of protective rage rose up in me.

"Hit what? Oh, wait. Was there a polar bear cub over there?" he asked, casting his eyes across the slope. He bent to pick up another rock.

Before he could toss it, I sprang forward and gave him a hard shove. He stumbled back against a large boulder. Maddox laughed, and when Dash got over his surprise, he started laughing, too. He drew his arm back, preparing for another throw.

"Stop! Stop! Stop!" I screamed, overcome by the possibility that a pika might be hurt right before my eyes if I didn't do something now. I threw myself at Dash again.

"Ginny—whoa," Brooklyn said, running over and grabbing my arms.

"Grab *him*," I said, nodding at Dash. "He's the problem."

All the boys were watching us now, riveted.

"He threw a rock at a pika," I explained.

"No, I didn't." Dash made a stupid smile. "What's a pika?"

"The awesome animal you just tried to kill."

"She's a nice kid, but she's hallucinating, Brooklyn," Maddox said, wadding up the granola bar wrapper in his hand. "Dashy didn't do anything."

"Then where did the rock come from?" I asked. My heart was still beating hard.

"Same place as all the rest of these rocks, I guess," Maddox said. He motioned behind him. "Uphill." His smile had never been more infuriating.

"You're a mother-spelunker, Maddox," Greyson said, speaking up from his rocky seat.

I gave him a grateful nod.

"Enough. All four of you are going to have to pump the water for the rest of the group tonight," Brooklyn said, easing up on my arms. "Together. Next bit of trouble, though, and you'll be doing it for a week. Got that?"

When I nodded, she moved off.

Maddox put on his sunglasses and I could see in the reflection just how unhinged I looked.

"I've been nothing but nice to you," he said to me. "I don't get why you can't be nice back."

"Forget her," Dash said. "She's a scary vegan eco freak."

I sat back down on my rock. It was possible that Maddox had done nothing worse than cover for his dumb brother, but it didn't matter. He was there and he hadn't tried to help. A pika's life had been on the line and he'd just laughed.

I ate my bar and looked around for more pikas, worried they wouldn't come back, worried they would.

"Five more minutes, guys," Kai called.

I didn't want to leave. When Kai called again, most of the boys started to line up on the trail, but I lingered till the last possible moment. What if I never saw a pika again?

"Ginny, you okay?" Greyson asked, pulling on his pack one boulder away.

"Yeah. Thanks. Just hard to leave, is all."

When I stood up, I spotted something shiny and green. It was Maddox's granola wrapper, wedged between two rocks. Before I could get to it, Greyson snatched it up and stuffed it in his back pocket.

"You can learn a lot about a dude by where he puts his trash," he said as we joined the line.

Maddox gave us a sideways glance, and then we all moved on.

I hiked hard for the next couple of hours. Exertion was good. The wild air and the sweeping views of distant peaks quickly blew the evil twins out of my thoughts. Before long, all I could think about was the pika. I'd seen one—an actual pika. Before the trip, I'd been so focused on how sad it would be to say my final good-bye that I hadn't appreciated how good it would feel to say my first hello. I dubbed the rocky slope Pika Peak in its honor and kept my eyes peeled in case another one popped into view.

I named more things. It kept my thoughts off the local delinquent life and on the trailside attractions. From Bead Lake and Pika Peak, the trail wound past Spruce Grove before following Skyline Ridge for what turned out to be a very long stretch of flat trail with jaw-dropping views in either direction. Kai pointed out little piles of rocks, called cairns, that marked the trail along the ridge. I counted cairns for the next half hour. A hawk circled below us, flaunting its freedom.

The boys didn't talk much until we spotted a small group of backpackers descending a trail on a far hillside.

"Yo, dudes!" Maddox shouted, trying to get their attention.

"Wait up!" Elijah called after them.

"We've been kidnapped!" Dash hollered.

"Drop your chocolate!" Elijah added.

"Take us to the city!" Vidal pleaded.

"Knock it off, guys," Kai said. "You'll give TrackFinders a bad name."

"You think it has a good one?" Greyson said under his breath.

We dropped down in elevation again, crossing a hillside I called Paintbrush Meadow that was dotted with tons of the red wildflowers. We took another snack break at Little Dipper Pond. Up in these peaks, you never knew when you'd turn a corner and see a mountain lake going all diamondy in the distance, but you always had to visit them when you did. I took off my boots and dipped my feet in the cold water until Brooklyn said we had to get moving again. Our milestone today was going to be another journaling exercise back at base camp before the next episode of Talking Truth.

Our trail was often a barely visible stretch of beaten grass or dirt. Despite the appearance of the backpackers, I didn't get the feeling people came through here very much. The traces of animals were much more visible, a ratio I'd never experienced before, even at my Vermont camp. Clumpy bird nests were tucked into tree branches and shrubs. Round holes pocked the side of a bank, and others appeared inside little volcano-like domes on the trail. As we hiked along, grasshoppers flung themselves across our path and little white butterflies fanned the trailside clover.

I was taking it all in when I suddenly got a whiff of something foul.

"Whoa. Who let one rip?" Dash asked.

"Something died," Elijah choked, covering his mouth.

He was right. Ten yards later we came upon a huge carcass splayed across the grass. I registered bones, blood, flies, and a brown hide, then turned away. I didn't want to see its eyes.

"What is this?" Dash asked, poking it with a stick.

"Elk," Greyson said, squatting close. "Mature bull, looks like. Check out those antlers."

"Where'd you learn that?" Elijah asked, sounding half curious, half suspicious.

"Hunting," Greyson told him.

"You *hunt*?" I said, unable to conceal my surprise.

He turned and gave me an even look. "You judge?"

"I'm not judging. I'm just... I don't know... disappointed."

He made a face.

"So what killed it?" Vidal asked, nervously searching the surrounding shrubs.

"Hard to tell at this point," Kai said.

"But whatever it is, it's still out here," Maddox said ominously, enjoying Vidal's reaction.

The boys—and even the counselors—seemed excited by the dead elk. I didn't get it at all. I hated seeing a dead animal. I hated seeing—or even imagining—when an animal was in pain without any possible source of relief. Was it because it was so helpless? Because I was? I'd never really known.

When we were back on the trail, Greyson spoke up from behind me. "So what's wrong with hunting, anyway?"

I sighed. Did we have to keep talking about this? "Well, it seems unfair, for one thing. Animals out here are just trying to survive. Don't you think they have it hard enough already?"

"What do you mean?"

"There are enough things making their lives miserable . . . and short. Why should they have to deal with you? You're just adding to their misery. You're not even part of their habitat."

"It doesn't feel like that when you're out there in it."

I didn't respond.

"I bet you have a room full of teddy bears and stuffed animals," Greyson went on. "I bet you've never touched a worm or caught your own fish."

"I've touched worms."

"Caught a fish?"

I didn't say anything.

"There's a big difference between plush toys and real animals. Real animals eat and get eaten. They're alive and then they die. That's reality."

Did he think I was an idiot? I wheeled around. "Is this what you tell yourself when you kill them—that you're keeping it real? Or are you just trying to make yourself feel cool? Because what I meant to say before is, killing animals for sport is pathetic."

He didn't say anything. Good. I turned back and hiked a few more steps, glad to be done with the unwanted debate. Then he spoke up again. "Who said it was for sport?"

I let the words sink in. Did Greyson really hunt for food? What did I know of his life back home? Maybe I was an idiot. I turned around, prepared to try again, but he'd already dropped to the back of the line to talk to Vidal.

I was left feeling weirdly hollow, but I couldn't tell if it was because of all the talk of dead animals or because Greyson was gone.

I started looking for signs of animals again, like the track finder I'd meant to become on this trip. If I saw a round burrow, maybe something would be peeking out from inside. If I saw fresh prints, maybe their owner would still be trotting near enough to see.

I was eyeing the droppings left on a rock by some local mammal—marmot? weasel?—when someone gave a loud shout from the front of the line. I looked up just in time to see an enormous black moose lumber across the trail in front of Elijah and crash into the trees. The surprise of it, the size of it, sent my heart thudding against my chest. But I didn't feel afraid, exactly. More like very, very alive.

"Whaaat?" Vidal exclaimed. "That cow thing was as big as a freaking dinosaur!"

"Moose," Brooklyn said. "Not a cow thing. A moose."

"It could have flattened me like a pancake," Elijah said, looking stunned.

"A male would have been even bigger," Kai said. "With antlers out to here." He stretched his arms to the limit on either side of his head.

"It was plenty big, whatever it was," Vidal said, sounding defensive.

Everyone went on high alert. We'd gone days without seeing anything bigger than a ground squirrel. The elk and the moose were a reminder that we weren't the biggest mammals on the mountain.

"It's like those hidden pictures," Elijah said, spinning in a couple of slow circles, taking everything in. "At first you don't see anything. Then all of sudden you realize what's there: the cup. The shoe."

"The poisonous snake. The deadly grizzly," Vidal added.

"The stone giant. The trogg."

They laughed and kept up the exchange. Maybe someone had made an actual friend. For the fiftieth time that week, I thought how much I missed Zinzie.

We ate our trail lunch on a fallen tree I named the Mono-Log after Kai gave us an epic lecture about the seven chakras, or energy centers, of the human body. Everyone munched on crackers and stared at the ground, willing him to run out of gas, and it didn't seem like pure coincidence that Brooklyn suddenly needed to completely re-lace her boots—several yards away from us.

By the time we reached a sweet tinkling spot I called Music Box Creek, we'd made almost a full loop without even realizing it. A half hour later we were back at our campsite, where we found two surprises waiting for us: freshly stocked food packs and a small sack of mail.

"Who brought this stuff?" Elijah asked, two letters in hand, looking as amazed as if a spaceship had just touched down beside us.

"Ray," Brooklyn said, passing me a letter. It was from Mom. "Vidal's friend with the horse."

"He's not my friend," Vidal said, eyeing the mail pouch from a distance, like he wasn't sure he wanted anything it contained.

Kai strode toward us with a fresh apple in his hand. "We love Ray. He works for TrackFinders and he keeps us alive. Anyone notice how light the food packs were getting?"

"So he brought everything in on his horse?" Dash asked.

"Seems like he did," Elijah said, wrinkling his nose at a pile of manure under the trees.

"He usually brings a pack mule, too," Brooklyn told us.

"Where does he come from?" Maddox asked. "Can I see the map?"

"Nope," Brooklyn said. "Not unless you want us to take your boots, too."

"Relax. I'm not going anywhere," Maddox insisted, putting up his hands. "I like you guys too much to leave."

"Good," Kai said, satisfied. "You can keep your boots."

Brooklyn handed me two more letters—one from Dad, one from Vivian. "But you still can't have the map. Camp rules."

I headed back to my tent with my letters. I ran my fingers over the handwriting, the postmarks from Lexington, but I couldn't bring myself to open the envelopes. The boys had been annoying with their stupid period talk last night and their behavior on Pika Peak. But my parents were still worse.

I slid the letters into the mesh pocket inside my tent and changed into my swim things. The little mustard-colored tent was growing on me. It didn't remind me of a coffin now so much as a butternut squash—bulbous, sturdy, reliable. The ceiling really wasn't so low. My sleeping bag and pad gave me a comfortable snooze spot. My backpack stored all my clothes. The mesh pocket kept my sunglasses, bandannas, and watch in easy reach. A loop from the top of the tent turned my flashlight into a ceiling light. And the rainfly staked out over my doorway created a covered porch for my wet boots and my ever-ready roll of toilet paper, stowed in a plastic bag. As I kicked my bare feet out of the tent and stood up on my wildflower lawn, I decided I'd have to explain it to Zinzie sometime—how camping in the backcountry really wasn't roughing it so much as finding a rough-edged corner of the world and turning it into home.

"I don't know why my parents complain," Elijah told the group at Circle Time that night.

We were back around the firepit, eating banana boats—a gooey combination of baked bananas, marshmallows, and chocolate chips. Elijah, hyper from sugar, had stood up on a log and announced he was ready to talk about himself.

"I get all my homework done. I'm doing Precalculus on Khan Academy."

"What's your typical day like, in terms of screen time?" Brooklyn asked him.

He scratched his belly. "What other terms are there?"

"Do you stop for dinner?" Kai asked.

"Why?" Elijah asked, dropping to a squat.

"Family time?" I suggested. "That one-hour-slot your parents schedule for spontaneous togetherness?"

Elijah blinked. "They get home kinda late. I usually just nuke a dinner and eat with Megabyte."

"Your cat?" Vidal guessed.

I pictured a big tomcat with fangs.

Elijah shook his head. "Betta fish."

"Betta fish," Dash repeated. He snorted loudly, then dug his finger into his nose like something had gotten dislodged in the process. Afterward, a patch of chocolate-marshmallow goo was left smeared on the rim of his nostril. You couldn't invent his kind of gross.

"You never hang out with a friend? Or go outside to a park or something?" Brooklyn asked.

I knew why she was asking. Elijah's life sounded incredibly lonely.

He shook his head and scowled. "You sound like my parents. And no. I would never voluntarily be that far away from an outlet."

"Dude, I totally get that," Vidal said, folding his foil into a neat square.

"You're a gaming addict, aren't you?" Maddox asked.

"No labels here," Kai put in.

"I am, though, I think," Elijah said, scratching his shoulder. "I miss my games so much my dreams have started getting pixilated."

"Well, let's see what a few more weeks at TrackFinders does for you," Kai said. He nodded at Brooklyn. "We have something special planned for tomorrow."

"Did Ray bring an Xbox?" Elijah asked hopefully.

"No tech talk, Elijah," Brooklyn told him. "And no."

"We're going to give you some time alone—far, far away from those outlets," Kai said cheerfully.

"Alone?" Vidal asked. I could hear the dread in his voice.

"Alone-ish," Brooklyn clarified.

"Like the way we're alone-ish when we go to the bathroom?" Maddox guessed.

Kai smiled. "Precisely."

Back in my tent, I finally opened the letters from home. "... *hope you're settling in ... trying to help ... lucky to find a place with openings ... counting on you to throw yourself in ... weather ... sunscreen ... tent ... bears? Miss you. Love you. Miss you/don't miss you ... write back soon.*"

They could have saved themselves the postage. Seriously. The letters were so predictable, I could have written them myself.

"Goodnight, Shepards," I whispered under my breath.

I glanced roofward. "Good night, skinny bugs."

I turned off my flashlight and lay down. I was here. Bundled in a lilac sleeping bag on a thin navy mattress on the hard soil of a high mountain in the western stretch of North America. I pulled an imaginary camera back farther and farther until I was only a miniscule form on a gigantic map. And somewhere across the continent, my family was sharing an evening inside a tidy little house in Lexington, Massachusetts, with its television and whooshing sound machine. The remoteness was surreal. And exactly how I wanted it.

CHAPTER
11

"One of our intentions at TrackFinders," Kai said over breakfast, "is for you to get to know someone better: yourself. And sometimes the best way to do that is to separate yourself from every other person for a little while so you can just be."

"Be what?" Elijah asked nervously. He was clutching his day-pack in his lap like it was a security blanket.

"Just *be*. Exist. Listen to your mind as it chatters and follow it where it takes you. Breathe into every chamber of your heart. Maybe even try to peer all the way into your soul," Kai said. "What color is it? What shape?"

"Dude," Maddox said, running his fingers back through his hair, "you're getting pretty woo-woo on us here."

For once, we all agreed. Maybe even Brooklyn. She took over.

"It sounds simple, but it's serious," she said. "You'll be sitting in one place alone for about two hours. While you're there, pay attention to yourself and the scene around you. Are you with me so far?"

Reluctant nods.

"We're calling this milestone Solo Souls. After you've spent some time absorbing the scene, capture something you see or feel with a piece of art. You have journals and pencils for drawing. But if you find another material you'd like to work with, go for it. You don't have to finish it all today, either. You'll be returning to this spot for several days."

We spent the rest of breakfast sorting out where each of us would be situated—away from camp, but within shouting distance of at least one other camper and of Brooklyn or Kai, each of whom would supervise half the group. Four of us would head up to where we'd started our hike yesterday. The other four would retrace our steps in the direction of Music Box Creek. For obvious reasons, I made a plea for the first option, and, as soon as we were within sight of Pika Peak, begged to make that my solo spot.

"So the talus slope is calling you, huh?" Kai said with a smile.

"Talus slope?"

He nodded. "It's a geological term for 'reposing rocks' that have tumbled down and collected on a slope."

"I like that."

"Then pick a boulder, any boulder, and find your own repose."

I laughed. "Dude, you're a poet."

I clambered up the rock pile until I reached a nice flat boulder, then threw down my backpack and turned to wave. The remaining trio continued on the trail and briefly disappeared into the nearby patch of trees I'd named Spruce Grove. Elijah must have opted to stay there; a few minutes later, Kai and Vidal emerged and hiked toward the ridge. I could just barely see Vidal's head as he settled into his ridgeline spot. Smart kid. He must have realized his chances of a bear surprise were small with open views in every direction. And in any case, Kai would be situated midway between the three of us, giving us added security.

I stretched out on the warm boulder and took in the sweetness of another Montana morning. Mega-blue sky. Morning sunshine. Cool breeze. Rocks dappled with black, white, and green lichen. The field of puffy white stalks—bear grass, Kai had told me. I pulled out my journal and tried sketching the scene, but it ended up looking like a bunch of random dots and lines. Art was never going to be my thing.

And then a high-pitched *eeep* filled the air.

When the second *eeep* sounded, I saw it: a pika sitting atop a nearby rock. It popped down and ran to a nearby patch of grass. Was it the same one I saw yesterday? Were pikas territorial like that? Were they loners? There was so much I didn't know.

The pika began nibbling on a pizza-size patch of grass, lifting its head from time to time to chew and scan the surroundings. I couldn't take my eyes off it. Reading about pikas, even seeing them in videos, was nothing like this—the difference between watching a romantic comedy and getting kissed by an actual boy. One was fluttery imagination; the other, the shock of life in all its awesomeness and awkwardness, too—like braces, elbows, onion breath or, in this case, a gnat flying into my eyelashes or the stiffness creeping into my legs because I was so afraid to move. But also, oh, the fluttery good part: Here was a real pika going about its daily routine right before my eyes. An impossibly adorable being. Fur and whiskers, wide eyes and busy mouth.

I wanted the moment to last forever. I thought about Kai's morning instructions and, when I peeked inward, I thought I really could see my soul. And it looked okay, actually. Better than okay. Sort of shyly, tentatively, momentarily... happy.

Intense. I pulled out my pencil and journal. I wanted to draw the pika in a way that would capture its poofy perfection, but I didn't even come close. My pika looked like a dustrag with six metal skewers poking out for whiskers. It did inspire a name, though. I decided to name the pika Bob. Short for Kebab.

"Yo, Ginny!" Kai was waving at me from his security post. "You good?"

I waved back.

"Fantastic morning, isn't it?" he called, biting into a carrot.

I nodded, hoping he'd remember that we were supposed to be "soloing" up here, in total silence. When I turned my eyes back to the grass pizza, the pika was gone.

"Elijah?" Kai yelled. "Everything all right up there?"

There was a moment of silence.

"Elijah? Hello?" Kai called, sounding slightly concerned.

"What? Yeah. Here," Elijah said at last, distracted or just waking up.

Kai looked relieved. "Vidal! Let me know you're there!"

Kai's shout-outs continued at regular intervals. I waited for Bob the pika to come back, and when he didn't, I blamed Kai.

He was loud, invasive, annoying. Why would a pika want to be around that? Even if it wasn't Kai's fault, the best part of my morning was over. My furry friend was gone, and I was left observing the thrilling antics of, well, lichen.

I started doodling and watched my scribbles take shape as a comic strip about me, the hungry pika, and the moment when Kai ruined everything with his obnoxious shouting.

After two hours, those of us in Kai's group joined up on the ridge for a late lunch. Vidal was humming. Literally humming. I couldn't tell if he was relieved to have survived his first solo or if he'd actually enjoyed being alone on Skyline Ridge, taking in the view. Elijah was just plain hyper. He snatched up his ration of six big rye crackers and ate them fast without putting anything on top.

"I never thought I could do that," he said triumphantly, brushing the crumbs off his mouth.

"What?" Vidal asked.

"Eat sandpaper straight-up."

It wasn't a bad comparison. The crackers were hard and dry with a rough surface that scratched your tongue if you didn't pile on enough toppings.

"Can you pass the peanut butter?" he asked Kai.

"What are you going to put it on?" Kai asked.

Elijah held up his index finger, but Kai nixed the idea, so he was left to eat raisins and chocolate and give Kai a hard time about his own meal.

"You eat more than any of the rest of us," he told Kai. "And more often."

It was something I'd noticed too, though I wasn't going to mention it.

"Yep. Have to," Kai told him, unperturbed.

"Why? Because being in charge burns up extra calories?" Elijah asked, wiping his hands on his cargo shorts.

Kai shook his head. "I'm diabetic."

"Wait, what?" Elijah asked. "Seriously?"

"Yeah." Kai laughed at Elijah's expression. "It just means I have to manage my blood sugars. It's a little trickier up here at elevation, but I've mostly figured it out. Extra food helps. And I keep a shot of my emergency medicine on hand in case things really get out of whack."

Vidal was watching an ant crawl toward him on his rock. "If I were diabetic, I'd stay close to a hospital all the time," he said, shifting out of the way when the ant got too close to his leg.

"Nah, man. That's no way to live. Who'd want to miss this?" Kai gestured at the view. I had to agree with him.

"What happens if your blood sugar gets wrong?" Elijah probed, palming a pile of raisins into his mouth.

"Elijah," I said.

"No, it's cool," Kai told me. "No reason to hide it. In fact, the whole group should know. Worst-case scenario is diabetic shock. Not pretty. If I show symptoms—dizziness, erratic behavior, rapid pulse, heavy sweating—I need a quick dose of sugar. A gulp of honey or a sugar pill helps. Or if that doesn't work, a shot of the serious stuff." He reached into his pack and pulled out an orange plastic box, a little bigger than a phone and with a medical label across the top. He slid it back inside. "Otherwise . . ."

"Yeah?" Vidal asked, moving to an ant-free rock.

Kai made the motion of slitting his neck.

"You die?" Elijah asked.

"Like I said," Vidal said, putting a square of cheese on a cracker. "Hospital parking lot."

"Don't worry, pal. I am well supplied. Not gonna happen." Kai popped a huge bite of his energy bar into his mouth and smiled as he chewed. "Now, who's gonna be brave and share their artwork from this morning?"

Elijah and Vidal stiffened, like they both had something to hide—probably that they hadn't done any artwork at all.

"I'll share," I said. "But you have to promise not to judge."

I tugged my journal out of my pack and flipped to the comic-strip page. The three of them leaned over and went silent. Elijah finally spoke up.

"I get the part about Kai talking too much . . . ," he began.

I glanced uneasily at Kai, whose face was a contemplative blank.

"Yeah. Hundred percent," Vidal said. He looked up at me, confused. "But what's up with the little talking potato?"

I clapped the notebook shut and shook my head. "I don't know why I even tried."

"It's cool, Ginny, really," Kai said. "It takes courage to share your artistic vulnerability like that."

"A lot of courage," Elijah giggled.

"I mean it, guys," Kai said. "Personal expression is really important. There's no such thing as bad art."

"Got it," Elijah said. He leaned in close. "But next time, maybe you should use an app."

We took a shortcut to Music Box Creek, arriving to find the rest of the group finishing up lunch beside an enormous pile of branches.

"What's that?" Elijah asked, ambling over.

"Greyson's art project," Dash snorted.

"Looks like it's waiting for a match," Elijah said, snapping off a twig.

"Bonfire! That would be awesome," Maddox agreed.

"Pyro," Dash laughed.

"Don't even think about it," Brooklyn warned with a nervous appraisal of the nearest trees. I had a feeling she was thinking about last summer's wildfires again.

Greyson took a sip of water, looking bored with the whole conversation.

Elijah nudged one of the branches with his foot. "Can I take a couple for the road?"

"Go for it," Greyson said. He stood up and went down toward the creek.

I had to rinse off my water bottle anyway, so I joined him for the view. Across the water was a green hillside with large boulders spaced out like stepping-stones for giants.

"Hogs. Chucks," Greyson said.

"Who, us?"

He shook his head and nodded toward the boulders. "The place is crawling with groundhogs, or woodchucks—whatever you want to call them. They've been watching me with their beady little eyes." "Beady" made it sound like he didn't like them, but his tone was halfway affectionate.

"Marmots," I told him. "Yellow-bellied marmots, I bet. They're groundhogs at altitude." I scanned the slope, jealous that he'd seen them first. "I need to meet them."

"Then come back again. Without them," he said, nodding toward the other boys.

Was that an option? My palms felt tingly, like they did before a big match.

"Ginny? Greyson? Time to go!" Kai called, making sure it didn't last.

➤·◄ ❦ ➤·◄ ❦ ➤·◄ ❦ ➤·◄ ❦ ➤·◄

All the boys were in a bad mood that afternoon. Brooklyn and Kai needed to do some work in their tents, so they gave us a menu of tasks and told us to start in wherever we wanted.

"'Tidy your tents,'" Elijah read officiously. "'Purify some drinking water and refill your bottles. Wash out your dirty clothes. Whittle a spoon. Braid a rope. Generate a spark (but if you do, stomp it out fast!).' What is this, *The Hunger Games*?"

"Ignore it," Dash said.

"We deserve some downtime," Maddox agreed.

It was the hottest day we'd had since we arrived. The boys draped themselves across the rocks and the ground, trading ugly jabs. I wanted to disappear into my tent, but it had turned into a bread oven in the sun. I dribbled some water over my head and plaited my hair into two French braids so at least my neck would stop sweating.

"You guys must be seriously bored," I told Elijah and Vidal when I caught them watching me braid.

"Girls are like, *spiders*," Elijah said. Then he lay down.

Vidal just nodded and turned away.

"What was your art project, Vidal?" Maddox asked, lying on the ground with his cap pulled over his face.

Vidal had rolled his T-shirt up over his shoulders—to cool down or even out his tan, it was hard to tell which. His arms were smooth and nutmeg brown. "Kai said we don't have to share."

"Why does it always feel like you're hiding something?" Maddox asked. "You training for covert operations?"

Vidal blinked. "Not really."

"Not *really*!" Maddox said, lifting his visor and sitting up. "So you kind of are?"

"Leave him alone, Maddox," Greyson said. He was absent-mindedly piling up pebbles on a rock to make tiny stacks, like cairns for the ants.

Dash whipped his flip-flop through the air. It struck two of the cairns and sent their pebbles flying. "Yes!" he said, throwing his hands into the air. His face was a mean, glistening gloat.

"What are you looking at?" he asked me.

I wondered how to keep myself from showing my disgust around Dash. It wasn't good to be that obvious. And then it came to me. The chicken trick. I plopped an imaginary rubber chicken right into his unruly mat of curls. It was, believe it or not, a significant improvement. I practically smiled.

"What?" he asked, noticing the change. "What?"

"Nothing," I said.

Maddox twisted himself around and stared at the tent where Kai and Brooklyn were working. "They're making phone calls in there, FYI."

Elijah woke up fast. "Wait, what? How?"

"They have sat phones," Maddox told him. "Satellite."

Elijah rolled his eyes. "I know what 'sat' means."

But Vidal looked curious. "How do you know?"

"I know everything," Maddox said. He returned to his prone position and pulled his cap back down.

"You're so full of it," Greyson said, shoving the last of the pebbles off the rock.

Tired of so much bad energy, I jumped up, seized with a sudden determination to mix things up. If I'd learned one thing from my dad—besides the beneficial uses of imaginary rubber chickens—it was that you didn't need regulation equipment to play his favorite sport. Dad could turn anything into a bat—a metal spatula, a golf club, a broom. Maybe I could, too.

"Who's up for baseball?" I asked the boys.

"Shut up," Dash moaned. "We're sleeping." He crossed his arms like a mummy and began to snort-snore. Elijah giggled.

I scanned the clearing. The branches Elijah had carted home from Greyson's stack—those would work.

"Elijah? Can I have these now?" I asked, picking them up.

"But those are my hiking poles!" he whined.

"I'll get you a new pair tomorrow," I promised.

Over by the campfire was a pile of pine cones Kai had collected on our hike. I made my way up to the edge of his tent.

"Kai? Would you be really mad if I used a couple of your pine cones as, um ... sporting equipment?"

"Not if no one loses an eye," he answered from inside.

"We'll do our best." I laughed, wondering if Kai was always funnier when you caught him off guard.

I had three bandannas in my tent—the green one, a pink one, and a navy one with constellations printed on top. I grabbed all three, then silent-pleaded with Greyson to let me borrow one of his. He pulled it from his back pocket and tossed it my way, then watched as I made a not-quite-regulation diamond on the rough grass.

"Okay, people," I called. "Pine cone baseball. Who's in?"

"This I gotta see," Maddox said, ambling over. One by one, the rest followed—out of blind obedience or dumb curiosity, maybe; no one looked actually enthused.

"So the rules are pretty much the same as regular baseball. Just with homegrown equipment, okay? Bandannas are the bases."

The boys still looked bored, but I kept at it.

"We'll play three on three. Dash and Maddox, you can captain." It was the best way I could think of to keep them off each other's backs.

They took turns choosing their teams. I ended up with Maddox and Vidal, and we were first at bat.

Greyson pitched. He had a good arm, but it took time to get used to throwing a pine cone. His first two pitches sailed right over Vidal's head. The third one fell two feet shy of the plate. Maddox heckled Greyson mercilessly and, worse still, Vidal swung each time.

"Those don't count," I assured him, hoping he wouldn't get discouraged. "Everyone needs to warm up a little."

"Aw, come on!" Elijah complained. "We'll be here all day."

"Yeah, well," Greyson said. "That's kind of guaranteed no matter what we do."

"Good point," I said.

Greyson's next toss flew three feet wide of the plate. "Don't swing!" I yelled to Vidal, to no avail. He thrust out the stick and spun in a complete circle. For a total fail, it was pretty graceful.

"Vidal, man, you sure you're not wearing a blindfold?" Maddox teased.

Dash snorted. "Dude looks like he's hitting a piñata."

To my surprise, Vidal just smiled. The kid seemed to be enjoying the whole pine cone baseball thing more than anything that had happened at camp so far. He seemed both oblivious to his own shortcomings and unaffected by the heckling.

Greyson threw the next pine cone softly into the strike zone. It was a total gift. Except Vidal missed again.

"Striiiike fifty-seven!" Elijah shouted. "Seriously—he's gotta be out by now!"

"Aw, don't make me go!" Vidal pleaded. He tapped his fingers on either side of his chest. "I was just starting to feel it. Right here! In my fourth chakra," he added, earning a few laughs.

"Uh-oh. He has a bad case of Kai," Maddox said, head shaking.

Vidal bent over the plate and shook his booty. "One more? Pretty please?"

None of us could help laughing now. Vidal just looked so ridiculously blissed-out.

Greyson nodded and threw a perfect fastcone that sent Vidal whipping around home plate in a complete 360.

"Now he looks like a windup toy," Maddox said.

"It's called a pirouette," Vidal said. And then, to my surprise, he did another—this time without the stick—and it was practically elegant. He handed the stick to Maddox. "Best sport ever," he told me.

"It's nature," I pointed out. "In case you didn't notice."

Vidal rolled his eyes. "I tried not to." But he was still smiling.

We ended up playing four innings. It took some time, but finally everyone settled into a rhythm—regular throws across the plate, some solid swings, a few serious hits, a lot of crazy scrambling, more laughs. It turned out that moving and sweating was better than just baking in the sun. Maddox struck out his first turn at bat, too, then hit a pair of triples. Elijah, Dash, Greyson, and I had a mix of singles, doubles, and strikeouts. And Vidal struck out over and over, but loved it the most. He was unpredictable, that kid. He could go from cranky withdrawal to full-on sunshine—and back again—in a matter of minutes. But for now, at least, he was in the good zone.

Dash was on the pitching mound when Vidal came up for his last turn at bat. He was still wearing his track pants, but he'd kicked off his boots two innings back, not seeming to care for once that he was barefoot on the grass and dirt.

"Strike one," Greyson said, when he swung at a pitch a mile from home plate.

"Read the cone, Vidal," I said. "Wait for the one that's yours."

He nodded.

The next pitch flew in fast and dropped right over the plate before Vidal could manage a full swing.

"Hey, batter batter batter," Elijah called. "Hey, batter batter batter."

Maddox shook his head. He walked over to Vidal and whispered something in his ear.

"What?" Dash said, paranoid. "What'd you tell him?"

I couldn't imagine what he could have said to help Vidal; maybe the whole thing was just a ploy to psych out his brother. Whatever it was, Vidal nodded, and Maddox walked away.

"What?" Dash said again.

"Just pitch it, man," Vidal said, shaking his butt again.

The pine cone flew straight toward home plate, and this time Vidal seemed ready. He swung at just the right time—a beautiful, even swing that would have definitely hit a baseball. Problem was, we were playing with a narrow pine cone that had been chipped away by three innings of play. His stick caught the bottom of the cone, sending it up and over his head. We all watched as it sailed toward the ground, struck the top of Greyson's water bottle, and ricocheted back up and into the lake, where it skipped twice before coming to a floating stop.

"No way!" Elijah called, cracking up. "That thing went in five different directions."

"That was insane," Maddox said.

"A thing of beauty," I agreed.

"But what's the call?" Vidal asked, putting his hands on his hips.

By any ordinary measure it should have been a foul. But nothing felt ordinary this afternoon.

Greyson eyed the pine cone, now bobbing on the water. "Home run. Definitely."

"Yeah, baby," Maddox said. He tossed his bat toward the campfire and whipped off his shirt. "Let's swim."

"Yes!" Dash agreed, following him toward the water.

Elijah tore after them, and play-pushed his way past. "Last one in has rotten chakras!"

We didn't really swim, of course. But we stood around in the water long enough to toss the pine cone and cool off, enjoying ourselves so much that no one seemed to notice who'd made it in last. I guess that meant all our chakras were just fine.

➤·◄ ✺ ➤·◄ ✺ ➤·◄ ✺ ➤·◄ ✺ ➤·◄

"We need to talk about trust," Brooklyn said at dinnertime. The playfulness of pine cone baseball was gone, replaced by a reminder that we were at TrackFinders and we needed to get back with the clipboard.

"We were trusting you to follow through with those tasks we assigned you. Did anyone do *anything*?" she asked in a semi-severe tone.

"We washed our clothes," Maddox said with one of his trade-mark winks.

"Yeah, like, inhabited," Elijah giggled.

I smiled. It was the most fun I'd had in a long time.

Brooklyn flashed us a warning look and continued with her lecture. "Trust is a powerful currency," she said, sounding weirdly like a Wall Street executive. "You do the right thing, it builds trust—just like building up coins in a piggy bank, like building credit. And if you earn enough credit, you can cash in on it."

"Cash in on it how?" Maddox wanted to know.

"Well, at home if you build up trust with your parents, they might let you stay out a little later. They might not jump to the worst conclusion the next time you miss a meal or a homework assignment," she explained.

"And around here, we might start relaxing some of our rules," Kai added.

"Which ones?" Elijah asked, looking eager.

"Which one are you closest to breaking?" Kai joked.

"Oh, I don't know. I didn't mean . . ." He scratched his head, looking nervous.

"Nah, it's cool, Elijah. This is probably a good time to tell you. Brooklyn and I were talking, and we both agreed that you and Ginny have built up some nice trust sharing your stories during your campfire sessions. Anyone else feeling ready to share?"

Vidal rubbed away a scuff mark on his sneaker and Greyson stared at the campfire, as closed up as he'd been on our first night of camp.

"I'll go," Maddox said, casually tossing something into the fire-pit. "More than happy to pop the lid off that can of worms. Dash, feel free to back me up here any time, all right, bro?"

Dash nodded and made one of his nervous sniffs.

"So, our parents are insane. Certifiably," Maddox began. "Dad makes so much money he doesn't know how to spend it all. All he can think about is how he could lose it. Or someone could cheat him out of a whole precious dime. Dude's totally paranoid."

Brooklyn cleared her throat. "What do you think, Dash?"

Dash nodded. "Insane and paranoid."

"Our mom's a stress puppy," Maddox went on. "She has some job, but her main job is self-care."

"'Some job'?" I repeated. I mean, I got that their parents were annoying, but they could at least name their mom's work.

Dash shrugged.

"What's self-care?" Vidal asked, like it was a phrase he'd never heard before.

"Making herself look and feel good," Maddox said. "Getting massages and manicures."

"She likes anything lavender," Dash put in. "Also podcasts. And white wine."

"Okay," Kai said. "Talk about yourselves now, guys. What's your relationship with your parents like?"

"What relationship?" Maddox asked with a crooked smile. When Kai looked confused, he added, "Twin boys and self-care? Not a good combo."

Dash nodded. "Dad works late and when he comes home he wants to chill. Grown-ups only. Mom's a little . . ."

"Self-involved," Maddox said, like he'd read articles.

"When I was little, I actually called our nanny Mama," Dash added.

"You had a *nanny*?" Greyson asked.

Dash nodded. "Consuelo."

Vidal shook his head. "Figures."

"She sewed a spacesuit for my teddy bear one Halloween. When I was Buzz Lightyear," Dash said, oblivious to their judgment.

For a moment I could see it—him—the cute little kid who had been there before the delinquent with the messy nostrils. Did everyone have a toddler inside them like that? Cute and perfect, like Vidal's little sister? I thought of the baby self-portraits Kai and Brooklyn had asked us to make of ourselves. Maybe there was a point to that milestone after all.

Maddox coughed, and Dash suddenly looked uncomfortable. "Anyway, Dad fired Consuelo 'cause her boyfriend was treating her badly."

"Wait, what?" I asked.

"Mom said it wasn't safe for us," Dash explained, "if she wasn't safe."

It was the kind of thing that made Mom furious—when the victim got victimized. "Did he pay her—" I began.

"Ginny," Kai interrupted. "Let's let these guys tell their story."

"That's pretty much it," Maddox said, folding his arms across his chest. "All they do is spend money on themselves. Dad's car. Mom's clothes. Their vacations. If they spend anything on us, it's to get us out of their hair. Like sending us here."

"Is that the only reason you think they sent you here?" Brooklyn asked.

Maddox pursed his lips. "Pretty much."

"Dash, you agree?" Kai asked.

Dash glanced at Maddox, then gave a half nod. "Mom says she can smell us for like an hour after we leave the room. So I guess she needed a full month off just to, what's the word?—de-fume the place."

"That's not the word," Elijah said.

"You don't think it had anything to do with your coping strategies?" Brooklyn persisted.

"Coping strategies?" Dash asked, his face a blank.

"Ways of dealing with your frustrations that they maybe considered inappropriate?"

"We don't hurt people, if that's what you mean," Maddox said quickly.

Brooklyn shook her head. "We're talking about risky behavior, unhealthy habits."

Dash suddenly got very busy digging into his chili.

"Hey, we're cleaner than the other kids in our grade," Maddox said defensively. "I mean, way cleaner."

"Mom and Dad always assume the worst," Dash added. "No matter what we do."

"That sounds hard," Kai said. "But trust is hard, too, and it usually goes both ways. I'd like you all to take a little time tonight to think about the building blocks of trust."

"There are certain questions we each need to ask ourselves," Brooklyn put in. "Am I being truthful? Am I taking responsibility for my actions?"

"Complaining's easy, see," Kai added, "but it rarely leaves you feeling better. Try self-honesty. Try thinking of your own personal responsibility. Try showing gratitude."

"For what?" Dash asked.

"That's a question we can't answer for you," Kai said. "But here's the thing: Every human is a human. You know? Even your parents."

He gave us a significant look.

And that meant . . . what? Everyone went silent. Did he think these were dazzling insights?

Elijah finally spoke up. "I mean, it's not like I ever thought they were gods."

"Well, give it some thought," Kai said, looking a little vexed. "And we'll talk more tomorrow."

Brooklyn nodded. "Now we'd like you to clean up," she said, standing up and tossing her Sierra cup into the cooking pot. "You know what to do."

176

"Every human is a human," Dash said when she and Kai were out of earshot. "Except us. We're just here to get ordered around."

CHAPTER
12

I woke up extra early and climbed out of my tent into the nip of morning. Nighttime was a giant reset button here in the mountains; I could hardly believe yesterday had been hot at all. I zipped up my fleece and pulled on my knitted beanie, then went to find a boulder to sit on. The sun was peeking above a peak and lighting up a line of rocks above camp, but it had a ways to go before it would be dropping its honey rays on me.

I hugged my arms around my bare knees and waited. The still surface of Bead Lake offered a perfect mirror to the spruces, straight-backed and sporting some excellent green fringe. Something stirred high up in one of their pointy tops, and the next thing I knew, two great brown wings unfolded and flapped, and a golden eagle lifted out into the morning sky.

"Gorgeous, huh?"

Kai spoke in a hushed voice and wandered toward me, wearing Tevas over his wool socks and cupping his water bottle like maybe it had warm tea inside.

I nodded. He sat down on a nearby rock and I braced myself for the usual chatter.

"Wanted to follow up on something I said last night, Ginny. And in your, er, comic strip. I'm a talker. Always have been. Can't help myself, apparently. But I don't want that to get in the way of your solo time. Seems like you really value watching wildlife, don't you?"

I nodded.

"Brooklyn suggested we extend a trust line to you and Elijah this morning."

"A trust line?"

"You know. Kind of let out the rope a little bit. Give you some more independence. What if I moved my post this morning over closer to Vidal and gave you guys a couple of hours without call-outs. Would that be nice?"

The feeling of sweetness was so strong, it occurred to me that maybe there was something legit about that trust talk. "That would be totally amazing," I told him. "I'd be so . . . you know . . . grateful."

He beamed. "Then this is progress."

My solo time that morning began as a long playdate with the world's most insanely adorable rock rabbits. Almost as soon as Kai left me, two of them popped up on the rocks and stayed in my sight for almost an hour. The pikas were in high gear, launching off the boulders. Dashing across the slope. Eating and collecting and *eeep*ing. After a while, I felt sure they'd gotten used to my presence. I didn't have to stay statue-still any more. Even when I sneezed, neither one of them went into hiding. Talk about progress.

I glanced at my watch. Kai said we needed to show up to Vidal's solo spot for lunch no later than noon. If we didn't, we'd be back to the regular shout-outs. No way was I going to let that happen.

The sun continued its hike up the sky, becoming stronger and hotter. Maybe that was why the pikas eventually went away. They'd be more comfortable in the cool of the rocks.

Wait. That wasn't quite it.

They'd *stay alive* in the cool of the rocks.

Damn, damn, damn, damn, damn.

Everything Mr. Stelling had lectured about in that awful class months ago was playing out again right in front of my eyes. Just because the pikas were alive now didn't mean they were going to survive longer than Mr. Stelling had predicted. In fact, this could be their last summer. Their last week.

I felt a wave of devastation. How could I have let down my guard and enjoyed myself the past few days—like pika survival was a spectator sport? I needed to do something. *Help* them. I had an overwhelming urge to scoop them up in my shirt and head for Canada.

But you couldn't outrun climate change. That was the thing—the sun was a formidable foe. Well, not the sun. Us. We were the ones ruining everything. Everywhere. A familiar grip tightened over my chest. I felt helpless and stupid. What was I doing? What was the point of being here, no matter how great the company or the scene? What was the point of anything?

I rubbed my head. It was hard having an existential crisis at high elevation, in sun this bright. I gathered up my things and headed toward Elijah's Spruce Grove. Kai would understand if I moved into the shade to avoid sunstroke.

As I approached the trees, I heard an unfamiliar noise—high and tinny. When it disappeared, I tried to re-create it in my head. Was it Elijah's water bottle bumping against a rock? Was it a new kind of songbird? I waited and listened, and when I didn't hear anything more I continued up the slope—at a measured pace so neither my steps or my breath would be audible. Soon I caught a different noise. A ping. This was not a Montana noise at all, at least not a natural one.

It sounded electronic.

Elijah was too absorbed in the action on the screen to notice my approach. He sat with his knees up, back against a trunk, playing a game on a genuine, real-life, totally illegal cell phone.

"What?" I shouted in surprise. "You are so busted, game boy."

He leapt up, startled, and slipped the device under his arm. It was too late; I'd already seen all I'd needed to.

"Oh my god—that's *my* phone! You have my phone!"

Like a scared squirrel, he panicked. And ran. Unlike a squirrel, though, he couldn't scramble up a tree, so he just ran as fast he could in the opposite direction. Away from Pika Peak, away from our trail, away from any place we'd been before. I followed him as fast as I could, but he had the head start and he was fresher than I was. He stumbled through the trees and headed up a hillside behind it.

"Elijah, come back!" I yelled. I could feel our trust line straining. If he pulled it any harder, it was going to snap. But he kept running and I kept chasing him, because the worst thing I could do, I realized, was lose him.

When I crested the top of the ridge, I saw him picking his way down a boulder field on the other side.

"Stop, you dork!" I yelled. "You're going to get us lost!"

He kept going.

"I don't care about the phone!" I yelled. "Just stop!"

He paused and bent at the waist, breathing hard. I hurried down the slope, thinking we were done with this foolishness, but when I got close, he took off again. He rounded a slope, but I had the momentum now and I caught up and grabbed him by the shirt. We stumbled at the same time and fell down in a field of rocks and grass on the edge of a broad valley.

"You little thief!" I said, sitting up slowly. I'd scraped my thigh against a sharp boulder. I pressed my hand against my skin and against the sting.

Elijah was too wiped out to talk at all. Gradually he sat up and brushed off his palms.

"You have a lot of explaining to do," I said. I put out my hand, and he reluctantly relinquished my phone. It felt hard. Cold. Alien. Wrong. I was almost disappointed the screen wasn't shattered. "I really wish you hadn't stolen this."

But Elijah was staring at something on the ground beside us. A string.

"What is . . . ?" I looked around us, trying to make sense of what I was seeing. Thin red string running in straight lines across the rocks. Well, almost straight. One of the strings was tangled around Elijah's foot, and when he stood up, he pulled down three of the stakes it was tied to.

"I'd appreciate it if you would freeze right there before you make everything worse," came a strained voice.

A woman was approaching us with a walking stick in her hand. She moved steadily, her lips pressed together in obvious displeasure.

"It took me a whole morning to set those up," she said when she reached us.

"I'm so sorry. We tripped," I said insensibly, shocked to encounter a new human for the first time in more than a week.

It was hard to see the woman's face under her wide-brimmed hat, but she looked older than my mom, with weather-worn skin and black hair streaked with gray. She knelt down and carefully guided the string off one stake and around Elijah's legs. She eyed the cell phone.

"Let me guess. You were taking selfies and didn't notice the plots."

"We weren't taking selfies," Elijah said irritably. "She was trying to kill me."

"Oh, well, that's better."

I stifled a laugh.

She set the first two stakes back in the ground, then began to knot the string around the third. I noticed that her hand was trembling. She didn't seem like the kind of person to be scared of us; maybe it was fury.

"Are you doing a study here?" I asked her.

"It's weird seeing an actual person," Elijah added, watching her with wonder.

She looked up fast. "Why? Are you two out here alone?"

I shook my head. "We're at a camp over on the other side of the ridge. TrackFinders?"

Her eyebrows went up in recognition, but not necessarily the right kind. She finished replacing the stake, brushed off her hands, and leaned on the walking stick to bring herself up to standing. "I thought you weren't allowed to stray more than a few inches from your counselors."

"We're doing trust solos," I said.

Elijah glanced at me uncomfortably. "Without the solo."

"Or the trust," I admitted.

I checked my watch and was startled to see that it was almost a quarter to twelve. "Shoot, Elijah. We have to get back for our check-in!"

We'd never make it without sprinting. Saying a quick goodbye, I took off with Elijah close on my heels. The panic made us fast. Halfway up the slope, I paused. I wanted to know what the plots were for. I turned around to call back, but the woman was already picking her way back across the rocks. In the distance I could see a couple of tents, a fire ring, metal boxes.

Elijah pushed my back. "Go! We have to go!"

It was a furious, panicked race up and over the ridge. When we stumbled into Vidal's solo spot, Kai held up his watch: 11:59. "Nice, job, you two. Did you enjoy your morning?"

Elijah dropped to his knees and wheezed melodramatically.

I gave a thumbs-up. "Sorry. We cut it too close. It's hard to keep track of time out here."

"You ran," Kai smiled. "I like that you ran."

Vidal pointed at my leg. "You're wounded."

The scrape had gotten a little uglier. Thin streaks of blood ran down my leg. "Did I forget to mention the grizzly?"

Vidal looked at me with faux resentment. "We do not joke about these things."

"Aw, come on," I said, giving him a playful nudge. "It's good to visualize our resilience."

"Hey, I like that!" Kai said, nodding eagerly.

"Resilience, yes," Vidal said, carefully arranging three crackers on his bandanna. "Bear attack, no."

Kai directed us down the trail after lunch, saying we'd pick up the others and then spend the afternoon on journaling exercises and maybe some lakeside yoga. As we approached Music Box Creek, Elijah, in the lead, came to a sudden stop.

"What the...?"

Greyson's heap of wood was gone. In its place was a large round ring of interwoven branches—like a giant crown, or a paddock for a pint-size pony. Stouter branches were arranged vertically about every two feet, providing the structure around which smaller branches had been woven in and out. It was dramatic. Mind-popping. Like something you might see in a sculpture garden, except it was here, in the middle of the Montana wilderness, which made it ten times more startling and a hundred times more cool.

"Greyson, you made this?" Elijah asked, running forward.

"No, he ordered it on Amazon," Maddox said.

The four of them were sitting on the ground around the remnants of their trail lunch—open jars of jam and peanut butter, glistening cheese, and a bag of cracker crumbs.

"Man oh man, Greyson. It's awesome," Kai said, gripping a section of the sculpture and admiring its strength. "Willow, right?"

Greyson nodded.

"How did you learn to do this?" Vidal asked as he walked the full perimeter.

Greyson shrugged. "Weaving's just weaving. You ever make one of those construction-paper mats in preschool?"

"Don't make it sound like less than it is," Brooklyn said, tightening the lid of the jam jar. "That's art."

Kai nodded. "Have you seen the work of Andy Goldsworthy?"

Greyson shook his head.

"Well, you should," Kai said. "He does art like this too."

"It's not art," Greyson insisted.

As I ran my hands lightly along the top edge of the sculpture, he stepped up beside me. "It's not done yet." His brown hair was falling almost across his eyes. This close, his freckles looked like dots in one of those puzzles, waiting to be connected.

"It's already genius," I said quietly. "What's it going to be when you're done?"

He shrugged. "A thing."

"What kind of thing?" I persisted. "A pen? A fort? A marmot motel?"

When he looked uncomfortable, I thought about our conversation from the other day. Wait. He wouldn't have made . . . "A hunting blind?" I asked, trying not to sound disgusted.

He squinted, then shook his head like I was out of my mind.

"Sorry—maybe that was dumb."

"Not dumb," he said, stepping away. "Disappointing."

➤•⦊ ❡ ➤•⦊ ❡ ➤•⦊ ❡ ➤•⦊ ❡ ➤•⦊

That night we stayed up extra late for Circle Time, sitting on the edge of Bead Lake to take in the view. A full moon lit up the sky and its reflection bounced on the water like a floating lantern. It was the kind of night that puts you in the mood for thinking deeply—even bonding. I stayed quiet, hoping if I did, somebody's secrets might come out of hiding, like pikas.

"Greyson, how 'bout you do some sharing tonight?" Brooklyn said. "I think we might be ready to hear more about the male line of your family."

I was glad she asked. I'd been curious about it ever since our first night.

"No, thanks," he said, taking a sip from his water bottle.

"What's going on?" she asked him.

"I just don't feel like sharing. Is that a problem?"

It was the kind of normal teen resistance I'd come to expect at TrackFinders; I just didn't like it coming from Greyson. Not now. I wanted to hear him talk, and I didn't want him getting on Kai's and Brooklyn's bad sides.

"You sure, Greyson? This is what we were talking about with the trust, remember?" Kai said.

Greyson lifted his face just enough to meet Kai's glance. "You could trust me to know when it's time to share."

"That sounds a little confrontational, buddy," Kai said.

"We're not buddies, though," Greyson pointed out. "That's the thing. You've been paid to spend four weeks trying to shape me into your idea of a functioning person, right? Don't get me wrong—I get that you're just doing your job. And I'm down with being here in the mountains. But the whole thing's totally messed up. Why do you two get to decide what functional looks like?"

There was a moment of collective stunned silence. I could feel the other boys taking in his words, turning them over, maybe wondering why they hadn't thought about TrackFinders in quite the same way.

"It feels kind of like brainwashing to me," Greyson continued before Kai and Brooklyn could say something to redirect the conversation. "Also, I don't know how much this thing costs, but I'm guessing it isn't cheap. And my mom? She has nothing to spare. So basically I think she put her whole financial situation on the rocks so you two could turn me into the kind of person *you* think the world needs. That's some crazy kind of trust."

I expected Kai and Brookyn to either ignore him now or start getting defensive. But to his credit, Kai just nodded. "That does sound kind of crazy, Greyson. I wish you'd believe us when we say we don't have a plan for what kind of person you're going to be after this."

"Sure feels like it," Vidal said quietly.

"Why else would you have all those milestones?" Elijah asked.

"Because they're what's keeping you on track," Brooklyn said. Her unquestioning faith in the milestones was really starting to get on my nerves.

"*Your* milestones. *Your* track," Greyson pointed out.

I nodded. He was totally right—Kai and Brooklyn weren't letting us choose anything for ourselves.

From the look in Greyson's eyes, I could tell he'd registered my agreement. "And what does 'functional' mean, anyway?" he went on, no longer sounding like he was speaking just for himself. "Being just like everyone else? Conforming to some kind of corporate, moneymaking plan for following the rules and getting ahead, even if that means ignoring what it does to everyone else? Like, poor people? Nature?" He caught my eye and then turned back to the counselors. "'Cause if that's 'functional,' I don't think any of us here wants it."

It was rebel talk. In a lot of ways, it reminded me of what I'd been feeling with my parents all spring. They thought I was messing up because I'd stepped off Dad's racing line, my supposedly certain path to success. But from my perspective, it was the racing line itself that was totally messed up.

"'Corporate' isn't a word that describes anything Kai and I have valued in our lives," Brooklyn began, choosing her words carefully, like she was stepping from rock to rock across a tumbling stream. "And we honor your unique identity and creativity—I promise. I do understand your distrust, though, Greyson, and I'm not going to argue with it. It's on us to prove that we're here out of genuine concern for your well-being. I just want to reassure you that we don't have a plan for what you look like when you come out. We don't want to change you."

"I believe that," Maddox put in, to everyone's surprise.

Dash looked like he couldn't decide whose side to take.

"All we want," Kai said, "is for you to find your authentic self." It sounded like more of Kai's woo-woo talk, and Greyson rolled his eyes. But Kai pressed on. "You're at a time in your life when you have a lot of choices. And an awful lot of them are self-destructive, or will eventually take you down the path to self-destruction. You guys know exactly what I'm talking about. And the bottom line is that none of us wants you to destroy yourselves. Not me, not Brooklyn, not your parents."

Greyson pressed his lips together, looked away.

"Thanks for sharing this much, though," Brooklyn said quickly. "We want to know what you guys are thinking, even if you don't think we'll like hearing it."

"That's right," Kai said earnestly. "Some say disagreement is the birthplace of truth."

"Okay, so anyway," Brooklyn went on hurriedly, "Vidal—if you'd like to share instead of Greyson, we probably still have time. What do you say?"

The moon surfed a couple of small waves on the water. Something hooted in the distance.

"Actually, my head hurts," he said, putting up his hood.

"I'm sorry to hear that." Brooklyn glanced at Kai. No one believed Vidal had a headache, but what else could she say? Trust was a funny animal.

"Okay, then," Kai said, slapping his hands on his knees. "Who wants to help me put away the food packs tonight?"

"I will," Maddox said, getting up fast.

"Thanks, guy," Kai said.

Brooklyn headed down to the lake with her water pump. Maddox settled in close beside Kai and they walked away like they were co-counselors, leaving the rest of us behind to be the kids.

"When did he get to be such a Boy Scout?" I asked Greyson under my breath.

"I don't know," Greyson said, gently tapping my arm like his index fingers were drumsticks. "But I don't trust it."

>-< ♥ >-< ♥ >-< ♥ >-< ♥ >-<

I had a hard time falling asleep. Being inside a sleeping bag felt too confining, so I tried lying on top of it instead. But that just left me cold.

Greyson's talk about TrackFinders had stirred me up, feeding a festering uneasiness about a lot of things—the program and what it was trying to do to us, that was part of it. But I was also still uneasy about the pikas and what I was doing here with them. I didn't want to go back to my solo spot for more navel-gazing, or soul-gazing, for that matter. What was the point? I wasn't even sure it made sense to be around them so much. I didn't want to get any more attached to something that was slated to die so soon. And what good did it do to squeal and call them cute, anyway? None. What a waste. What an embarrassment to my DNA.

I thought about my cell phone, too. Should I turn Elijah in? Take a chance of keeping it, at the risk of getting caught? As I deliberated, it felt like the phone was ticking away in my backpack like the telltale heart in that spooky old story by Edgar Allan Poe. Of course it wasn't really ticking. In fact, when I peeked at it, I saw that it had run out of juice. That wasn't a big surprise. The real mystery was how Elijah had managed to get any use out of it at all. He must have really rationed out the battery power just to get it to last this long.

Back in my sleeping bag, I rolled over three times, unable to get comfortable. I was never going to fall asleep.

I replayed the evening's conversation again, only this time I ended up in a different place: Greyson playing a drumroll on my arm. That had stirred me up, too.

How could one body contain all these crazy feelings? No wonder the sleeping bag felt too small.

I flipped myself over two more times. Enough. I was like a pancake that was never going to turn out right. I needed to change things up and start over.

I stepped out of my tent, pulled up the stakes of the rainfly, and yanked it away. Now the mesh top of the tent was exposed to the full night sky and whatever elements it might decide to deliver. But who really cared if it rained?

Inside my tent, the effect was immediate. The air blew in, the moon loomed, and the universe stretched on and on. I stared out for a long while, following the stars as far as they would take me, then drifted into sleep.

CHAPTER
13

"I found out why Vidal's here," Maddox said to me the next morning.

We'd been assigned to wash breakfast dishes on the far edge of the lake. I scoured a chunk of oatmeal that was stuck to the bottom of the cooking pot, then moved on to the lid using the same cloudy water. Out here in the backcountry, you only got one rinse.

"You curious?" Maddox asked.

I glanced up, which was all the encouragement he needed.

"Shoplifting," he said with a knowing lift of his brow.

"He told you that?"

"I overheard Kai and Brooklyn talking. Started with small stuff—you know, stupid drugstore junk. Then he moved on to clothes. Leather. Furs. Jewelry. Bet he sold it all for a heap of Benjamins."

I got up and poured the dirty oatmeal water into a hole we'd dug under the trees. When I came back, I added a spoonful of water and wiped the pot clean.

"I told you he had something to hide," Maddox said, dropping a metal mixing spoon into the pot.

"Well, doesn't everybody?" I set the pot on a rock and moved on to the Sierra cups.

I didn't want Maddox messing with my mind, but it was hard not to think about what he'd said as I watched Vidal hiking ahead of me later that morning. I hardly knew anything more about him than I did after the three-legged races: He was moody, a little anxious. He didn't like nature and he had a baby sister named Lola, and something had made his parents enroll him in TrackFinders. But a criminal record? That didn't seem right.

Then I remembered his gear, with the price tags still on. Were those stolen goods? No, that wouldn't make sense. Taking off the tags would be the first thing he'd have done.

Anyway, if Vidal was a thief, he wasn't the only one here. As soon as I could, I climbed up to Elijah's shady Spruce Grove.

"So 'fess up," I said, putting on a tough-guy voice. "How'd you get it, anyway?"

"Your phone?"

"What else?"

He leaned back against a tree, his lips a pout. "I stole it from your tent the first day—before Brooklyn got there."

"Seriously?" I said. "That was bold. There were so many people around. And what if she'd asked me where it was? Or I'd asked her?"

"I was looking at four weeks without electronics," Elijah said, as if that answered everything.

"But how much did you even use it? I mean, the battery didn't run out till yesterday."

"Mwah-ha-ha," he said, sticking his teeth over his lower lip, vampire-style. "You underestimate my need." He reached into his daypack and pulled out a small rectangular box. "I had this."

"Is that a solar charger?"

He nodded. "I hid it before she could get it too."

"Where?"

"In my underwear." He waggled his eyebrows.

"Okay, gross."

"And thanks for telling me your passcode, Pikagirl," he said, practically cackling. "It only took me a few minutes to figure out which letters to leave out."

He must have registered my look of annoyance. His smile faded and he looked me up and down. "Are you going to turn me in?"

"Maybe."

"Really?"

"Probably not. I just wanted you to squirm."

"Can I have it back then?" he asked. "I hurt."

"Not a chance."

Here we were, going at it again. But it felt different. More like siblings. I was almost enjoying myself.

"But if I get caught with it," I said, "I'm going to kill you."

"Again?"

I laughed.

"I miss my games, Ginny," he said in a pitiful whine.

His hiking boots were as dusty as Brooklyn's now, and there were pine needles clinging to his shirt.

"Looks to me like you're turning into a nature boy, actually. Try sitting still and being quiet, minus the electronics. Maybe you'll learn something."

"Like how boring nature is? Oh wait—I already knew that."

"Very funny."

Back on the talus slope, there was no room for joking, though. A couple of pikas scrambled into view but stayed out for only an hour. I imagined them racing back to the rocks and panting like dogs trapped in a hot car. Or maybe when they reached the shade, the cool was immediate and they recovered fast. Curiosity made me want to go investigate, but I didn't want to disturb them.

I wasn't sure how I was supposed to learn anything about animals without doing what so many humans had done before me: meddle, disrupt, harm. So instead I just waited and wondered.

Kai picked us all up early and said we should head down to Music Box Creek for lunch with the rest of the group. The ridgeline was too hot and too exposed.

"The clouds are gathering," he told us. "We could use a thunderstorm this afternoon, and we definitely don't want to be up high when it arrives."

"Why not?" Vidal asked.

"The last thing you want when lightning strikes is to be the tallest thing around," Kai explained.

As we followed him down the trail, Vidal's eyes darted from the top of Kai's head to the top of mine.

"Kai's taller," I whispered. "He'll get zapped first."

"That's not how it works, Ginny," Kai called.

"Joking!" I said.

Vidal shot me a look like I was so busted, and we somehow managed not to laugh. Elijah plodded behind us, quiet and cranky in what seemed like a clear sign of tech withdrawal.

When we reached Greyson, he was still arranging willow branches on his paddock. The others hadn't yet arrived.

"Now it looks tall enough for goats," I told him, putting my hand on a high branch.

"Not goats," he told me, wiping his brow. "They jump."

"How do you know?"

"Just do."

I was intrigued, impatient. I was about to ask him if he was ever going to tell me about his life back home when Dash arrived, making farting noises in his armpit.

"There's purple-and-white bird poop on my rock," Elijah griped.

"Dipping sauce, dude," Maddox said, waving a package of rye crackers in his face. "Eat it."

Elijah normally would have laughed, but instead he stuck out his tongue at Maddox's back.

"It's on all the rocks. I'm getting water to scrub it off," Vidal said, heading for the creek.

"You can make bird-poop smoothies," Dash suggested.

These guys sure knew how to spoil a person's appetite. "Can I have lunch in here?" I butted my forehead against the side of Greyson's paddock.

"Goats do that, too," Greyson told me.

"They can join me," I said.

A cry of horror broke through the air. It was Vidal, frozen in place at the edge of the creek and pointing at the ground.

The rest of us hurried over. There, in the mud, were two enormous paw prints, each topped with the marks of five long claws.

"Grizzly, right?" Brooklyn said as Kai used a twig to draw a line across the top of the print.

"Yup." Kai tapped the mud. "See the way the toes are all above this line? That's a dead giveaway."

"Did you have to say 'dead'?" Vidal asked.

"They're freaking ginormous," Elijah added.

Kai nodded. "Probably a full-grown male."

Vidal frowned.

"Greyson should get a new solo spot," Dash said, eyes darting across the creek.

"I'll be fine," Greyson insisted.

"We better get a new campsite," Elijah said.

"It's a mile away, Elijah," Brooklyn said. "We'll be okay. Besides, we always knew there were bears around here. We'll keep following our precautions, and if we do that, it's the rare bear that won't leave us alone."

"How rare?" Vidal asked.

"Give us a number," Elijah pressed.

As everyone drifted away, Greyson knelt on the ground and placed his hand inside the paw print, like a baseball player trying out a new glove.

"How's it fit?" I asked him.

He put his other hand in the second track, then rounded his shoulders, showed some teeth.

"It's a good look," I told him. Better than I wanted to admit.

Everyone was in a weird mood when we came back to camp. Clearly the tracks had been unnerving. The boys all sat close together by the lake, trading grizzly bear attack stories that may or may not have been true. I sat on a nearby rock, only half-listening. A small rustling sound came from below the rock, and a few seconds later a chipmunk scurried into view. It looked kind of like the chipmunks back home except it had bold black-and-white stripes on the sides of its head, not just on its body. It froze when it saw me, checking me out like it wanted to know if I had snacks on me, and if I'd share.

"Sorry, friend," I told it. "No feeding the bears. Camp rules."

I swear it looked disappointed. Then it turned and skittered away.

➤·◄ ❤ ➤·◄ ❤ ➤·◄ ❤ ➤·◄ ❤ ➤·◄

Vidal and Greyson were messing up the milestones. After dinner, they both still refused to Talk their Truths about what had brought them to camp. Brooklyn shook her head and started to warn them about consequences, but Kai interrupted her and suggested a conference by the tents.

"They're fighting," Elijah said, watching them.

"Stop staring, Elijah," I said. "They'll get mad."

"They already are. With each other."

I didn't know about mad, but they were definitely disagreeing. When they returned, Brooklyn was quiet. Kai took charge, saying we were going to do a special activity he'd thought up the day before.

He began by giving everyone a piece of paper and a pencil.

"Here's what we're going to do," he said. "Write down the words 'I want to be _____' and then finish the phrase. But make it something the rest of us don't even know. There won't be any names here. So it's trust with a wide safety net."

"Who's reading them?" Dash asked.

"We'll put them all in a bag and I'll take out one at a time to read to the group. After that, we'll make a little wish fire and toss them right in. So our dreams can sail up with the ashes."

"Perfect," Maddox said, pitched just right so it was impossible to tell if the endorsement was genuine or sarcastic.

"And if we get a single blank space or joke or swear word, no one gets chocolate for the rest of the week," Brooklyn warned, betraying her skepticism about the whole exercise.

I thought for a while about what I most wanted to be. Scrawled it down in block letters, folded it up. Kai passed around an empty stuff sack and we dropped our slips of paper inside, one by one. Kai shook them up and started to read.

"I want to be ... bigger than everyone here."

A couple of the kids chuckled, glanced at Elijah. "What?" he said defensively, but Kai was already moving on.

"I want to be in Vegas."

"I want to be where the bears aren't."

A few more laughs.

"I want to be reincarnated."

There was a momentary pause. You had to think about that one for a minute. Did the person like the idea of coming back to Earth as something or someone else, or did they want to hurry up and get this one over with? Probably the former. I guessed it was Kai's.

"I want to be a happy sister."

Dash snorted. "Kind of easy to guess that one, Ginny," he said, rolling his eyes.

I gave him a look. "It could be Brooklyn's."

"Please, Dash," Kai said with a warning glance. He read the next slip of paper.

"I want to be a pile of rocks."

The boys burst out laughing, making comments about how someone must have been really sick of the food. Or hiking. Or doing stupid activities like this one.

I waited for one of the counselors to read the next slip, but Kai stood up and said, "Great. It'll just take me a sec to get this little wish fire going. Then we'll throw them in."

I looked up, confused. "You only read six," I pointed out. "Didn't you two do one?"

Brooklyn shook her head. "No. This was just for campers."

"Oh," I said dumbly.

"Ha! Told you!" Dash teased. "Pretty stupid mistake for an honor-roll geek."

"Trash duty, Dash," Brooklyn said.

When Kai was ready, the counselors tossed the slips into the fire and we watched them flame up. Someone joked about the ash of someone's dream getting in their cocoa. But I was still thinking about the happy sister comment. It was like we were playing a game of Clue, in a way, and only two of us knew the key piece of information: That comment wasn't mine. I wanted to be the pile of rocks, so I could give the pikas a cool home whenever they needed it.

I glanced at the faces around the firepit. Everyone seemed preoccupied watching the fire consume the paper scraps and trying to snag a passing piece of ash. But not Vidal. He just sat there, hands stuffed in his sweatshirt, staring ahead. When he noticed me looking, he held my gaze for several seconds before turning away.

Now that was trust.

CHAPTER
14

"Aren't you happy?" Elijah said on our way up to our solo spots the next morning. Vidal and Kai were hiking behind us, in a long, one-way conversation about the beauty of the lightning bolt.

I hesitated. What could I say?

"Sometimes," I told him. "But this climate stuff hangs over me like a constant cloud." It wasn't a lie, and it preserved Vidal's privacy. That felt right.

I was still replaying Vidal's words from last night. *I want to be a happy sister.* He adored his little sister—did he just sort of envy her, too? Did he want to be as bright and innocent as that again? Or was the sister part the key thing here? I knew kids at school who were finding new pronouns to reflect their true identities. Is that what Vidal wanted, too? I thought back over everything I knew of Vidal so far, but it didn't add up to much at all. I'd been given my first big clue, and it only made the mystery of Vidal bigger than ever.

"I thought you liked being here, though." Elijah wasn't letting the subject go. "Outside. Looking at animals."

"I do. Or did." We'd arrived at the talus slope. I planted my foot on a boulder and pulled myself up, then crossed the rock, thinking. "You ever build a sandcastle at the beach—with a moat around it?" I asked finally.

"Um. Maybe once."

"You fill the moat with water and it looks amazing, but only for a couple of seconds. Then all the water sucks down into the sand and you're left with an empty trench. No matter how many times you fill it, you know it's not going to last. The completeness. The awesomeness."

"What does this have to do with anything?"

"It's how I feel about the pikas."

"Huh?"

"Look at what we've got here right now," I said, gesturing up and around. "The blue skies, the peppy pikas. Pretty great, right? But it's temporary. The pikas are going extinct. That's what my science teacher says, anyway. Because of the way things are heating up. I want to grab them—hold on to them so they never leave us—but they're just going to slip through my fingers and disappear. Like the water in the sand."

Elijah looked up the talus slope. "Can I see them sometime?"

"The pikas? I didn't think you were interested."

He shrugged. "Got no phone now, so . . ."

Twenty minutes later he was sitting beside me on the rock when one, then two, then three pikas began to scurry around the slope.

"Hey," he said under his breath, "they look kind of like Pikach—"

"Don't say it," I interrupted. "Pikas just look like pikas. Lagomorphs, if you want to use their scientific name. Cousins of rabbits. Some people call them rock rabbits."

"Cute," Elijah said.

"That's better," I said, bumping his shoulder.

He rubbed the spot but didn't move away.

Either Elijah was good luck or the pikas enjoyed an audience, because they ran through all their best routines: staying statue-still (with an occasional *eeep* of communication). Zipping over and around the rocks with lightning speed. Finding a patch of lichen and becoming absorbed in happy grazing. Best of all was watching them gather grasses and wildflowers. They'd bite off a big bunch of stalks right at the base and then drag the whole heavy load with their heads tilting to one side. Little goofballs. They looked hilarious running lopsided like that, but I was sure they had their reasons.

At one point, a pika sat and watched us from a rock only a few feet away. We could see its fur up close, mottled with browns and grays just like the lichen-covered rocks. We could see its fluffy round toes. We could even see it breathe and, for one long moment, we made sustained pika-to-human eye contact.

"Cool," Elijah said with a nicely quiet voice when the pika moved on. "I had no idea."

"Of their utterly fantastic adorability?" I asked.

He refused to say the words, but I could tell he kind of agreed. I smiled. In a weird way, Elijah had cheered me up. He started back up toward his Spruce Grove, then stopped and turned back.

"You should film them," he said.

"What?"

"You should make videos."

I shook my head. "I've seen some wildlife documentaries with pikas in them, but it's not the same as being here."

"I never have. Post them on YouTube. For kids like me."

It was hard to believe that filming the pikas would do a bit of good, but I wouldn't say that to Elijah right away. *An open mind is a beautiful mind.* I hadn't forgotten Ms. Arocho's favorite expression.

"While you still can, right?" he added.

I nodded noncommittally. Elijah peered out at the valley, lost in thought. "It stinks, you know," he said after a while.

"What?"

"The air. At home. When the fires are burning."

"The wildfires?" I asked, surprised he was bringing this up.

He nodded. "It's not safe to go outside. Even if you wanted to." He gave me a look. "You'd totally hate it."

I'd heard about the wildfires in California, but I'd never met anyone who was living through them. "Ugh," I said.

He nodded. "Mega ugh."

The pikas scattered soon after Elijah left. It didn't take long, sitting there alone with the heat radiating off the sun-doused rocks, to start reconsidering his idea. Almost no one in my entire science class had heard of a pika. Charlotte from school mixed them up with rocks, and that college kid on the Common had thought they were fish. Nobody at TrackFinders seemed to have known about them either, except maybe Kai and Brooklyn. What chance did we have of saving the winners of the NCAA creature cuteness championships if most people didn't even know they existed? And anyway, I had my stupid cell phone. Maybe there was a reason it had survived Brooklyn's search and seizure.

At 11:45, I tucked my belongings into my daypack and climbed up to Elijah's solo spot. He was stretched out on the ground with his open journal beside him. I peered in for a closer look and saw that the page was blank.

"Is that a picture of your soul?"

"Very funny," he mumbled. "What do you want?"

"I'm heading up to lunch. I thought we could carpool."

"Whatever."

He wasn't in the mood to laugh. Maybe it was still the tech withdrawal. He got up grudgingly and started packing up his things.

"You know, I think I'm going to do it," I told him. "Film the pikas. But I'll need to borrow the charger."

"Oh yeah?" He pulled the charger out by its clip and let it swing back and forth like a dead rat. "*My* charger?"

"Yeah. So?"

"I'll let you use it." He gave me a sly grin. "But it'll cost you." For a short Californian middle schooler, he could do a pretty good imitation of an old New York mob boss.

"Okay, whatever," I told him.

We worked out a deal. I'd use the phone for the first hour of our solo time. Then Elijah would take it back for the afternoon. I wouldn't ask how much he used it, but he had to return it to me the next day fully charged. If either of us got caught, we'd take full responsibility and not turn the other one in—even if it meant earning one of Brooklyn's harshest "consequences."

"She'll probably make us clean the peanut butter jars for the rest of the trip," Elijah said.

"Or carry her scary clipboard," I said.

"Or wash Dash's snot-rags!"

"Ewww. Still want to risk it?"

"Of course."

I dug my cell phone out of my backpack and shoved it into his hands. "Here. Take it. I didn't like having it in my tent anyway."

Elijah looked ridiculously happy—emphasis on "ridiculous." He held the phone to his chest and patted it affectionately.

"Omigod, it's like an emotional-support animal for you," I said.

"Mmm-hmm," he purred, closing his eyes and smiling.

"How fun is a phone without Wi-Fi?" I asked him.

"You have apps," he said.

"Like, two." I felt a little bad about contributing to his affliction, but then again, it was for a good cause. "You're weird," I told him.

"Am not. I'm just trying to make sure you're a happy sister."

Not that again.

"You *are* kind of like our sister," he continued, pulling on his backpack. "And if *you're* not happy, *we're* never going to be happy." He hiked a few steps, then paused. "Actually, you're more like our Snow White."

"Very funny. And you guys are the seven dwarfs?"

He shrugged. "Pretty much."

"There are only five of you."

"Not if you count Brooklyn and Kai."

I laughed. "Okay. Who's who?"

"Well, Dash is Sneezy, obviously."

"Obviously."

"And Brooklyn's Doc."

"The bossy one. Fair."

"Vidal's probably Bashful, right?" Elijah asked.

"Sure." I tried to think of the other dwarfs. "Who's Happy?"

"No one," Elijah said, giggling at his own joke.

"Ha. Kai's pretty happy."

"I'd say more like Dopey. The chakras? The seeds of wisdom?"

"We can come back to Happy, then. Who's Grumpy?"

"Greyson," Elijah said. "Definitely Greyson."

I didn't argue. I understood why he'd say it, even if I didn't exactly agree. "We still haven't figured out you and Maddox."

"Maddox is Sleazy—don't you think?"

"Totally!" I said, relieved he had the same feeling I did. "But that's not a dwarf."

"It is now," Elijah said.

We were still laughing when we reached Kai and Vidal, starting in on their lunch.

"You guys are in such good spirits," Kai noted. He beamed. "That makes me happy."

I caught Elijah's eye. "Bingo."

That afternoon at base camp, Brooklyn put us to work doing extra chores—shaking out our tents, washing our dirty clothes, organizing the food packs. It didn't even matter that we hadn't done anything wrong; she just seemed to like it when we were accomplishing something.

"Do we really need to be this clean and organized?" Elijah asked.

"Yes," she said.

"I miss baseball," Vidal said.

"I miss sleep," Dash said, dragging himself up off the ground.

Maddox insisted on helping me with my job, then offered to pump water for everyone—for no reason at all.

"We see you, Maddox," Kai said, putting his hand against his heart. "Good stuff."

"It's cool," Maddox said. He was wearing a button-up shirt over his hiking shorts while his T-shirts dried in the sun. Between that and the sunglasses, he still gave off a strong whiff of "country club," even perched on a lakeside boulder, filling up water bottles.

"Maybe I'm being unfair," I said to Greyson, eyeing Maddox across the water. "What if he's genuinely trying to be helpful and I'm too biased against him to believe it? People can change, right?"

We each had a nylon bucket filled with water and a tiny bit of biodegradable soap. The idea was to put our clothes in, swoosh them around a bit, give them a quick rinse, and call them clean.

"Give yourself more credit than that," Greyson said. "He's definitely slippery."

I smiled. "That would be a good dwarf name."

"What?"

"Oh, nothing. Just something Elijah and I were joking about earlier," I said, shaking my head.

So far, Greyson and I seemed to bond best by complaining about Maddox. Was that wrong, too? When he looked down at his washtub, I found myself admiring his sprinkling of freckles again. If I looked long enough, maybe I'd find a constellation.

"Did you give *me* a dwarf name?" he asked, pulling up a pair of socks that had probably been white in another life. The kid was too quick.

"*I* didn't."

He waited.

"But Elijah said Grumpy."

He wrung out the socks one at a time. "Because of the way I talked to Brooklyn and Kai the other night?"

"I think maybe it's more because you've been holding back."

"No more than anyone else," he said, dropping a couple of pairs of briefs into the bucket.

"You sure?" I asked.

It was less awkward to look at his face than his underwear. He held my gaze. It turned into a stare-down, which I won, thanks to years of practice with Vivian. The key is to make your eyes wider and wider until you look so freaky they can't help but laugh or, in Greyson's case, allow the merest trace of a smile.

"What do you want to know?" he asked me.

"Same thing everyone else does. Why are you here?"

"There are giant mutant spiders in my tent!" Elijah shouted from across the campsite. "I need a dustbuster!"

"Use your own power, buddy," Kai called back.

"Clean your own dust, Buster," Elijah mimicked, before laughing at his own joke.

Greyson pushed the laundry bucket aside and leaned over his knees, then pulled a pine needle out from between his toes. "It's a long story. Epic, really."

"I got no place I need to be," I said.

The problem wasn't time, of course. It was getting any kind of privacy from the other six dwarfs. I wanted them to go whistle and work far away from here so Greyson could tell me his epic tale. Instead, he had to wait till they were semi-preoccupied with their chores again. Then he started. At the beginning.

"Like I said the first night, my family's basically cursed. My great-grandfather died in his twenties. And my grandfather. Then my dad. It was all related to stupid addiction stuff, one way or another. But when my dad died, Mom decided something had to change fast or Justin and I were doomed."

"Justin?"

"My older brother. So after Dad died, she moved us out to live with her dad. On his farm, twenty miles outside of town. She thought Pops would be a better influence. Realign our stars or whatever."

"Did it work?"

"Well, living on the farm kept us in line, definitely. We worked our butts off, followed the rules. Justin was an Eagle Scout, actually. Total goody-goody. Then he started dating Ellie, the daughter of our high school principal."

"Uh-oh. Bad news?"

Greyson shrugged. "Not like you're thinking. But she made him act crazy. I mean, not her exactly. But the love or whatever. He slept on his phone so he wouldn't miss a single text. Spent twice as long getting dressed. Stuff like that. Last winter she pinged him awake one night saying she and a friend needed a midnight donut run. So he went, obviously. All the way back to town and then another town over, where there was a place that stayed open twenty-four seven. Even though the roads were completely covered with ice. He'd just gotten his license and wasn't even supposed to be driving other kids yet."

"I thought he was an Eagle Scout."

"Yeah, well. I'm sure he thought he was being a hero." Greyson looked at me, his face hard. "You probably don't need me to tell you they crashed."

I didn't, but it was still awful to hear it spoken. "He died?"

Greyson poured the water out of his laundry bucket and we watched as it ran down in little rivulets between the rocks. "They all did."

It was the worst story I'd ever heard. I wasn't sure there was anything I could have said to him then that would have felt right.

"Greyson," I said, trying anyway.

"Don't even."

Before he could say more, Kai called out from the firepit. "Guys! Time to start chopping the tofu!"

"We should go," Greyson said.

I nodded. It was a lot to take in at once, in the middle of an afternoon of camp chores. And he still hadn't told me what this had to do with him being here.

Brooklyn had strung a rope between the tops of our two tents and told me I could use it as a clothesline. I hung my socks and then my T-shirts and was just starting to hang up my sports bra when I noticed Vidal standing by his own tent, watching me.

"You okay, Vidal?" I asked.

"'Course," he said quickly. But he looked a little twitchy.

"Happy to talk any time."

He shook his head. "Just *don't* talk. Ever."

I made a zip motion across my mouth.

He lingered, looking at my wet clothes dripping onto the ground. "I mean, I'm not even sure."

"Okay." The reassuring was easy; I would never tell a kid's secrets—especially not big ones. But was that what this was—a secret? I felt like I was being asked to guard something without even knowing what it was.

He ducked away and I finished with my laundry, then went back to the firepit. Brooklyn was kneeling over the camp stove, pumping the gas.

"We never do campfires anymore."

"It's too dry. Not safe."

"Oh," I said, glad we were doing it right, but sorry for the reason.

The boys straggled in one by one.

"Is it true we're having tofu tonight?" Elijah asked.

"Rehydrated dehydrated tofu," Kai said, coming toward us with a big pot in his hands. "It's practically gourmet."

"Sure it is," Maddox said, lifting the lid and peering inside.

"I miss hot dogs," Dash added.

"We won't have meat again till the next resupply," Brooklyn told us.

"When's that?" Elijah asked, making a face.

"We like to keep you guessing," she said matter-of-factly. "It's a TrackFinders tradition."

Dinner took a very long time to prepare. The camp stove was on the blink and it took twice as long to bring the water to a boil. To keep us busy while we waited, Kai had us make a timeline of our lives from elementary school to middle school, highlighting the best moments in green and the worst moments in red. Afterward, we were supposed to circle every situation we thought we could have changed, and underline everything we thought was out of our control.

"Can we burn this afterward?" Elijah asked.

"Funny, but no."

Bored by my own timeline, I glanced at Greyson's. Sometimes people got weird ideas about what was their fault. At least that was what Mom said after years of defending people who'd been dumped on for too long. But from what I could see, Greyson hadn't written anything at all. Fortunately, dinner was ready before they asked us to share.

When we'd finished eating and cleaning up, Kai asked for volunteers to put away the dinner supplies.

"I'll go if Ginny goes," Greyson said, to my surprise.

"I think Ginny's in charge of her own volunteering," Brooklyn put in.

"No, it's fine," I said, trying to sound chill. I stood up and started collecting the remains of the food.

"Be good out there," Maddox said, holding out a bag of marshmallows. When I reached for it, he held on.

"Don't know any other way." I gave the bag another tug, and this time he let go. I shook my head. I couldn't believe I'd ever thought Maddox was gentlemanly.

The food packs were stowed inside a cluster of trees on the far end of the campsite. Greyson and I filled them with everything we'd collected, then closed them up tight.

"You doing okay?" I asked him.

He nodded.

"Can you tell me what happened next?" It felt easier to talk in the near dark with no one to eavesdrop but the trees. "After the accident?"

Greyson took a moment to collect his thoughts.

"Well, Mom fell apart. Completely. So being home sucked. But school was just as bad. It was my first year of high school, I was a total mess, and everyone avoided me. Like I was a leper. Like tragedy was contagious. Nobody checked in. Not the Eagle

Scouts. Not the scholar-athletes." Even in the dim light I could tell he was giving me a pointed look. "And obviously not our principal. Mom thought he blamed us for killing his daughter."

"But it wasn't your fault! That's so stupid."

"Small towns always are."

Greyson began piling the pots and pans around the food packs. I helped him finish, and then we closed up the fencing.

"I finally gave up and started hanging out on the Tray," Greyson told me.

"The Tray?"

"An old field next to the high school. I think the name's from 'ashtray.' It's where the undesirables go—the Tray kids—to do undesirable things."

"You became one of those?"

"Don't judge," he said, catching something in my tone. "They didn't judge me, and that's what I liked. Those kids figured out a long time ago that the world's screwed. They're smarter than other kids, if you ask me. I mean, think about what happened with Justin. He did everything perfect, and he crashed and burned."

Well, he *had* snuck out for a drive on a dark, icy road, but I wasn't going to mention that now.

"When Mom found out I was spending time on the Tray, though, she went double nuts. Didn't even ask what I was or wasn't doing. Just said something had to change. Fast."

"That's when she decided to pack you off for TrackFinders?"

"Guess so. Kind of ironic, too. Because you know what? I still thought I was going to college. And now we'll never be able to afford it. She went into debt so I could draw pictures of my soul, and now I'll probably end up working at a meatpacking plant and get killed by a giant cleaver. Pretty funny, huh? I guess that's what happens when you try to outrun your fate."

"I wouldn't say funny."

"Ginny? Greyson?" We heard a snap of twigs, and Kai emerged from the campsite clasping the red and green pens. We'd been gone for about ten minutes, but that was an eon at this place. "You guys good?"

"Er, uh-huh," I said, even though it felt wrong to say it when Greyson was standing there with his heart laid out, raw and exposed.

"Excellent," Kai said. He nodded toward the fence. "Is it on?"

Greyson put his palm on my back and guided me out of the way, so I wouldn't get shocked. But his warm hand was a shock of its own. He flipped the switch on the fence and gave Kai a nod.

"Thanks. Come on back for Circle Time. I'm thinking we could try some campfire songs tonight—fun, right?"

"You haven't heard me sing," I told him.

"Can't miss it now," Greyson said, mustering a smile.

CHAPTER
15

The world was too full of sad stories. I was beginning to understand why people found ways to tune out the news. You could obsess over your GPA or you could check out on the Tray, but in the end it all came down to the same thing: denial. Distracting yourself from the overwhelming, crazy pain of being a human in a world where so many things went wrong.

In the morning I was almost envious of the pikas and their blissful ignorance. I held my phone up and hit "record."

"For the last five days I've been hanging out with the woolly mammoth of the Rockies. Well, not a woolly mammoth, exactly, because it's more furry than woolly. And okay, it's also a LOT smaller than a mammoth. But it's like a woolly mammoth because by the time you see this video, it may be one of those animals you can only see behind glass at a natural history museum, stuffed and stiff. Awesome Animals of North America You'll Never See Alive. Mothball Gallery. Hall of Extinction. Something like that."

I took a deep breath.

"Sorry. It's not a joke," I told my imaginary listener. "I think I do that sometimes because the facts hurt too much."

I switched off the video. I'd never done this kind of thing before. I wasn't sure I could pull it off.

Then a pika let out a high-pitched *eeep*. It was perched on a nearby rock, giving me a look.

I smiled. "I need to do this. Is that the idea?"

The pika's nose twitched. I took it as encouragement and hit "record" again.

"So, anyway. Meet the pika. See it there? I'm going to stop talking for a few minutes so you can just watch it. Hopefully you'll hear it, too."

I panned the camera around the slope to set the scene, then focused in on the little pika cheerleader. It bolted down the slope to an area of tall wildflowers, grabbed a mouthful, then sprang back up the rock. Maybe someday I'd figure out how to put parts of the video in slow motion. The pika's movements were such a zip of speed, you almost lost sight of the acrobatics. A tiny creature flinging itself off a boulder, landing on hard rock, bounding up and on. It reminded me of Olympic gymnasts, hurling themselves on and off the vault.

I stopped filming again and just watched for a while. I'd missed something before. My pika friend had a notch in one ear, like maybe a weasel had taken a bite out of it. Or maybe there'd been a lovers' quarrel that had gotten a little rough. In any case, it was just a scar now, and it gave me a useful point of reference. A way to distinguish this one pika from all the others.

The next day, I pointed out the pika to my nonexistent viewing audience.

"This is Van Gogh. She's had an interesting day. You know how yesterday we saw the pikas gathering flowers to store under the rocks? Well, today, Van Gogh did something sneaky. Instead of gathering fresh flowers, she stopped halfway down the slope and snagged some out of someone else's storage spot. That's right, she's a furry little shoplifter. Let's see if she does it again."

Van Gogh started down the hill. Paused to scratch her good ear. Was it my imagination, or was she watching the pika downslope to make sure it wasn't paying attention? And yep, sure enough, she made a beeline toward the other pika's cache and emerged with a stolen bouquet.

"Omigod, she's shameless!" I said.

In a few seconds she was above her favorite rock. She dropped out of sight, and then emerged flower-free. She looked calm. Almost smug. I laughed out loud.

"What's so funny?"

Elijah was standing on the edge of the slope, trying to follow my gaze. I gestured toward Van Gogh.

"One of my pikas is stealing from her neighbor."

He made his way over to my rock and sat down, flouting the rules again. He scratched his head, sighed.

"What's up?" I asked.

"It's boring under the trees."

"Okay, but you don't get the phone for another fifteen minutes."

"Whatever. Your apps suck—you were right. I got so sick of Candy Crush yesterday, I spent most of my time with your thesaurus."

"That must have been fun."

He shook his head. "Boring. Tedious. Dull. Blah."

I laughed. Then I pointed out my notch-eared friend. "That's Van Gogh. The sneaky one. She's hoarding wildflowers right now."

Elijah watched her cross the rocks and disappear. "You should attach a GoPro to her head so you can see inside her house."

"No technology talk, Elijah," I said, making an X with my fingers.

"Shut up."

"Seriously, I would never do that to a pika."

"Why?"

"Why not tie a camera to her head? It's gross. Invasive. Undignified—for her, I mean." I handed him the phone. "Here, film her the regular way. You're probably better at it than I am."

He climbed over to a different rock and sat down. For a little while he filmed the pikas, then a beetle, then his boot. Then he put the phone away. Van Gogh stood on a rock, frozen as an ice sculpture. When the shadow of a hawk crossed the slope, she *eeep*ed extra loud and dove out of sight.

Elijah was resting his chin on his knees, watching with half a smile.

"You should name the next one after me," he told me.

Greyson's structure had grown to be more than shoulder height, with rounded sides like an oversize nest. He'd left an opening in one wall so we could climb inside. Everyone wanted a turn, of course. When mine came, I felt embraced by the woody walls, and more deliciously alone than I ever did in my tent or even in my solo spot—though I couldn't have explained why. I lay on my back and counted clouds. Imagined just staying here for the rest of my life.

"Ginny? You coming out?" Kai called.

"Possibly." I got up and made one last circuit of the nest, dragging my hands along the walls. There were spaces between the branches where you could press your face and peer out. I saw the creek. I saw the opposite hillside and finally glimpsed a fat brown marmot waddling over a rock. I saw Brooklyn looking hot and impatient.

"Sorry," I said, popping out. "It's just so nice in there." I looked back at the hill but the marmot was gone.

"You should start a business," Maddox told Greyson. "People would pay serious money to have you make these for their yards."

"That sounds like something your dad would say," Greyson said.

"Shut your face," Maddox hissed, viciously and so quietly that no one else heard.

"Greyson, seriously, have you ever thought about a start-up?" Kai asked. "Maddox is right. You could do a real business with these."

"Maybe," Greyson said.

"It's something you should all think about," Kai told the group. "You never know when that quirky interest—that thing you've gotten totally hooked on—could turn into your life's work. It's a really beautiful thing when that happens."

"Depends on what you're hooked on," Maddox smirked.

"I was addicted to my fidget spinner for a while," Elijah said. "If I didn't have it in my hand, I'd scream."

"I was addicted to lime popsicles one summer," Vidal said. "First my lips turned green. Then my face."

"I think I'm addicted to sleep," Dash said, making everyone nod.

It went on for a while. I saw a pine cone on the trail and stopped to pick it up. For some reason, it reminded me of the cristata cactus I'd given to Zinzie. I ran my finger over the brainy bumps.

"What about you, Ginny? You ever been addicted to anything?" Maddox asked me, something mocking in his tone.

"Sure," I said. I slid the pine cone into my pocket. "Zoo webcams."

The boys laughed derisively, but I didn't care.

"It was at the start of quarantine. I started watching all the animals being born and then I couldn't stop checking on them."

"Did you learn anything interesting?" Kai asked. He seemed relieved we'd moved on from fidget spinners and lime popsicles.

"Panda moms lick their babies a lot."

Greyson's eyes were on me, like he knew there was more.

"For a little while it felt like everything rested on that one little pink panda," I told him. "Whether it lasted another day. Or didn't."

"You're insane," Dash said.

"Lockdown made everyone crazy, right?" Vidal said, running a hand through his uneven hair.

"And some people never recovered," Maddox said, cuffing Dash behind the head.

They were just throwaway comments, but they struck a nerve.

"My grandparents *died*," I said. "Two weeks apart."

"Whoa," Elijah said.

"And my stupid dad said it'd never happen," I added, sharply. "That the virus didn't stand a chance against a 'perfectly executed Shepard family game plan.'"

Maddox whistled through his teeth.

"That's really hard, Ginny," Kai said.

I nodded. I was surprised at how angry I felt again, just talking about it.

Greyson looked angry now too, which was why I fell back and walked beside him the rest of the way. We didn't talk, but it felt like he was sharing the weight, and that's what made it bearable again.

Back at base camp, the heat mounted and we all took quick dips in Bead Lake. The water seemed more tolerable every day, or maybe we were just getting tougher. The conversation continued about life back home, food back home. From the way everyone talked, you would have thought we were being starved. Dash said he wanted a root beer float and Elijah said he'd handle trash for the rest of the trip if he could just have a pepperoni pizza and a chocolate milkshake with whipped cream and sprinkles. After a while, Greyson and Maddox padded over to the firepit in their bare feet, looking for snacks. Dash and Elijah followed.

Vidal waded back into the water, then dipped his hair below the surface the way we all did when we wanted to get it clean.

Actually, not quite the same way. When he bent forward, he folded himself almost exactly in half, graceful as a flamingo.

"Are you a dancer?" I asked him.

He stood back up, and the water streamed down his shoulders.

"When no one's watching," he said with a hint of a smile. He whipped his head, making his hair stick out in funny angles, then stepped onto shore and began toweling himself off.

I still had so many questions about this kid. About the things he'd said. About the things the other kids had said.

"What?" he asked.

I must have been staring.

"Maddox says you're here because you shoplifted," I said, a little bluntly. It was that kind of day.

Vidal gave me a startled look, and for a moment I thought he was going to go dark on me again.

"Half true," he said after a few seconds.

Half true?

"He said you stole furs."

Vidal rolled his eyes and sat down on the rock.

"Leather?"

He looked out across the water.

"If I guessed, would you tell me?"

He didn't say no.

"Money?"

He shook his head.

I thought about his tent—all those price tags. "Camping gear?"

A jay landed on a branch a few yards away. We both watched as it ruffled its wings, dabbed at its feathers.

Vidal shook his head again.

"Jewelry?" Maddox had said that, too.

He didn't move at all at first. Then he gave the slightest of nods.

So not furs or leather or money. But yes, jewelry. Maddox had mentioned cheap drugstore stuff, too.

An idea came to me.

"Did you ever take makeup?"

He hesitated, then gave another nod.

The stuff he couldn't ask for.

"Just to … try it out?" I asked him.

He gave me a shy look. "When no one was watching," he said. "Just like the dancing."

We went back to bird-watching, though I figured he wasn't much thinking about the jay.

"You got caught, though? At some point?"

"'Course. Mama told one of the priests at church. Then the church ladies took up a collection. To send me here."

"Harsh."

"Mama said I was lucky. She said some people went to jail for stealing. It wasn't really the stealing that upset them, though. She started, like, obsessing about my long hair. Dad even threatened to give me a buzz cut. So, well, I did this first."

"Oh," I said. That explained the uneven hair—cut in anger, or shame, or maybe revenge.

"I could totally see you with long hair."

Vidal smiled. "Thanks."

"Do Kai and Brooklyn know? I mean, the whole story?"

"Doubt it."

I knew better than to pry too much with Vidal, but there was something I'd been wanting to know since the first day of camp.

"Can I ask one more thing?"

He tugged a strand of hair and a few last water droplets fell to the rock. "Go."

"Why do you hate nature?"

It was hard even to say it out here, in the company of the jay and the boulders and the wildflowers I loved so much. Like—what was that word my parents used?–like sacrilege. "I mean, I know the insects get to you…"

He scrunched up his face. "You can't trust bugs."

I smiled in spite of myself. "Is that all?"

He reached for a T-shirt and slipped it over his head. "The thing is, out here I got no options. I'm Vidal in the camo sweatshirt and track pants his parents bought him. That's it."

"I didn't think about that."

He rolled his eyes, like he was sick of educating.

"Are you sure it's nature's fault, though?" I asked him.

"Positive. Nature put me in this body. And nature will not let me out."

After dinner that night, Kai and Brooklyn once again invited Greyson and Vidal to talk more about themselves. It had become something of a nightly ritual now, and it always ended the same way. They shook their heads or gave a quick "No thanks." This was no exception.

Maddox cleared his throat. "I have some stuff I'd like to talk about, if no one else is going to."

"Go for it," Kai said, with an appreciative smile.

Maddox ran a hand through his hair and pressed his lips together, like he was thinking carefully about his words. "So, I haven't been fair to my parents."

Everyone went quiet. Stiffened. Waited for the other shoe to drop.

"I feel like I've been judging their choices—you know, about their money and how they spend it—instead of taking responsibility for my own actions. I don't think I've done enough to earn their trust."

There was a hoarseness to his voice that wasn't normally there. Was it because he wasn't used to speaking this way? Was he actually reaching deep, and getting emotional?

"What do you think you could do differently in the future?" Kai asked gently.

Maddox cleared his throat. "I could help out more. Show more respect. I mean, they're our parents, right? They love us. They deserve better."

Dash was watching his brother the way you'd watch an unfamiliar dog—sizing up its body language and bracing for it to turn.

"I'm sure they'd appreciate that, Maddox. You want to tell the group about your artwork?" Brooklyn asked.

"Oh yeah. Sure. I call it my 'heartwork,' actually. Brooklyn caught me one day and she thought I was ignoring the assignment and just working out."

"Well, you were working out," she said, tugging off her headband and shaking out her hair. "It just wasn't that simple."

"Right. It's about transformation more than training. I'd gotten really out of shape before camp. I had some, er, bad habits—back home, I mean. Made it hard to haul my butt—uh, sorry, backpack?—uphill when we first started. But I felt really different after that first week. I decided my heartwork would be about continuing the transformation, like I said. I wanted to purify my body so my mind would be clearer, too."

"The mind-body connection," Kai chimed in, pressing his fingertips together. "That's big."

Maddox nodded. "I feel like I'm seeing things really differently now."

"That's awesome, Maddox. And I just want to add that Brooklyn and I have really appreciated your helpfulness around camp," Kai added. "You've become a real leader here."

"Thanks." Maddox folded his arms across his chest. "I've been trying."

Brooklyn cast her eyes around the circle. "Any thoughts from the rest of you?"

"About what? Him?" Dash asked.

"Well, about this kind of shift—from complaint and defiance to shouldering some of the responsibility for the patterns you get into. With your parents. With yourself."

No one said anything. Maybe it was small of me, but I didn't like it that Maddox seemed to be getting credit for going through a conversion here. Which was better—feeding the counselors back their own lines or being genuine, even if it didn't fit their wishes?

"I've been pretty frustrated with my parents, too, obviously," I admitted. "But I'm not sure I'm ready to forgive them yet."

"Interesting," Kai said, dropping his hands to his knees.

"Have you thought about your own actions and how they've affected the situation?" Brooklyn asked me.

I hesitated. "A little. But it hasn't changed anything. Is that bad?"

Brooklyn looked uncomfortable, and zipped up her Track-Finders fleece. "Well, there's still plenty of time."

No one seemed interested in continuing the conversation.

"Speaking of time, we'd like you all to turn in early this evening and finish up your next letters home," Brooklyn told the group. "We've got big plans for tomorrow."

"Early plans," Kai said eagerly.

"To do what?" Elijah asked.

"We'll tell you in the morning. Now hurry up and get ready for bed."

Back in my tent, I stared at a blank sheet of paper for five minutes. Finally I drew a potato shape in the middle of the page. I added ears and whiskers, and the outline of a rock below. It was hard to believe that at the time of my last letter home, I'd never seen a living pika. I considered giving my family a detailed report about all that I'd seen and felt and learned, but the thought exhausted me. I made an arrow pointing to the pika. And next to that, just four words.

Mammal of my soul.

It was five syllables—just like the first line of a haiku. Maybe I could write a pika haiku. A paiku? I was too tired to think, but I jotted down two more lines.

Mammal of my soul.

Calling eeep, eeep eeep eeep eeeeep!

The futile alarm.

CHAPTER
16

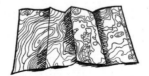

Kai and Brooklyn woke us at sunup with the clang of their metal Sierra cups and more exclamations about what a big day it was going to be. I stayed nestled in my sleeping bag as long as I could, but eventually their noise had its intended effect.

"Everyone have a full bottle of water? Sunscreen? Hat and gloves? Journals?"

Kai was at his chattiest, jumpy and excited. Brooklyn seemed to be running through a long mental checklist and hardly said a word. Eventually they sat us down and told us about the day's milestone: The Peak Is You. We were going to spend an early hour at our solo sites and then take a daylong hike up Jumping Jack Mountain, one of the highest peaks in the area. I think we all guessed that this was going to be another resupply day, and they were getting us out of the way so Ray could do his thing. I wasn't looking forward to more mail from home, but the thought of some fresh fruit and actual bread had me salivating.

My hour with the pikas provided the day's first surprise. For reasons I couldn't explain–habituation? the direction of the breeze?–Van Gogh did something she had never done before.

She visited me.

I was filming her as she scurried down the slope, when she paused on a rock and peered in my direction. She leapt from rock to rock, coming closer and closer. I almost forgot to track her with the camera because the next thing I knew, she disappeared around a boulder and reappeared inches from my foot. I could have reached out and stroked her fur. The temptation was real. One of my bootlaces was untied and she gazed at it like she was calling me out on being such a slob. I resisted the urge to retie it, and kept my foot still. The next thing I knew, she leaned forward and grabbed the lace in her mouth.

"Hey," I said softly.

She chewed it once, then let it drop, apparently unimpressed by the flavor. But she didn't immediately bolt. For a minute, I filmed her. And then I just watched as she wandered around my feet, sniffing and scratching—as if a human and a pika sharing a morning sunspot was an everyday event and not, as it felt to me, a gift from the gods.

When she finally scrambled away, I stared at my feet, still deep in the awe. I wasn't sure I'd ever want to tie my laces again.

➤·◄ ❥ ➤·◄ ❥ ➤·◄ ❥ ➤·◄ ❥ ➤·◄

Our hike up Jumping Jack Mountain wasn't fast-paced and we didn't have our heavy packs. But it was still the hardest hike of the whole trip. Part of it was the length. Part of it was the steepness of the ascent. Part of it was the fact that we often didn't have trails to follow. Kai and Brooklyn taught us how to create our own switchbacks up the steep hillsides, saying that our muscles would last much longer that way than if we tried to climb straight up. So we were picking and choosing our way, trying to balance the urge to put the climb behind us with the need to do it at a sustainable pace.

"Aren't you getting hot in those?" Dash asked Vidal as we paused for a water break. Vidal was still wearing his polyester track pants, even in the blazing heat.

"Kinda."

"So why'd you wear them?" Elijah asked.

"They protect me. From the bugs."

"What bugs?" Elijah asked.

"Flies. Mosquitoes. Ants that climb on me while I'm trying to enjoy a nice picnic lunch." He gestured toward Dash and Maddox. "Don't have those fancy pants that zip off into shorts."

As we climbed up higher, the wind picked up and the few remaining trees looked like they'd been blown—and shaped—by it their whole lives. Their trunks were twisted and bent, and their stubby branches grew all on one side and pointed away from the wind, like ragged green flags on contorted brown poles. We hiked on, leaving even those trees behind as we crossed a broad, rocky slope where nothing grew taller than our knees.

Coming around the side of a high peak, we reached our first snowfield. I wondered if this was a good sign, seeing this much snow so late in the summer. We had to stop and have a snowball fight, of course. We packed balls and walloped anyone we could hit until our fingers got frozen. Then Kai stomped out a level trail about two-thirds of the way up the snowfield, and the rest of us followed in a line. It wasn't so different from walking on a dirt trail, but it was still a bit harrowing if you weren't fond of heights, like Elijah; or didn't trust your innate balance, like Dash; or had never set foot on snow in your life before this morning, like Vidal.

When we finally reached the other side, I expected Brooklyn and Kai to reward us with an announcement of lunchtime. But Kai said we were going to push on for the summit. We'd leave our packs on the last plateau, pop up for the view, and then come back down to eat so there wouldn't be any chance of exposure during the afternoon thunderstorm hours.

"But we never have thunderstorms anymore—haven't you noticed? And I'm starving," Elijah moaned. "Famished. Deprived."

I gave him a look. I'd created a thesaurus-saurus.

"Here. Go crazy," Kai said, flinging two energy bars in Elijah's direction. "Anyone else? We'll have plenty more by the time we get back to camp this evening."

The last plateau was like a moonscape—all barren rocks with no signs of life except for one small cairn. We tossed our daypacks in a heap beside it, grabbed hats and jackets against the elements, and climbed on. Fifteen minutes later we reached the pinnacle, with a dizzying view of peaks extending out in every direction. Everyone whooped and crowded around the marker showing our elevation—11,514 feet. It felt like we should have a flag to pop in the ground.

"We need a picture," Vidal said, clinging to the marker like he might blow away if he didn't. "No one will believe I've been here."

"You'll have to take a picture with your mind," Kai told him. "Sorry."

"If I'd brought my journal, I could have sketched you. But it's down on the plateau and I have no intention of running back," Brooklyn said with a laugh. She looked relieved, happy—like the mother goose who has successfully herded her goslings across a busy road.

"I didn't know you liked to draw," I told her.

"I was an art major in college, actually."

"How come you never told us that before?"

She shrugged. Brooklyn never talked about herself. She was the opposite of Kai in that way, but at this point it made her seem more interesting than him. I would make a point of asking her more on the way down.

"A group portrait would be so cool," Elijah said. "We could have them made into T-shirts when we get home. My mom knows how to do that."

"Next time," Brooklyn said, pulling an anorak over her head.

"I could run back for you," Maddox offered. "I'm not tired."

Greyson and I did synchronized eye rolls. That Boy Scout thing again.

"That's okay," Brooklyn told him. "No one wants to wait that long for lunch, I'm sure."

"Seriously. I bet I can make it there and back in, like, seventeen minutes. Twenty-five, tops. I'll put my heartwork together with your artwork and we'll end up with"—he flashed his winningest smile—"a masterpiece."

Enough, I thought. I was getting sick of his smarm. At least when he'd been acting cool and arrogant he hadn't seemed so fake.

"It's a nice thought, but . . . ," Brooklyn began.

"Elijah's too hungry to wait," I pointed out.

"Actually not. Those two energy bars sank like the *Titanic*," Elijah said, sticking out his tongue.

"Brooklyn," Kai said, "maybe Maddox is ready for us to extend him a trust line."

Maddox waited expectantly. Was he flexing his muscles? In that moment, he looked so buff I had the feeling he could do a couple of handsprings down and pole vault back up.

Brooklyn finally relented. "Okay. As long as the rest of you don't mind sitting and letting me sketch you after that. It might take another fifteen or twenty minutes."

"Works for me," Dash said, flopping on the ground.

It was true. We were worn out, and the idea of sitting seemed nice, even if we had to fight over the most comfortable perches.

"You can bring my whole pack. It's not too heavy," she told Maddox.

He nodded and took off. Brooklyn stood at the top of the trail to watch his progress as long as she could. The rest of us stretched out wherever we could fit ourselves. The wind was whipping in spirited gusts, but when I lay down all I felt was the warmth of the sun. I began to get sleepy—I think everyone did—and closed my eyes.

"Hey, look there," Kai said softly.

I pulled myself up on my elbows. I couldn't tell how much time had passed. Five minutes? Fifteen? I really might have been dozing. Kai was gesturing across the valley to the next peak. It looked like a rocky slope with some blobs of snow on it, but then the snow moved.

"Mountain goats!" He kept his voice quiet, but his excitement was clear.

Brooklyn left her post and came to join us. Everyone else sat up and watched as the mountain goats picked their way along the edge of the peak, shifting up and down the crags with quick little steps. I couldn't believe what we were seeing. I couldn't believe what they were *doing*. I glanced at Vidal, expecting him to look like he was having a heart attack on the mountain goats' behalf. But he was completely riveted, like how Dad looks when he watches a brilliant triple play.

"They've got the *moves*!" he said under his breath.

"You guys are crazy lucky to see these," Kai said.

"A lot of people never do," Brooklyn added.

Maybe this was some kind of karmic reward for the effort we'd put into getting here. For lingering long on the peak instead of hurrying back down like overscheduled commuters. I guessed we had Maddox to thank for that.

I glanced over my shoulder. "I hope Maddox gets back in time to see these."

"He won't care," Dash mumbled.

Brooklyn glanced at her watch. "He's taking a lot longer than he thought he would."

"So much for his 'heartwork,'" Elijah said, making quotes with his fingers. "He's just an out-of-shape slob like the rest of us."

Brooklyn stood up. "Should we all just head down?" she asked Kai. "It's getting late."

"Let's give him five more minutes," Kai suggested.

"I bet he stopped to eat his lunch," Dash said. "All our lunches."

"Maddox wouldn't do that," Kai said.

"You don't know Maddox like I do," Dash said.

Brooklyn was still unsettled. "I can get a good view of the plateau if I jog down a little ways."

We were only too happy to extend our viewing time with the mountain goats. There were two of them. Wherever the first one chose to go, the other followed behind several paces. They were like a pair of rock climbers, with an invisible safety line tethering them together.

Pika. Moose. Eagle. Marmot. Mountain goat. The list of wildlife I'd seen on this trip was growing, and it made me happy—not the list, but the seeing. A teeny sprout of gratitude rose up through the layers of resentment that I'd been holding on to for the last couple of weeks. If my parents had been really stubborn, I'd be coding in New York City instead of sitting here, seeing this. Maybe they figured this part was the gift and the milestones were just the packaging I had to rip through to get to it.

"Hey, Kai," I said, thinking he'd want to know.

"What is it?"

But before I could say anything more, Brooklyn came bursting up onto the peak, panting, her face moon-white. "He's not there! Maddox is gone!"

>-< ⩔ >-< ⩔ >-< ⩔ >-< ⩔ >-<

We stood in front of the pile of daypacks trying to piece together the story.

"He got eaten by a grizzly," Vidal said.

"He did not get eaten by a grizzly," Brooklyn said.

"At least not yet," Elijah said.

"You think he will?" Dash asked, and by his tone it wasn't clear which answer he wanted to hear.

Maddox's absence was a shock, a hole. Without him there, the vastness of the wilderness loomed ten times larger. Where would one person be in a space this big?

"He took my pack, like he said he would," Brooklyn said, after moving the rest of ours out of the way. She was trying to be deliberate, but her eyes looked a little panicky. She peered up toward the summit. "Do you think he went back up a different way?"

I squinted at the peak. "You'd have to be really confused to do that."

"Maybe he's just going to the bathroom," Elijah said, glancing across the moonlike plateau.

"Where?" Greyson asked. Up here there was no easy place to hide.

We were still holding out hope for a responsible Maddox just taking a bathroom break or finding a different route up, when Kai interrupted.

"Brooklyn." He was squatting beside our pile of belongings. "He took my pack, too."

No one said anything. For the first time since the trip began, I heard fear in Kai's voice. He sat down and looked at Brooklyn with a dawning sense of doom. "We don't have any food."

"What? He took our lunch? But I'm starving!" Dash moaned. "I only got one bar."

"Do you have anything on you?" Brooklyn asked Kai.

Elijah, Vidal, and I knew exactly why she was asking. It was what Kai had told us. About his diabetes.

Kai reached in his pocket and pulled out a plastic bag with a few raisins in it.

"Will that get you down?" Brooklyn asked.

He nodded, but I would have had an easier time believing him if he'd used actual words. And what about his medicine—was that gone, too?

Vidal must have had the same thought. "We gotta go! Quick!" he said, stamping his feet.

But Brooklyn stood where she was, thinking. "You snacked before the summit, too, right?"

Kai nodded.

"Then we'll go—but not fast."

We began our descent. Climbing down a boulder field, we soon learned, requires at least as much effort as climbing up, and much more concentration. It was something about resisting gravity as you shifted down the rocks; my leg muscles were trembling after just half an hour. And we had a lot of downhill left.

When we reached the snowfield, Elijah let out a yelp.

"I know it looks a little scarier this way, buddy," Kai said, turning back. "Just keep your eyes on the trail in front of you, and don't look all the way down. One step at a time."

But Elijah wasn't looking at the snow. He was focused on something on the ground near his feet. "Sandpaper!" he exclaimed triumphantly as he snatched up a rye cracker and held it in the air. "Maddox was here."

"Nice spotting," Brooklyn said.

Kai nodded, looking relieved. Even I was relieved to know Maddox really had started down, that he was running from us and not hurt or lost. Now I wouldn't have to waste any energy feeling worried or sympathetic.

Dash moved closer to Elijah and hovered over his shoulder. "Can I have it?"

"Gross," Vidal said. "Who knows where that's been?"

I looked around us at the rugged rocks, the wild sky. Which part was gross?

"Give it to Kai," I suggested.

"Thanks," Kai said. "Let's go."

On the way up, I'd thought we'd taken a level path across the snowfield, but I could see now that it had angled subtly up the slope. Coming down was harder; Kai was right. He told us to put our weight on the inside foot and lean into the hillside so we wouldn't feel like we were pitching out over the drop. It worked, but the snow below us was icy, and the one time I accidentally stepped off Kai's trail, I was surprised at how fast my boot skidded out. I pulled it back quickly, glad I'd listened to Kai's advice about planting the other foot well.

"That was graceful," Greyson said.

"That's one word for it," I told him, my heart racing. I called up to Elijah, hiking in front of me. "Hey, Elijah, be sure to follow Kai's path so you don't slip," I said. "I speak from experience." I was afraid the kid would go sliding the full length of the snowfield if he wasn't careful.

"The section up here is even more slick," Kai called back. "Take it slow."

Elijah stopped and backed into the hill. "You go first," he said, giving me room to pass.

It wasn't the easiest thing to get around him, but I managed to do it. When I took my next step forward, though, I felt a tug behind me. I peered back. Elijah was clutching the ends of my backpack straps.

"If you stay up, I'll stay up," he explained.

"Or if you go down, you'll pull me with you."

"I've always wanted to be an influencer." He smiled and whipped the straps like reins. "Giddyap!"

I planted my boots a little harder and moved on. We'd nearly made it the length of the snowfield when someone behind me yelled out a curse word. I turned to see Dash slipping straight down the slope at a breakneck speed.

"Drop to your butt!" Brooklyn yelled.

"Dig your heels! Elbows! Anything!" Kai yelled.

Dash sat down fast, but he was like a spastic crab, desperately flinging out his limbs and clawing the snow as he sped down the slope, screeching. The end of the snowfield was close. The only thing to catch him was a lot of very hard rocks.

"I can't look," I said, squeezing my eyes shut.

"He's okay, he's okay," Brooklyn said, slipping past us. "He didn't hit his head."

I opened my eyes and saw Dash at the bottom of the snowfield, hugging his knees.

"You okay, bud?" Kai called.

He nodded.

"Stay there," Brooklyn called. She'd reached the boulders on the far side of the snowfield and was beginning to climb down.

Kai made the rest of us sit and have some water while Brooklyn carefully worked her way to Dash's side. Once there, she did an assessment of his ankles, wrists, neck. She was very thorough, and it felt like a lot of time passed before she helped him to his feet. When he managed a couple of steps, she gave us a thumbs-up. Then we waited for them to climb back to us.

Now it was Dash's turn to sit down and rest.

"This is why we stick together," Brooklyn said to Kai.

He nodded. "You sure you're good?" he asked Dash.

Dash held out his hands. "Kinda scraped up from trying to grab on to something. But I'm okay."

"You were like a Winter Olympian out there," I said, thinking he might appreciate a little levity.

"Totally," Elijah giggled. "And you definitely didn't get the gold."

"Maybe it was a new event," Greyson suggested.

"Yeah. Interpretive butt slide," Dash said, cracking everyone up.

It was the best joke he'd ever made, but the fact was, his fall had been scary to watch. And Maddox was still gone. And we'd lost a whole lot of time. At this point, Maddox had an hour or two on us, minimum. If he was determined to ditch us, I figured our chances of finding him were getting very small.

We didn't hit any terrain as difficult as the boulders or the snowfield after that, but our progress was slow—and it was because of Dash. Vidal noticed it first: His stride looked off. He tried to keep up, but he kept falling farther and farther back.

"Dash, you still good?" Brooklyn called.

"Yup."

"He's not," Vidal said. "He's walking funny. I think he's hurt."

We circled up again, and this time Dash admitted that his leg felt sore. When he rolled up his pant leg, his knee was puffy, swollen. Brooklyn ran through another set of checks and said she was worried he'd sprained it on the fall.

"Did you hear a pop?" she asked him.

"I couldn't hear anything over my screams," he admitted.

Brooklyn frowned. "I can't believe we don't even have a first-aid kit," she said to Kai.

"What would you give him?" Elijah asked.

"Some ibuprofen. A stretchy wrap for the swelling."

"And that was all in your packs?" I asked.

"Everything was in the packs," she said.

"You can use my track pants," Vidal declared suddenly.

"What?"

"To wrap his knees. They're stretchy. They'd be perfect, right?"

"Thanks, Vidal. That's super helpful," Kai said.

"You gonna hike in your underwear?" Dash asked him.

"I got shorts too," Vidal said. "Just don't remind me about bugs, okay?"

Vidal handed Brooklyn the pants, and she wrapped them around Dash's leg in careful circles. She tied the two leg sections together and Dash stood up. "Let's go."

"You feel ready for this?" Kai asked him.

"Will there be food at camp?" Dash asked.

Kai nodded.

"Then I'm ready."

The next two hours of hiking were draining—especially on an empty stomach. It reminded me of our first days on the trail, when no one spoke, when the only objective seemed to be to put one foot in front of the other and not give up. Our pace had slowed drastically to accommodate Dash. I was sure he must be in real pain by now; at a certain point, he'd started leaning on Greyson's shoulder and half-hopping along. But nobody wanted to talk about it, especially him. Walking slowly was harder than our normal pace. We weren't going easier on our bodies; we were prolonging the agony of staying upright and on our feet, resisting gravity's hard pull down the slope.

After another half hour of trudging along, Kai raised the possibility of sending some of us forward at a faster clip. It made sense to me. We needed food, and the counselors needed to get the search for Maddox underway. This time, Brooklyn agreed. Greyson and Vidal would stay back with her in case Dash needed more physical support. Elijah and I would move forward with Kai.

Freed from Dash's slow pace, and with a smoother stretch of trail, we covered the remaining miles twice as fast. When we reached Vidal's solo spot on the ridge, we knew we were on the home stretch. We passed Elijah's Spruce Grove, and the trail across my talus slope. And then we were back—light-headed and exhausted. Our campsite really did look like home.

"Maddox? Maddox, are you here?" Kai called as we approached the tents.

I was prepared for Maddox to pop out with a bagel and cream cheese in his hand, smiling as if this whole thing were a big joke—not because I really believed it, but because it was worth imagining such an easy end to the day's stress. But the only answer to Kai's calls was the chatter of squirrels, squabbling under the trees. The campsite was bare.

"Do you think Ray came?" Elijah asked.

Kai wiped his brow and nodded toward a familiar blue sack by the campfire ring. "There's the mail pouch."

"Awesome. Let's go get the food!" Elijah exclaimed. He glanced at Kai. "You need it, dude."

Elijah was right: Kai did look a little off. His olive skin had a white cast to it and his forehead shone with sweat.

"Have a seat," I told him. "We'll open up the fence and bring everything to you."

Kai put his fingers on his chest like he was feeling for his heart rate, then nodded. Elijah and I pushed our way through the trees to the clearing where the food packs were stored.

Except they weren't stored.

The electric fencing was half-toppled, and the food packs were on the ground, overturned and trashed. Food was strewn every which way, and a crowd of ravens and jays was gobbling up every bit they could reach. As we shouted and approached, the birds flew up into the nearby branches and stayed there, squawking at us for interrupting their feast. A squirrel dove into the trees, dropping part of a potato behind it.

My eyes absorbed the scene fast; my brain processed it more slowly.

"Ray refilled the packs . . . ," I began, because I saw new food—or what would have been new food if it hadn't been reduced to crumbs and globs. "But then what? He didn't turn on the fence?"

"Maybe not," Elijah said. He peered to look at the switch. "Yep. It's off. Definitely."

"But how did the animals get into the food packs? You think he forgot to close them up?"

Kai had told me once that even though rodents and birds might be able to get past the bear-proof fence, they couldn't get into the big food packs. They were called critter-proof for a reason.

"Maddox," Elijah said decisively. "I bet Maddox did this."

"You think he'd turn off the fence? Leave everything open?"

It sounded extreme, even for Maddox.

"You got a better explanation?" Elijah asked me.

I thought for a moment, then shook my head.

It was a stupid thing to do in the wilderness—like leaving the refrigerator door open in a kitchen packed with hungry football players. I squatted down and picked up a shredded section of plastic wrapping. Hot dogs. It had been filled with hot dogs. Another package had held ground beef—I recognized it from our first resupply night—but it too was destroyed, empty. All the meat had been ravaged. The fresh stuff that we normally ate for the first couple of days—and pretty much all our trail food—was just plain gone. There was no sign of the bagels or the crackers or the chocolate or the raisins or the apples or the oranges or the energy bars. The best we could figure it, Maddox had grabbed everything he could stuff in his pack to eat on the trail, and then fled. Between him and the animals, we were left with half a bag of rice, salt, and several dozen oatmeal packets. A jar of oil. A punctured tube of pesto.

"I didn't know these guys could eat that much," Elijah said, eyeing the birds unhappily.

"The squirrels helped," I said, nodding in the direction of the one that had bolted into the trees.

Then I turned over the biggest food pack and saw five long claw marks slashed into the side. I gulped. "Or maybe not just the birds and the squirrels."

Elijah's eyes widened. "What did that—a bear? We need to go tell Kai."

"Oh gosh! Kai!" I'd almost forgotten him. I grabbed two oatmeal packets and a Sierra cup. When we reached Kai, he had his head on his knees. I dumped the oatmeal into a cup and poured in the last bit of water from my bottle, hoping the stuff would dissolve.

"Here. Oatmeal," I said to him. "It's the best I can do right now."

He ate it clumsily, then put his head back down, mumbling.

"What's he saying?" Elijah asked me.

"No idea." I leaned closer. "Kai, what else do you need?"

He shook his head. "I'm okay. I'm okay."

"He's not okay, is he?" Elijah said.

"He needs the medicine," I said. "From . . ."

". . . his backpack," Elijah said despondently.

I took another look at Kai. He was sweating like crazy now. My heart raced.

"Kai. Is there more medicine here someplace? Tell us what to do. Everything. Including what to do if you can't tell us what to do anymore."

He mumbled something unintelligible. We were already there.

"Come on," I said, grabbing Elijah's arm. "Let's go look."

We raced back to the clearing. I scanned the spilled contents on the ground and saw nothing that looked like medicine. I picked up the big food pack and turned it upside down. Three silver packages of freeze-dried chili fell onto the ground. But no orange box. I started picking up every shredded bag and box in sight, but it wasn't there. I already knew it wasn't there. I took a deep breath. "Elijah?"

I heard a scuffling sound in the trees.

"Elijah?" My heart was racing again. Why had we been so quick to assume the bear was gone? "Elijah, where—"

He burst out from behind the trees waving an insulated pouch over his head like it was the winning ticket. "It's in here— two of those boxes! There's more food back there, too. We can get it later."

Kai looked so dazed, we didn't even ask him to help us. Inside the orange box was a vial of white powder, a liquid-filled syringe, and an illustrated set of instructions that Elijah used to guide me through the mixing and refilling. After I tapped out the bubbles, I held up the syringe for Kai's inspection. He gave a vague gesture like a nod and half-rolled, half-fell onto all fours. Elijah yanked down Kai's trail pants and I took a breath and jabbed the syringe right into his butt. It was only after I pushed in the plunger and pulled the syringe back out that I realized how much I was shaking.

"Kai?" Elijah asked, crawling down to look at his face. "It's in."

Kai lay down on the ground and curled into a fetal position. The next ten minutes were the scariest of my life. Then Elijah looked back at the instructions. It took fifteen minutes on an unconscious patient. Kai had never been unconscious. There could have been seizures. It could have been worse. We just needed five more minutes for the medicine to get into his bloodstream.

A few minutes later, Kai pulled up his pants and sat down on the ground. He still didn't look so good.

"Are you better?"

"Not yet," he said, swallowing hard. "But I will be."

We sat with him quietly while he sipped some water. After a while, he turned to us and shook his head.

"What is it? Did we do something wrong?" I asked.

He waved me off, then pushed himself back up onto the log. He still didn't speak right away. When he finally did, it was clear he was frustrated.

"Shoot," he said, shaking his head.

"What?" I asked again.

He rubbed his eyes. "I'm not supposed to moon the campers."

Elijah laughed shakily. I let out a gigantic breath I hadn't realized I'd been holding.

"Now are you better?" Elijah asked.

"Getting there. Go find me some more food."

⇥⇤ ⩔ ⇥⇤ ⩔ ⇥⇤ ⩔ ⇥⇤ ⩔ ⇥⇤

Elijah and I collected every last bit of food we could find and dumped it at Kai's feet. It wasn't much—maybe enough to feed our group for another day. But Kai would be okay, and we could make a decent dinner, and that's all I wanted to think about now.

Kai still looked unsettled, though, and now it wasn't because of his blood sugars. He told us we had a new problem. "We have to leave this place, guys. Tonight."

"Because of Maddox?" Elijah asked.

"Because of the bear. It knows it can get an easy meal here now. It isn't safe."

"Let's *eat* all the food, then. So it won't have anything to tempt it," Elijah suggested, pleased with his reasoning.

"Um, except us," I pointed out.

Kai nodded. "We need to find another campsite. Before dark."

"When will that be?" Elijah asked.

"When. The. Sun. Goes. Down," Kai said, his enlightened pep finally subsumed by genuine New York City sarcasm.

I glanced at the sky. Good thing the sun didn't set till almost ten. We still had a chance.

"Start packing," Kai said. "I'll make dinner. If you finish with your own tent, work on someone else's. We'll pack, eat, and get everything ready for the others. And guys?"

We looked up.

"Watch out for bears."

Elijah and I scanned the campsite and our eyes met back in the middle.

"*Rahr*," I said.

"Walk me to my tent," Elijah told me.

"We got this," I said, locking elbows.

For once, he didn't pull away.

We managed to pack up almost all our things by the time Kai was ready with our meal: a big pot of rice and peas smothered in the pesto. We ate what we needed to think straight, then went back to work. Elijah disappeared into Dash's tent. Moments later, I heard a shout.

"Whoa! Look what I found!"

"A note?" I guessed.

He leaned out, holding up a large chocolate bar. "It was on his pillow!"

"A parting gift from a loving brother," I said.

"Some gift. Now the bears will smell chocolate on his head."

I laughed in spite of myself.

A movement across the lake caught my eye. It was Brooklyn and Vidal, covering the last few yards to our campsite. They came to a stop in front of us, taking in the scene with bewildered expressions.

"What's happening?" Brooklyn asked, sounding almost angry.

"We're moving," Elijah said. "To get away from the bear."

"Bear?" Brooklyn spotted Kai by the fire and strode over to talk to him directly. We trailed behind, not wanting to miss a word.

"Where are Dash and Greyson?" I asked Vidal.

"Back at Elijah's solo spot, resting. Greyson was practically carrying Dash the last bit."

For some reason it helped to hear Kai tell Brooklyn the whole story of what had happened since we arrived. Everything had felt surreal until then; hearing the words spoken out loud made it really true. When Kai mentioned the incident with the syringe, Brooklyn looked at me and Elijah with an all-new expression that I was pretty sure was respect.

I peeked at Vidal, expecting him to be a total stress puppy now that he had this long-dreaded calamity actually before him.

A bear at our campsite. A near-death experience. But the kid seemed strangely calm, even fascinated.

"I thought you'd be freaking out more," I whispered.

He turned to me with a small nod. "Me too! I mean, this day has been a total nightmare. But have you noticed—we're, like, alive anyway!" He laughed out loud, clearly amazed.

It was Brooklyn who looked more overwhelmed. For the first time that I could recall, she didn't move immediately into planning mode. Instead, she sat down on a log and stared ahead, like she had completely run out of gas.

"Would it be weird of me to suggest you have some dinner?" I asked, afraid I sounded like my mom.

"Excellent idea," Kai said, reaching for a clean Sierra cup.

"I have to get back to Dash," Brooklyn said without moving.

"What did you make?" Vidal asked, sniffing the air.

Kai took the lid off the cooking pot and scooped up a cupful of rice for each of them. He promised Brooklyn we'd take only five minutes to eat and plan and then get straight back to Dash. Greyson was with him, after all. They were probably sleeping on woven branch beds by now.

Brooklyn only started talking again when her rice was nearly gone.

"Okay, Kai. New campsite. Any ideas? We could head back toward the parking area, except what's the point? It's eight miles away, right? And I assume the van keys are in . . ." She hesitated, not wanting to finish the sentence.

"My daypack," Kai confirmed, rubbing his temple.

"So what do you think? There's probably another road closer to here, right?" Brooklyn asked.

"I think there is," Kai said. "But I'm not sure I could find it without a map."

"Both your maps were in your packs, too?" Elijah asked.

The counselors nodded grimly.

"We messed up," Kai said. "If it's any comfort, we'll probably get fired when this session is over."

"I wish there were a ranger station near here," Brooklyn said.

"Or a manned fire tower, even," Kai suggested.

A thought came to me. I caught Elijah's eyes. He didn't understand why. I made a gesture of a big brimmed hat but he still looked confused. Then suddenly he got it and shook his head. I gave him a plea with my eyes. *Come on.* This was no time to worry about getting in trouble. We already were in trouble—the real kind.

"What about a field station?" I suggested.

Brooklyn looked at me funny. "This is a wilderness area, Ginny. No one's allowed to build a field station."

"I mean, like a research site."

"You know of one?" Brooklyn asked, sounding dubious.

"There's a scientist working just over the ridge behind Elijah's solo site. Or there was a few days ago, but I'm guessing she's still there. She has a camp, and maybe she has a satellite phone and stuff, too. I'm sure she's got a map, at least. She seemed like a total pro."

"Wait, you *went* there?" Brooklyn asked.

"Yesss," I said slowly.

"Accidentally," Elijah added.

"You too?" Brooklyn asked.

He shrugged, rolled his eyes. "I said accidentally."

"Can you find your way there again?" she asked us.

I nodded. Elijah did too, and now he looked relieved, almost proud.

"It's only about ten minutes from Elijah's site. Well, running. Maybe twenty if we walked."

Brooklyn nodded. "Let's do it."

Kai and Elijah left first, loaded with their packs and carrying the whole pot of food plus the bar of chocolate for Greyson and Dash. The rest of us kept packing. When Kai returned, he had Greyson in tow and we all settled into work. Within an hour, the campsite was completely packed up and swept clear of trash. Greyson, Vidal, Brooklyn, and I put on our packs, and Kai doubled up, with Dash's pack on his back and what remained of Maddox's belongings on his front.

It was a sad way to leave Bead Lake, but there wasn't much time to focus on my goodbye. I patted my wildflowers on their purple heads, took a mental picture of the ring of trees and the jumble of white rocks, then blew a kiss to the water—the first gem of my trip. How strange to think that the next visitor here might be a bear. I hoped they'd love it as much as I had.

We trudged slowly behind Brooklyn and Kai, aware that they were talking about Maddox. They seemed as concerned about finding him as they were about getting the rest of us safely settled for the night.

I glanced at Greyson. "How much are you worrying about our hero the runaway?"

He made his hand into a big zero. "Happy to have him go, actually. What a jerk. How long would it have taken him to close the food packs and switch on the fence? Ten seconds?"

"He wasn't thinking about us."

"Yeah. Good point. I don't think he's ever thought about any-one but himself."

"He's a narcissist," I said.

"Sociopath."

"Loser."

"What's his dwarf name again?" Greyson asked.

"Sleazy or Slippery. We never decided."

Greyson shook his head. "Let's say Scum."

I nodded.

Elijah and Dash were propped up under a fir tree looking like a pair of scarecrows that had lost half their straw. Dash looked especially subdued, but there was a chocolate smear around his mouth. So at least I knew he'd eaten his food.

Brooklyn eyed Dash with concern. "Think you can walk if we help you?"

"Check this out," Dash said. He shifted his weight and pulled out a pair of long branches with Y-shaped ends. "Greyson made me crutches!"

Of course he did.

"Nice job, Greyson," Kai said.

I held up my hand and Greyson reluctantly returned a high five.

"Let's get you up and on your way, then," Brooklyn said to Dash, helping him stand up.

The daylight was fading. We needed to push on or we'd be camping on a rocky slope. Brooklyn said she'd be Dash's wingman in case he needed extra support. Greyson took Kai's pack. And then we headed out of the tree patch the way Elijah had run on that fateful day when we'd snapped our first trust line. It took much longer to mount the hill with packs on, and Dash and Brooklyn quickly fell behind. But they waved us on, and we continued up to the top. From there, we immediately spotted a new set of string lines set out across the rocks. Sweet relief. In the distance, I could just make out the little encampment at the end of the valley. It was worth waiting for Brooklyn and Dash to make it to the top of the hill so we could share the good news.

"See?" Elijah said, pointing.

Kai nodded. "You said she was friendly, right?"

We hesitated.

"I wouldn't put it that way," Elijah said.

"Kai, no one in the wilderness refuses to help a fellow camper in need," Brooklyn said. She gestured at our line. "Especially when we look as pitiful as this."

Kai started down the trail and the rest of us followed, one after another. Once we were closing in on the scientist's campsite, everyone got a little punchy. Elijah started it.

"Hey, I think we reached a new milestone today, you guys. Bear-ly Made It. Get it? *Bear-ly!*"

"Good one," I said.

"Don't forget Interpretive Butt Slide," Vidal said.

"And Shoving in Shots," Elijah added.

"And Creating Crutches," Dash put in.

I was glancing at Kai and Brooklyn, trying to gauge if they found the exchange funny or infuriating. "What do you think, you guys? Any other milestones we can check off?"

We'd reached the edge of the site. Kai unclipped his shoulder straps and threw his pack to the ground.

"Yeah. Seriously Screwed."

CHAPTER
17

I woke in the morning to hushed voices and the scuff of footsteps on gravel. They were trying to be quiet, but there's no way to keep noise from penetrating a nylon tent. I peeked out, curious. Brooklyn and Kai were talking with our new best friend. Her name was Theo.

Dr. Theodora Jurek had been gracious when we'd stumbled into her quiet campsite the night before, listening to our tale and telling us that of course we should set up our tents beside hers and join her for the night. She had no devices to help Brooklyn and Kai alert the Outlands staff about Maddox. She said she hadn't started her career with satellite phones and she wasn't going to end it with them, either. The best she could do was give the counselors a map and point them in the direction of civilization.

"But not until morning," she insisted. "Neither of you is in any shape to hike through the night." When Brooklyn voiced her concerns about Maddox, Theo was unmoved. "That boy sounds crafty enough to make it out just fine on his own. And if he spends the night alone in the woods..." She gave a small chuckle. "Well, it might just do him some good."

See why she was our new best friend?

I climbed out of my tent first, followed soon by Elijah and Greyson, then Vidal, and finally Dash. Yesterday's exertion had taken its toll. We were wrung out to the core. We sat on the logs in a bleary clump, not moving or talking, just listening. I leaned my head on Elijah's shoulder. The kid had almost dragged me down a snowfield yesterday; the least he could do was give me a headrest.

To Brooklyn's immense relief, Dash's knee hadn't gotten any worse in the night. She told us a mild sprain like this one just needed the RICE plan—rest, ice, compression, and elevation.

"Ice?" Elijah asked. It wasn't a regular commodity at camp.

"The water over there will put you in mind of a glacier," Theo said, gesturing to the rushing creek that was her nearest water source. She turned to Dash. "I can give you a little camp chair to sit in while you soak it. Sound good?"

"Awesome," he said, which I was pretty sure was the first positive thing I'd ever heard him say.

Kai and Brooklyn ran through their different options for getting the word out about Maddox and getting us resupplied. Theo said one of her research assistants was due back in a couple of days and would have a truck at the parking area, if that helped. But if they wanted to go out now, their best bet was to make a call from a granite outcropping about two and a half miles down the trail.

"You know the signal issues here in Montana," Theo said. "Miserable. But if you perch yourself out on the far right side of the rocks, you can usually catch enough bars from a tower in Dawson to get a text out, maybe even a call. It's either that or hitchhike!"

"I guess we'll hitchhike," Kai said.

Brooklyn nodded. "Maddox took our phones, too."

They had no phones? I lifted my head from Elijah's shoulder. Once again, he and I were sitting on a magic key. I rubbed my sleepy face and pressed my nose into my cupped hands.

"Wuh hah a fuhn," I said.

"What's that, Ginny?"

"You're not," Elijah said under his breath.

But he wasn't going to deter me. I lifted my hands away from my face. "We have a phone. Elijah and I. We have a cell phone."

The entire group was staring at me like I'd just admitted we were Russian spies.

"Since when?" Brooklyn asked.

I swallowed. I wanted to be honest, but I didn't feel like ratting out Elijah's whole criminal record.

"Since we got here, okay?" Elijah said. "But it doesn't count as technology. I mean, without Wi-Fi it's pretty much an Etch-a-Sketch."

"You don't have to explain, Elijah," Kai said gently.

"Yet," Brooklyn added.

"Do you have a charger?" Kai asked him.

"Duh."

"Be nice," I said, nudging him with my elbow.

Greyson was looking at us with an unreadable expression.

"What?" I mouthed.

He shook his head.

"We'll take the phone, Elijah," Brooklyn told him. "Thank you. And hopefully the spot on the rocks can actually pick up a signal today."

"I'll draw the location of the overlook on the map as best as I can remember it," Theo said.

"What are you going to do when you reach civilization?" Dash asked the counselors.

"We'll alert Outlands. The police. Search and Rescue. Try to figure out if Maddox left the wilderness or if . . ." Kai hesitated. "Does your brother know how to drive?" He looked like he didn't want to know the answer.

"Dad's given us a few lessons," Dash said.

Brooklyn shook her head in wonderment. "This is a total nightmare."

Vidal's eyes lit up. "Yo! We're all having nightmares!"

Someone's stomach growled, reminding us how much we needed breakfast. I tried to remember how many oatmeal packets were left, but Theo said she had more pancake mix than she knew what to do with. "Do you all like pancakes?" she asked. "With chocolate chips?"

Dash was staring at her with puppy-dog eyes. "Will you be my mom?"

"I take it that's a yes."

Kai and Brooklyn headed down the trail after breakfast, taking Elijah with them for tech support. He looked delighted to have the responsibility—puffed up, but in a different way from before. In fact, come to think of it, the kid had added some actual muscles since the day we'd first arrived.

Greyson, Vidal, and I helped get Dash set up by the stream. The water was as cold as Theo had promised, and while he soaked his knee, the three of us splashed off enough to clear the last of the cobwebs from our brains. By the time we'd put on dry clothes, Theo was out working at her study plots.

Without the counselors or a plan for the rest of the day, it felt like we'd entered a strange state of suspension. I didn't mind, actually. In fact, it gave me an idea.

I glanced toward Theo's research site. "I think I might go see what she's up to," I told the others. I'd wanted to ask her about her work the first time we stumbled into her plots. Now I could finally get an answer.

I assumed Greyson and Vidal would take a nap in the shade with Dash, but instead they followed me up the trail to where Theo was working. For a little while we stood there awkwardly, peering from a distance as she jotted down notations on a clipboard.

"I hope we're not bugging you," Vidal said.

"You're okay," she murmured.

"Then can we bug you?" I asked.

She looked up warily.

"I mean—I'm just curious. About what you're studying here."

She gestured toward a rock covered in splotchy gray growth. "Lichens."

"Those weird plants that scratch my track pants?" Vidal asked, looking doubtful.

Theo turned back to her clipboard. "They're not all scratchy. And they're not plants."

This was news to me. "Then what are they?"

Theo tipped her hat back and regarded us thoughtfully, as if trying to decide how much of the story to share. "It's complicated."

Greyson had his fingertip on top of a little wooden stake, the kind Elijah and I had toppled the week before. It wobbled under his touch, like a loose tooth. "If we offered to help, would you tell us?" he asked.

Again the look of assessment. A squint of the eye. Theo didn't hurry things.

"It's a deal," she said at last.

Theo taught us that lichens weren't plants or animals: They were three kinds of organisms coming together to make a whole new one. One of the three organisms was often a cyanobacteria, one of the very first living things to colonize Earth and make it livable for everything else.

"One of the first to arrive," she said, "and who knows, maybe the last to go after everything else has sizzled away."

My heart skidded to a momentary stop. You couldn't get away from this kind of talk. "You mean after climate change kills everything else?"

She studied me like I was the scratchy organism now. "Lichens live a very long time. I'm not talking about next month."

It felt like truth and a peace offering, rolled into one. I had a lot more questions, but I held on to them for now.

"Is that why you're studying them?" Vidal asked, tiptoeing around the plots.

Theo watched him approvingly. "Lichens get their sustenance directly from the atmosphere, which makes them good indicators."

"Of?"

"Air quality, for one. But also climate change—something all of us are trying very hard to understand."

"All of who?" I asked.

"Ecologists. The scientific community." She paused. "Anyone with a heartbeat."

Man, I liked this person. "Will you be *my* mom?" I said. I was going for the laugh, but my admiration was real.

"I don't know what they're doing with you at that camp," she said, shaking her head.

"We're okay," I told her.

"You should put us to work," Greyson added.

➤⋅◄ ❦ ➤⋅◄ ❦ ➤⋅◄ ❦ ➤⋅◄ ❦ ➤⋅◄

We spent the rest of the morning learning how Theo laid out her study plots across the rocky hillside and in a nearby clump of trees. She'd taken inventories of the lichens here decades ago and was assessing how much or how little things had changed. Between the rocks and the trees, there were more lichens than we could possibly learn in one day. But she introduced us to them anyway, saying we could at least make a start. There was frosted rock tripe, gray and crumbly at the edges, like a charred piece of paper. Theo called it friable. There was sunken button lichen, ashy and riddled with lines like a sun-dried mud puddle. There was brittle horsehair, whiskered jelly, brown-eyed wolf lichen, deadman's camouflage, cowpie crater, and sugared sunburst.

"These names!" I said, feeling like you could arrange them in any way and end up with a poem. But it wasn't just the names. Starting to zoom in on the wildly different lichens growing around us made the whole scene sharper, richer. Lichens I'd been hiking past and sitting on for more than two weeks now shouted out for my attention from every surface. It reminded me of how Zinzie had said the world looked the first time she wore glasses, how the treetops went from a blur of green to thousands of separate sparkly, sharp-edged leaves.

Vidal traced the edge of a sugared sunburst lichen, as brilliant and orange as its name implied. "Is this a male one or a female one?" he asked, sounding tired.

"Vidal?" I said. I was surprised he was asking at all.

"What? It's the first thing they tell us. Every time," he said grumpily. "You haven't noticed?"

Theo laughed. "Well, with lichens it's much, much more complicated than that."

"Oh," Vidal said, giving the orange splotch another look. "Huh. Cool."

Greyson studied him quizzically, and then blinked, like he'd finally figured something out.

I turned back to Theo. "So. How can we help?"

It wasn't clear that we really could be useful to Theo right away, but she gave us small jobs anyway, probably just to make us feel included. My favorite one was trying to identify and count up the different species in her plot. Greyson helped her measure how much area they covered. Vidal recorded the results of Theo's calculations. He seemed to love note-taking, writing down every detail with beautiful, precise handwriting that almost looked like a font.

"Where'd you learn to write like that?" Theo asked, peering in for a look. "An architecture class?"

He shook his head. "Catholic school."

Greyson was still focused on Theo's plot lines. "So as soon as you finish counting up the lichens, you move the stakes?" he asked her.

She nodded. "The most tedious part of my job."

"If I had a new idea, would you be interested?" he asked.

"What kind of new idea?" she asked, sort of gruffly, sort of not.

"This guy's a genius with wood," Vidal volunteered.

"How are you with string?" she asked.

"Worth a try," Greyson said. He nodded at Theo's measuring tape and she handed it over. He did some measurements, asked a couple of questions, scribbled some notes, and stood up. "I'll see if Dash wants to help me. He looks lonely."

When Greyson was out of earshot, Theo turned to Vidal and me. "I get the feeling that kid's a keeper."

"He's been told he's fated to die before he's twenty-eight," Vidal told her.

Theo frowned. "Fate is a construct of very small minds."

＞－＜　＞－＜　＞－＜　＞－＜　＞－＜

We circled up at lunchtime, though without Brooklyn and Kai, our geometry was freer than usual. I plunked down beside Greyson and checked out his morning's work. Where Theo's plots were made from planted stakes connected by string, Greyson had devised something more like frames: wooden *L*s with the string already attached to them. They collapsed in a small bundle, then could be stretched out easily and placed on top of any surface—even rock—without fear of toppling.

"Nice," I said, picking up one to try it out. "I think she'll like it. FYI, she says you're a keeper."

"A leper?"

"Oh, stop. *Keeper*, I said." I looked at his freckles and finally saw it. "Hey, the Great Bear," I said, pressing each freckle. "I knew you had a constellation."

He closed his eyes. "I didn't know you knew the stars."

"Only from my bandanna," I admitted. "But we could look at them sometime. I mean, the night sky's pretty awesome here."

"They'll take away our boots," Greyson pointed out.

"I have socks."

He gave me a long look. "There's nothing going on between you and Elijah?"

"What?" The question took me totally by surprise, mostly because I still thought of Elijah as the little kid of the group. How could anyone think we were an item? But maybe things looked different from the outside. "Um, no," I told Greyson. "Nothing going on between us . . . except breaking a lot of rules."

"Okay," he said, so quietly that only I could hear. "Then it's a date."

>·< ♥ >·< ♥ >·< ♥ >·< ♥ >·<

Brooklyn and Elijah didn't make it back to camp until mid-afternoon. The phone call had dropped out half a dozen times before they finally got hold of someone at Outlands. Even then, it took another couple of hours for a staff member to make the long drive out and meet them on the trail.

But none of us was complaining. The staffer had come equipped with some excellent emergency rations: a bag of trail mix, crackers and chips, and a tin of our trusty powdered orange drink.

"We gave her Kai; she gave us snacks," Elijah said cheerfully.

"Why did Kai have to leave?" I asked.

"To help with the search for Maddox. Share where we've been, what kind of equipment he took," Brooklyn explained.

"So he'll be gone a long time?" Dash asked.

"Depends on what happens with your brother," Brooklyn said. "I figure Ray should be able to get up here tomorrow morning. And"—she anticipated Dash's next question—"we won't starve. We have three packages of freeze-dried chili, plus new snacks to get us through till morning."

"I'm not worried," he said with a goofy smile. "Mom has bacon."

➤◄ ❦ ➤◄ ❦ ➤◄ ❦ ➤◄ ❦ ➤◄

"You're acting different," Elijah said to Dash after dinner.

Dash was sitting with his back to a log, his bad leg propped up on Kai's stuffed sleeping bag.

I nodded. We'd all noticed.

"And not because of the knee."

"And not because of the bacon."

"You're not snorting like you usually do."

"It started when Maddox left."

Brooklyn looked at Dash. "Pretty interesting to get that kind of feedback from your fellow campers, don't you think?"

He fished out a couple of M&M'S from his trail mix, popped them in his mouth. "Yeah."

"Maybe you want to start off tonight's sharing?" Brooklyn suggested.

"I can leave," Theo said, reaching for her walking sticks.

Dash shook his head. "It's cool. You can stay. I mean, if you want. But...I snort?"

"And sniff."

"All the time."

"When Maddox is around, anyway."

"Or maybe it's allergies?"

Dash was quiet, thinking. If brains had wheels, it seemed to me that his had really big, slow-moving ones, like on a rusty tractor. It took a lot to get them started.

"I guess I am allergic," he said. "To my brother."

We laughed a little, Dash included. But then his smile collapsed. He glanced over his shoulder like he half-expected Maddox to be lurking in the shadows, listening. When he turned back to us, his face had gone serious. "He's not a good person, you guys."

"Tell us something we don't know," Greyson said.

"No, you don't get it," Dash said, shaking his head fast. "It's even worse than you think. I mean, with other people, he pretends to be nice, at least for a while. But he gave up pretending with me a long time ago."

And then the tractor was hurtling down a hillside and his words came out fast, almost desperately.

"He told you it was hard for me to grow up in his shadow, but that was messing with words. It's hard growing up under his . . . his rule. Seriously, it's like living with a tyrant. He got the good looks and so no one sees the nasty stuff on the inside." He bit into another M&M, then had a thought and held out the broken half. "Like if this had poison instead of chocolate inside the pretty candy shell, that's what Maddox would be."

"Whoa," Elijah said.

Dash nodded. "He fools everyone. Even my parents. If they needed to send me off to therapy—I mean, not-really-therapy— camp, fine. Whatever. Send me. But *with* Maddox? What were they thinking? Out here, there's no way to get away from him."

"Till now," Elijah pointed out.

"Is that why you tried to run away the first night?" I asked him. He nodded.

"But the coyotes were scarier?" I asked.

He looked confused. "They weren't wolves?"

I shook my head.

"Dash, this sounds hard," Brooklyn said. "And we'd like to help you however we can. But I do want to put it out there that Maddox is just a kid, too. I bet deep down there's a hurt. Some reason he feels such a need to dominate."

"Dad loves how strong Maddox is, actually," Dash said, like he hadn't really heard. "He's always telling me to be more like him."

"Has anyone ever taken your side?" Theo asked quietly.

When Dash looked up, his face had that tender little-boy look I'd seen only once before. "Well, one person."

I could have guessed it.

"Consuelo. My old nanny. She always tried to make everything better for me."

I pictured little Dash in his Buzz Lightyear costume, longing for the power and protective helmet of a plastic astronaut, and it made me want to cry.

"I hope we can make things better, too," Brooklyn said. "Let's talk about this some more tomorrow, okay?"

Dash nodded, but I could tell he didn't have a lot of hope.

If Kai had been with us, I'm sure he would have tried to say something deep. Instead it was Elijah who piped up next. "So, wait, does this mean you're not actually a jerk?"

"Dude," Greyson said under his breath.

"What? I'm seriously confused."

"Elijah, please apologize," Brooklyn said wearily.

Elijah sighed. "Sorry, Dash."

"And you can help him with his nighttime routine, too," Brooklyn added. "I think it's time we all turned in."

Evening was settling around us. Seeing the first planet appear in the sky, I thought of my date with Greyson and wanted to hit the tent fast so I could sneak right back out. Then, for no reason I could explain, I did something crazy. I asked permission.

"Could Greyson and I spend half an hour looking at the constellations tonight?" I asked Brooklyn.

"Alone?" She sounded shocked.

Well, that wasn't exactly it. "Together?"

"No way."

"Oh."

"If you really want to look at stars, we could make it a group activity," she suggested.

"That's okay." I started for my tent. Now it would be doubly bad to sneak out. I should have kept my stupid mouth shut.

"I appreciate that you asked, though," Brooklyn said.

I flashed her a thumbs-up.

"And I never want to punish a kid for doing the right thing. So, listen. How about twenty minutes?" she suggested. "With no . . ." She stopped short, looking incredibly awkward. "You know . . . consorting."

"'Consorting'?" I couldn't help smiling. "Did your grandmother teach you that word?"

She gave me a look. "You know what I mean. Just twenty minutes, Ginny. I'll be timing you."

I nodded. "Thanks, Brooklyn."

After everyone seemed to be settled in for the night, I went out to Greyson's tent and made scratchy noises on the nylon. When nothing happened, I scratched again.

"What took you so long?" I asked when he finally appeared.

"I thought you were a chipmunk."

"Ha—nothing that adorable."

He climbed out and closed the tent behind him.

"I don't know about that," he said, making my palms tingly again.

Greyson and I crossed the meadow until the ground softened underfoot and there was space to stretch out fully on our backs. The black sky was already salted with so many more stars than when we'd left the fire ring.

"Is the stargazing this good in Kansas?" I asked him.

He put his hand on top of mine. "No."

My stomach did a funny little drop, like on an elevator, only nicer.

I smiled into the dark. "What do you think—does this qualify as consorting?" I whispered.

"What?"

"Brooklyn said no consorting."

Greyson shook his head. "Brooklyn needs to get over herself with those rules."

"Yup," I said, relishing the moment too much to believe it could be wrong.

We let the silence take over again. I was supposed to be looking at the stars, but all I could focus on was the square footage of our shared personal real estate: shoulders, hips, hands, feet.

"Show me a constellation," Greyson said.

I shifted my attention from his hand to the sky, but there was almost too much to see now: the layers and layers of stars. The bright planets. The swoop of the Milky Way.

"Well, there's the Big Dipper...," I began.

"Tell me something I don't know," he said.

But instead of searching for more constellations, I found myself doing a mind meld with the giant sky, growing dizzy with stars—their number, brilliance, persistence. These same stars had been here before the dinosaurs, and they would be here long after we were gone. From their perspective, we were just worthless specks of dust.

It was almost comforting.

"Still waiting," Greyson said.

His hand felt steady and warm, and when he gave mine a squeeze, I had to catch my breath before I could speak.

"Okay—see there?" I said, waving my free hand at the sky. "That's Puffy Q-tip. And that one? That's the S'more."

"Huh. It's strange I haven't heard of those before."

"Oh, well, you know. They sound different in the original Greek."

"Riiiight. I hear those ancient Greeks really loved their graham crackers...."

I laughed. "Okay. I give up. I guess I'm a useless astronomer, especially without my handy bandanna."

I expected him to tease me, but he didn't. Instead, he turned onto his side, so close our noses almost touched.

"Then we should probably consort," he said. And this time the word didn't sound ridiculous; it sounded ... irresistible.

My heart went *blip-blip-blip*, and I did not think about Brooklyn or the rules or the twenty-minute time limit, only the overwhelming awesomeness as this keeper of a boy kissed me now, in an alpine meadow, in the landscape of my soul, under a canopy of prehistoric solar-powered lights. It was entirely delicious, without a single awkward distraction at all.

Until Brooklyn's flashlight swept over the grass like a searchlight. We sat up just in the nick of time.

"Tomorrow I'll find the Great Bear," I said.

"In the sky or on my nose?"

"Oh, definitely both," I said, and I sneaked in one last kiss.

CHAPTER
18

Ray and his pack mule delivered the food first: frozen meat and fresh bread, vegetables, fruit, crackers, cheese, chocolate. He'd even brought a small cooler to hold extra fresh stuff, because Kai had told him we would probably have to stay at Theo's research site for at least the next few days.

While Brooklyn and Ray filled the food packs, Greyson and I stood nearby, getting to know the tough little mule that had helped haul everything up. He had a dark-brown coat and a scruffy black mane and a tail that was twitching constantly against a hovering trio of flies. Ray said his name was Scooter. Greyson stroked his neck and scratched him behind the ears. He didn't have to tell me that his grandfather's farm had a horse or two.

"Have you found my brother yet?" Dash asked, coming up from the creek on his branch crutches.

Ray shook his head. "The van is still in the parking lot. They're combing the mountains."

So Maddox had indeed spent a night alone in the woods—no, two nights. Theo was right: It probably would be good for him.

But it was hard to joke now, because every hour of absence was another hour that things could go really wrong. I didn't mind thinking about Maddox getting in serious trouble. But I would never wish actual harm on anybody, no matter what kind of jerk he'd been.

"Can we have lunch now?" Elijah asked, eyeing a couple big loaves of bread sitting on top of the cooler.

I was totally with him. After two days off our regular meal plan, I was craving a full-on feast. Something to get us reenergized and back into camp mode after these two days of crisis and recovery.

Brooklyn nodded. "You'll join us, I hope," she said to Ray.

"Maybe a quick bite." He rubbed his chin and looked my way. "You must be Ginny Shepard."

I nodded, surprised at being singled out.

"We got a message from your parents this morning." He turned to Brooklyn. "Looks like they've decided to pull her out."

"Pull me out?" I asked.

"Of the program."

"What's this?" Brooklyn asked, as confused as I was.

My mind went into hyperdrive. "Are they okay? Is Vivian—"

"As far as I know, your family's fine. But you can ask Dr. Hilton for the full story when he comes to get you this evening. I'm just the guy with the mule."

"Dr. Hilton?" I asked Brooklyn.

"Jed Hilton. The executive director of Outlands. My boss." Brooklyn looked a little sick. She turned to Ray. "Maybe I should talk to the office. Can I borrow your sat phone?"

"You can have your new one," he said, digging the instrument out of one of the packs.

Brooklyn stepped away from the group to make her call.

"This is messed up," I said to Greyson.

"TrackFinders is messed up," he said. "Or did you forget?"

A few minutes later, Brooklyn put the phone down and gave me a look—half apologetic, half confused. "It sounds like they were very insistent, Ginny. They have your airline ticket and everything."

"My airline ticket?"

"The plan is for you to spend the night in town and fly out tomorrow."

"*Tomorrow*? Why?"

She shook her head. "I didn't get the details."

At first I was too surprised to respond. They were seriously sending me home? Now? I hated the idea, which surprised me, too. Here I was at a program I'd been tricked into attending, that had an agenda I hated, and which was imploding by the minute— and I didn't want to leave. Not at all.

I glanced at Elijah, cradling a big loaf of bread. Dash with his halo of overgrown hair. Greyson stroking the mule's neck. Vidal, whom I was finally getting to know. How was it that my parents had decided to pull me out of here at the very moment things had started getting good?

"Brooklyn." I turned to her. "Don't make me go."

"Ginny."

"I don't know why they're doing this, but it's not right," I said insistently.

"You can pack your things while we put lunch together," she said tightly, glancing over at Ray. "That'll give you the afternoon to relax around camp and get in your goodbyes."

I made my way to my tent and ran my hand over the nylon like I'd done with Scooter's coat just moments before. This was my butternut bedroom. I wasn't ready to give it up.

Inside the tent, the air was warm and stuffy, which only made the packing more miserable. I unclipped my flashlight, emptied the mesh pocket, then started shoving a few loose items of clothing into my backpack. My mind churned. This time tomorrow I'd be sitting on an airplane. Really? The rest of the group would get to stay on the mountain helping Theo and watching the stars and bonding with wildlife, and I'd be headed home to fight with Vivian over the remote? The more I thought about it, the more desperately I wanted to stay. I wanted to throw myself on the ground and have a whopping temper tantrum.

Instead, I shoved my backpack out of the tent and started stuffing my sleeping bag. I didn't even try to shake out the pine needles and dirt. If I arrived back home bearing Montana detritus, it would be a good thing.

By the time I lobbed my sleeping bag out of the tent, I could see that everyone but Greyson had gone back to lunch preparations. He still had his hand on Scooter like it was his new job.

I sent him a pained look and he nodded back. It could have meant a million different things: *This sucks. I get you. I'm sorry. You'll be missed. Hop on the mule and we'll ride off into the sunset. Run. Stay.*

If I ran, they'd have no chance of catching me. Ray was a bowlegged fifty-year-old in cowboy boots. Theo needed a walking stick. Brooklyn was five times stronger than me but she couldn't sprint like I could. And none of the kids would have any interest in stopping me—or at least that's what I told myself.

But of course I didn't run. That was Maddox's coping strategy, and I wanted no part of his delinquency.

By the time I got to lunch, I'd lost all interest in a feast. I nibbled an apple and watched everyone else enjoy the spread. Ray finally left, and Dash went to soak his leg.

"Why don't you four go be useful to Theo again?" Brooklyn said to the rest of us. "Jed will like knowing you put in some community service hours."

"Brooklyn." Now that Ray was gone, I felt freer to complain. "I know you said there's a whole plan in place—the airline ticket and all that. But I don't get why we're giving in so easily here."

"Simple, Ginny. I'm not in the position of telling parents they can't have their children," she said flatly.

"But it has to be a mistake, right?"

"That's what you said when you got here," she reminded me. "And no, I don't think so."

"Can't we at least ask?"

"Rules are rules, Ginny," she said edgily.

"Come on, Brooklyn," I said, throwing up my hands. Greyson was right—she needed to get over herself. "Forget about your stupid rules for once. We need to talk! Sort things out! I'm sure they'll—"

"Stop! I'm not interested in sorting things out!" Brooklyn had lifted her head sharply at the word "stupid," and now she was actually yelling. Her face, normally so calm and Cheerios bland, was contorted with fury. "Our so-called stupid rules are here for one simple reason: to keep you kids safe. I'm not some boring capitalistic authoritarian trying to ruin your summer fun. I'm here to help you! And if you guys weren't so busy finding a way to go against everything we do, you might notice that!"

I blinked, taken aback by her tirade. "We're not going against everything you do, Brooklyn. I promise."

"Oh really, Ginny? Are you sure? Let's think for a second. You snuck a phone into camp. You shared it with Elijah—which is basically like handing a slot machine to a gambling addict—"

"Hey!" Elijah said.

"We extended you a trust line and you bolted from your solo site at the first possible chance. In fact, you spent most of your solo time hanging out with Elijah—another violation. You never made an art project…"

"Actually—"

"And after explicitly promising you would do no such thing, you completely broke my trust last night… and consorted!"

I flinched, but no one had time to laugh. I was pretty sure there were tears forming in the corner of Brooklyn's eyes.

"We kept heaping you with trust and all you did was throw it away, like it was worthless to you. You haven't been thinking about anybody but yourself. And you wonder why I'm not so interested in breaking the rules on your behalf?"

I wanted to fold myself up over and over until I was a tiny square, too small to see. "No. I get it now," I said, chagrined and sorry.

"Good." She dabbed her eyes. "Damn. I can't believe I cried on the job."

"And swore," Elijah pointed out.

She shook her head and strode after Dash.

"Wow," Elijah said. "First we get mooned by Kai. Then we get a hissy fit from Brooklyn. These people need their own therapy camp!"

"Don't say 'hissy fit,'" I said irritably.

"What?"

"Just don't."

I headed out to Theo's study site. Work. I wanted to do some work.

Seeming to understand, Theo handed me a clipboard and a pencil the moment I arrived. I made my way to the far edge of the plot, hoping no one would follow me this time. Then I sank my butt beside some sunken button lichen and got started.

No one found it easy to focus on lichen research that afternoon.

"Your pikas are a lot more interesting than these things," Elijah called across the plot.

I nodded and pretended to be absorbed in a tricky identification.

"I mean," Elijah went on, spinning his pencil in his fingers, "if I'm stuck here and the lichens are stuck over there, then where exactly is the action supposed to be happening?"

"In your brain," Theo said, wandering over and placing a hand on his head. "Like in an art museum. You ever lose yourself in a painting?"

"Nope!" he said cheerfully. "I got lost in a museum one time, though. They found me crying under one of the mummies."

"Here's a secret," Theo said, lifting her hand. "Ray brought Popsicles on dry ice. If you want to take a break, Dash will show you where they are."

"Cowabunga!" Elijah said, leaping to his feet so fast his clipboard banged to the ground. "You guys coming?"

I shook my head, but Greyson and Vidal scrambled up like they'd been waiting for the first excuse to get away. No one had said a word about my leaving. But I couldn't exactly accuse them of avoiding me; I hadn't given them much of a chance to talk.

Theo crossed to my corner of the plot and took a seat on a rock beside me.

"Can I take a look?" she asked.

I handed her my clipboard.

"I didn't get very far," I admitted. "I like doing this kind of work—more than it shows. I'm just a little distracted today."

"I imagine."

It was probably silly to have tried to do anything useful. I should have gone back with everyone else or walked around the fields and rocks saying my goodbyes, like Brooklyn had suggested.

Theo adjusted the brim of her hat. "What did Elijah mean by 'your pikas'?"

"The pikas I was getting to know. At my solo spot—Pika Peak. Well, that's just the name I gave it. Kai called it a talus slope. It was pika heaven. I mean, not exactly heaven." I hesitated. I was rambling, my edges frayed; I hardly knew what I was going to say next. "I wouldn't want it to be pika *heaven* in the literal sense, of course, because I want them alive. Which they are. For now, anyway. But my science teacher says they'll be gone before I'm done with college. Followed by a landslide of other species. Which is basically an unbearable blot on the whole of my existence."

I maybe shouldn't have skipped lunch. I felt trembly and friable myself.

When I looked up, Theo was staring out across the rocks. A light breeze swept across the hillside, making the grass stalks ripple and turn.

"It's an almost unspeakable pain, isn't it?" she said in a voice of quiet anguish.

It was not the response I expected. I stared at her, not quite breathing.

"You want assurances—you deserve assurances—and no one can honestly give them to you. The world is so battered right now." She turned to me. "You really see it, Ginny, don't you?"

I nodded, slowly. Exhaled. And dissolved.

"I'm sorry," she said, offering me a handkerchief. "This might just be the worst time in the history of the world to be a kid who loves nature."

Theo stayed quiet while I cried. I was crying for so many things—a battered world and the doomed pikas and my helplessness and her empathy and even the ways I'd disappointed Brooklyn and was now being sent home to two parents who might never really understand me again. I didn't realize how much I'd been needing someone to see me, affirm me—especially someone as wise as Theo. But her understanding also made the ache go deeper. A tiny part of me had maybe been holding out for the possibility that I was wrong, because then at least the animals and plants—and lichens too—would be okay. They were not okay. She knew it and I knew it. We were part of a club of grief I didn't ask to be a member of—a club of grief for the world we knew.

When I quieted down, she handed me her water bottle. I took a grateful sip.

"Tell me what you love," she said after a while.

I wiped my face with my hands and took a breath. "Here? Pretty much everything." I sighed. "The sparkly lakes and the paintbrush meadows and the trees that smell like Girl Scout cookies. The marmots with their cute beady eyes. The pikas with their mouths stuffed with flowers. I love the way the mountain goats mosey along a sheer cliff edge looking like they're daydreaming about whether to have moss or grass for dinner. I love the skinny bugs that bump against your tent, begging to be let inside. I love the fact that these crazy crusty lichens all have names that sound like ways of describing really bad hair."

Theo chuckled.

"I just don't understand how people can feel okay about wrecking it all, Theo. Or why they think saving it means you don't care about humans. Aren't we all part of the same package? And don't these other things have as much right to be here as we do?"

"*I* think so. But I've found that when you try to tell people in power that plants and animals should have any kind of standing, they look at you like you're naïve and childish. Like it's not what I think it is: a profound recognition."

"Of … ?"

"Of how widely dispersed intelligence is on this planet. You spend time with any life form—pikas, woodpeckers, ants, elms—and you only emerge with more appreciation of their capacities, even sentience. Not less."

"Lichens too?" I asked.

When she smiled, there were matching lines etched into her cheeks. "Three organisms that have figured out how to work together peacefully to colonize the most barren places on the planet? Let's see three world leaders try to do that."

I managed a smile back. "Van Gogh—she's one of my pikas. She steals from her neighbors. I don't know if that's intelligence or just plain old naughtiness, but it definitely makes me think of her as"—I hesitated, trying to find the right words—"her own self. A being who counts."

Theo nodded. "My biologist friends tell me the animals they study have as much individuality as their children. It's something so few people get to see."

"I know. I can't believe I got to see it," I told her. "Van Gogh felt like she was becoming my friend. For a few days, anyway."

"This may sound like a crazy thing to say right now," Theo said to me then, and hesitated. "But lucky you."

Maybe I was kind of lucky, even now, after all this. Theo pushed herself up to standing. She had work to get back to.

"Theo," I said, before she went away. "How come you get this stuff so much better than my parents do?"

"Do I?"

"When I got upset about climate change, they freaked out and sent me here—to be reprogrammed!"

She let out a sputter of a laugh.

"They're crazy, right?" I said.

She brushed her palm with her fingers, pondering. "Or maybe just really afraid."

➤·◄ ❤ ➤·◄ ❤ ➤·◄ ❤ ➤·◄ ❤ ➤·◄

"I need foodage," I said to Elijah when I returned to camp.

"We saved you a couple of Popsicles."

"Thanks."

Everyone was sitting on logs around the firepit and talking about Maddox—taking bets on where he'd gone and when he'd be found. I focused on my Popsicle, savoring every bit of fake berry sweetness even as it dripped like a bad faucet straight down my wrist. I would need to wash up well before I headed back to civilization.

"Where's Brooklyn?" I asked, licking the last red drops off the stick.

"In her tent."

"She okay?"

"Girl looks like she needs a beach vacation," Vidal said.

As if on cue, Brooklyn emerged from behind her tent, hair rumpled and cheek skin creased.

There was a lot I couldn't fix, but I could at least make one thing better.

"Brooklyn, I'm sorry about all that stuff I did. I didn't mean to make your job harder than it already was."

"Thanks, Ginny. I appreciate that."

"But wait, I'm the one who stole the phone," Elijah piped up. "That part wasn't your fault."

"Nice try, Elijah," I told him. "But I didn't exactly turn it back in."

"And actually, it was me who ran off to Theo's site, too," Elijah continued. "Ginny followed me there because she was afraid I'd get lost."

I didn't know whether to tell Elijah to shut up or give him a hug.

The other kids were listening intently.

"Did you consort with her, too?" Vidal asked Elijah, suppressing a laugh.

Greyson shot him a look.

"Didn't think so," Vidal said with a knowing smile.

"So basically Ginny didn't do anything. It was all you guys," Dash pointed out.

"No, it was me too. Totally me too," I said.

Brooklyn looked bewildered, like this wasn't a situation she'd ever witnessed before. Which it probably wasn't.

"I think," she said, "if Kai were here, he'd say something about how he really appreciated all the honesty."

"Totally," Vidal agreed.

"Don't you?" Elijah asked her.

"Yes," she said, smiling at the realization. "Actually, I do. A lot."

"Good."

She sat on a log and rubbed her eyes. "I don't suppose there are any Popsicles left?"

"I'll get you one," I told her, jumping up.

I dug out the last Popsicle from the dry-ice pack and handed it to her. "It's having a meltdown," I said. "So be careful."

"Meltdowns are my specialty," she said wryly.

I made my way down to the creek to wash the stickiness off my hands, then ended up walking straight in and letting the icy cold seep into my bones. I leaned my face down to the water and blew bubbles on the surface, wishing it were deep enough for a full plunge. When I looked up, Elijah was jogging down toward me, holding a white cardboard envelope in his hands.

"I almost forgot. I found the mail pouch when I was looking for the Popsicles," he told me.

"Mail pouch?"

"Remember? We saw it two thousand years ago when we arrived at the campsite looking for Maddox."

"Right." It did feel like two thousand years ago.

"You got the biggest envelope," he said, handing it over.

"My parents say their law firms are singlehandedly keeping FedEx in business."

"Aren't you going to open it?"

"I hate their letters," I said, tossing it onto the shore.

Elijah looked at the envelope longingly, like he wanted access to everything it represented: city life, speed, rattly white trucks. That kid. It may have been Greyson who made my heart go *blip-blip-blip* in the alpine meadow, but Elijah was my guy. The little brother I never had. The person I might actually miss most of all.

"It was nice of you to bring it over," I said, not wanting his effort to seem wasted. I stepped out of the creek and dried off my hands on my shorts, yanked the cardboard tab, and pulled out two letters. One was a silly card from Vivian and the other was a typed letter that both my parents had signed, like a contract.

"Want to read with me?" I asked Elijah, sitting on the stiff grass.

He sat beside me, crisscross applesauce, like we were two preschoolers sharing a picture book.

"Remember. They're lawyers. This could put you to sleep in two sentences."

"Just read," he said.

Dear Ginny,

We've been feeling guilty and miserable ever since your letter arrived. Neither of us is sure we can last another week for an update on how things are going. Before we signed you up, Mom spoke for over an hour with the Outlands director, who assured her you'd find the camp enjoyable and thought-provoking. We didn't think it was worth getting you worried about the milestones and mindfulness because they sounded harmless. But we see now that we

*were wrong. We didn't know there'd be quite so many rules. And
they told us nothing about your being there with only FIVE BOYS.
We're very sorry. Dad's at DEFCON 1 with worry. He's lost all trust
in the program. Mom's closer to a 4 and believes in the possibility
of 1) a misunderstanding; and 2) you being able to handle even
the Lords of the Flies with your typical grace. We asked the folks
at Outlands if we could call you, but it's against TrackFinders
policy. According to your counselors, you're doing okay, but we
don't know what to believe now. We're waiting on pins and needles for your next letter and your own assurances. All that matters
to us is your safety and your happiness, Ginny. We love you from
here to the moon.*

"Wow," I said. "They freaked out."

"What did you write?" Elijah asked.

"Normal complainy stuff. Didn't you?"

"Yeah. Your second letter must have been worse."

"It wasn't. It was just a picture of a potato and a paiku. And
what does that matter anyway?" I asked, ignoring Elijah's
confused look. "The mail only went out—what?—two days ago?" It
still felt more like two thousand years.

"Maybe they gave Outlands one of those," Elijah said, pointing at the FedEx envelope. "So they'd get it sooner."

I laughed. "It's like you already know them."

"Does this change anything?"

I slid the letters back into the envelope and sighed. "It only
makes me want to stay here more."

Jed Hilton, the head of Outlands, was a blue-eyed guy with salt-and-pepper hair, dressed in a polo shirt and khaki shorts. He arrived just before dinner, with Kai by his side. Jed introduced himself to each of us in turn with a solid handshake; Kai gave us high fives and warm greetings, but he didn't seem like his usual self. At first I thought maybe he was just cowed by the presence of his boss. But it was more than that. He seemed demoralized.

"Dr. Hilton wants to assess your knee," Kai told Dash. "That's okay, right?"

Dash nodded.

"You can call me Jed," the director said as he knelt down to take a closer look.

I turned to Kai. "You know I don't want to leave, right? I don't really understand any of this."

"Your dad was pretty insistent," Kai told me. "He's a lawyer, huh?"

"Uh-oh. Did he threaten to sue?"

Kai raised his eyebrows. "Let's just say Jed got an earful."

Jed stood up and gave Dash a reassuring nod. "It doesn't look too bad." He turned to Kai and Brooklyn. "If someone can take his pack, he should be okay for the hike out tomorrow."

"Tomorrow?" Brooklyn asked.

Kai sent her a meaningful look.

There was no time to find out more. Dinner was already waiting—four different courses we'd prepared with our freshest ingredients. We'd invited Theo to be our guest of honor and made her promise not to help; it was the least we could do after all she'd done for us. Only after the last fork was set down did Jed clear his throat and announce that he wanted to say a few words.

"It's a scary thing to have a camper run away, a brother run away. I'm very sorry you've had to go through that. It's also not fun to get hurt, though none of us enters the backcountry unaware of such risks. And then, of course, there was the bear. . . ." He gave us all a knowing smile. "That was a big mess, I know. But worse for the bear than for you."

"How come?" Vidal asked.

"If a bear shows signs of associating humans with food, then wildlife officers may have to step in and remove it. Or worse."

"What?" I exclaimed.

"Kill it, you mean," Greyson said, looking unhappy.

Jed nodded.

"That's insane," I said loudly, not hiding my disgust. "It was Maddox's fault. The bear was just being a bear."

"Unfortunately for bears, they don't get a chance to argue their case in court," Jed said. "But let's hope it won't come to that."

I shook my head. Theo's frown went inches deep.

"I'm proud of the way you handled these adversities," Jed continued. "You rose to the occasion in a way that shows real grit, growth." He puffed out his cheeks, exhaled. "But we've had a consultation as a staff and with your parents, and we've decided to bring you all back into the front country tomorrow—not just Ginny. We can keep you busy in town until we've made your travel arrangements home."

"Home?" Dash asked, as stunned as I'd been feeling all day. "Is this because of Maddox?"

"Partly," Jed said.

"I bet it's mostly my dad," I said. "He stirred things up, didn't he?"

"He . . . well, it's what I call a perfect storm, Ginny," Jed explained. "Dad gets worried, calls the office, demands to speak to you. He can't—because there's no sat phone at your site, remember? They've both been stolen. And one of your counselors isn't with you; he's in the home office. Why? Because the kid who took the phones is on the run." He shook his head. "If I were a worried dad, I'd think we were incompetent, too."

It was easy to imagine the whole scene playing out. Dad, quick to anger and distrust, throwing all his legal threats their way. The staff trying fruitlessly to reassure him I was well. Annoyed as I felt, Theo's words were still ringing in my ears. *Afraid.* He was just really afraid. And this news from Outlands would have given him more than enough material to feed his paranoia.

"Did he really call you incompetent?" I asked, mortified.

"Don't worry about it. We've heard worse. Well, actually, we did hear worse," he said, turning to Dash. "From your parents."

"I bet you did," Dash said.

"I'd tell you the exact words, but it would violate camp rules," Jed chuckled. His honesty surprised me. I could tell he wasn't a bad guy, no matter what Dad thought.

"So," he said, with a decisive nod. "We'll pack up in the morning, and by this time tomorrow you'll be eating brick-oven pizza, splashing in a heated pool, and watching movies at the Bozeman

Marriott. I'll even treat you to the best ice cream in town. How's that sound?"

I was sure it sounded dreamy to the other kids. Personally, I hated the way things were falling apart, though there was some consolation in not being the only one heading out. I looked around, expecting smiles. But all I saw was resentment. On *everyone's* face.

"What's up, folks?" Kai asked, noticing it too.

"If you want the honest answer…" Dash cleared his throat. "I'd rather stay here."

Jed looked momentarily surprised, then gave an understanding nod. "You worried about hiking down on that knee?"

"It's not that. I just…" Dash shrugged uncomfortably. "I like it here. Especially now."

Without Maddox. That made sense. With a new mom.

"I don't want to go, either," Elijah agreed, surprising me more.

"I thought you were craving a pepperoni pizza and a chocolate milkshake with sprinkles," I said to him.

"Well, yeah. But I can have pizza and milkshakes in SF any old day."

Kai and Brooklyn exchanged looks.

"We paid for a month in the wilderness," Greyson said, his eyes as dark and accusing as they'd been at our first campfire. "We didn't pay for a pool party."

"Oh, that reminds me," Kai said. "If it helps, it wasn't your mom who paid for you to come here, Greyson. Right, Jed?"

Greyson and Jed both tried to respond at once, but Vidal broke in over them. It was his turn to vote.

"Don't send us home," he said, his voice thick with emotion, "and pretend it's the safe, happy choice."

I think we were all taken aback by his words and his tone.

"They know what I mean," Vidal went on, nodding at the rest of us. "We had two years of things getting canceled. Just let us finish something for once."

Jed and the counselors looked astonished.

"No one wants to leave?" Jed asked, making sure.

"None of us," Elijah said. The other kids nodded resolutely—all except Greyson, anyway, who had looked distracted and agitated ever since Kai's comment.

I looked past everyone's heads to the glowy show of another Rocky Mountain evening. I took in the distant peak we'd climbed two days ago, the high ridgeline, the lichen-spangled rocks of Theo's research site, the staccato motion of two jays on the edge of the eager creek. The scene felt untamed and uncontained, big enough for all of us and any questions we still had left to ask.

"What is it?" Jed asked, catching my eye.

I gave him a small smile, hoping he'd understand.

"Maybe *this* is the front country now."

We'd given it our best shot. Now we just had to let Jed and the counselors decide if the plan could be changed. They conferred together while we paced and waited. Then Jed's phone buzzed and he went off by himself to talk. When he hung up, he looked extra focused. He called Kai and Brooklyn over for a conference, then gave us the news.

"It's Maddox," he said. "He's been found—at a truck stop in Utah. Trying to hitch a ride to Vegas."

"Vegas," Dash said, sounding impressed.

"His dream almost came true," I said, remembering the wish fire.

"Well, it sounds like he was pretty happy to be found, as it turns out," Jed said. He glanced at the sky and said he needed to go, pronto, before it got any darker. He told Kai and Brooklyn they could make as many calls as they wanted and he'd be in touch in the morning. Then he said goodbye and strode quickly down the trail, leaving them in charge again.

"I bet he was going to play the slot machines," Elijah said, sounding amazed.

"And stay in a five-star hotel," Dash added. "He had one of our dad's credit cards, you know."

Brooklyn shook her head. "That may have been his original plan. But you heard Jed. Sounds like he got in over his head—and knew it."

Greyson had pulled Kai aside and was talking with him in hushed tones. Their conversation ended abruptly, and Greyson whipped away and into his tent.

"Can I check on him?" I asked Brooklyn. She'd been watching, too.

"Okay," she said reluctantly. "He could probably use a friend. But leave the tent flap open, will you?"

"For sure."

Greyson was curled in a ball on top of his sleeping bag. It was too shadowy to see if he was crying, but that's what I sensed, so I pushed off my shoes and climbed inside.

I didn't know what to do. I wanted to hug him. I wanted to be a labradoodle he'd want to hug. But in the end, I lay down opposite him, listening till his breath was slow.

"Someone else paid?" I asked finally.

He nodded.

"Who?"

"Mr. Lund."

I racked my brain but it was no name I'd heard before.

"The principal. Ellie's dad."

"Oh."

"He used her college savings account. To send me here."

"Oh," I said again. I expected him to be relieved, but he just seemed sad. "Did he say why?"

Greyson didn't answer at first. I heard him swallow. "He said Ellie and Justin would have wanted the money to go to me." His voice cracked. "And . . ."

I waited.

"He said I was a good long-term investment."

A good long-term investment. The kid who was convinced he was fated to die by the age of twenty-eight.

We didn't talk for a while after that. I slipped one of my hands between his forearms, and the other one over the top. His arms were lean and hard, but you could feel the way they could soften, cradle, embrace. A person like this needed to last. The world needed him to last.

A good long-term investment.

A keeper.

"Make it true," I told him.

CHAPTER
19

Turns out, my parents thought I was the pika. If it hadn't been the source of so much trouble, it would have been hilarious. They'd taken one look at my haiku and decided it was a secret message to get past the TrackFinders staff, in case they were censoring camper mail. I was the pika *eeep*ing out a futile alarm. That was what had clinched Dad's worry. "Futile alarm." It sounded like desperation.

It took me five assurances, plus a secret code word to show I wasn't being coerced into speaking against my wishes, for him to believe that I was really truly fine.

"And the boys? They're not a bunch of stinky trouble-makers?"

"Of course they are," I said. "But I kind of like them like that."

"What about that kid? The one who ran away?"

"They found him, Dad. They're super professional, super careful. Stuff just happens sometimes."

The whole mix-up felt like an extension of the communication problems we'd had all spring. Here I was, warped with worry about our big, bruised, blue marble and everything on it. And for some reason, all my parents could see to worry about was . . . me. Not even a single species—a single organism. Maybe it wasn't so good to become a parent. Maybe it made you so insane about your own gene pool that you couldn't make room for anything else.

And then I paused. And thought again about what Theo had said.

"Dad, I know I made things sound really awful in my first letter. I'm sorry. I wasn't thinking about how you guys would feel, sitting with a letter like that for so many days before hearing more. And then, well, the haiku wasn't exactly a helpful communication, was it?"

"Nope." He went quiet for a moment. "But thanks, Ginny. That was a very mature thing to say."

There was a brief pause while he and Mom conferred, and then they both got on the phone. They'd made their decision. If Jed was willing, I could stay.

Before we said goodbye, I asked a favor. "I know you guys are the rabble-rousers who got all the other parents worked up. So can you please be the rabble-rousers who get them to chill out? The kids here are all desperate to stay."

"I don't know, Ginny," Dad began. "That's their parents' call. And I know for a fact that those twins' parents are out of their minds about—"

"I'll do it, Ginny," Mom broke in.

Of course. She was used to negotiating with immigration officers and drug lords. This was nothing.

"Just give me a couple of hours. I can do this for you."

"Thanks, Mom. I love you guys to the moon, too." I paused. "And back."

Even through the sat phone, I could hear the relief.

➤·◄ ❦ ➤·◄ ❦ ➤·◄ ❦ ➤·◄ ❦ ➤·◄

Over breakfast, Kai and Brooklyn sat and ate their oatmeal, as subdued as they'd been when Jed was around. I was surprised. I'd expected them to be overjoyed at everyone's determination to stay at camp, but they seemed listless and uncertain, even after every family had come around to the new plan. It was like we'd strayed so far off the map that they couldn't get themselves oriented again.

"So," Kai said, putting his palms together in a soft imitation of a clap. "Group check-in. Everyone doing okay?"

"We're good," Greyson said, giving Kai a watchful once-over.

"What about you?" I asked.

Kai sat up straighter. "Good. Fine. Great."

"So, what's the plan then?" Elijah asked. "You got a new milestone for us?"

Kai looked over at Brooklyn. She shrugged at him and took another bite of oatmeal.

"Why don't you guys, uh, clean up your breakfast dishes and check back with us when you're done," Kai said.

Elijah swiped his finger around his Sierra cup and popped it into his mouth, then licked his spoon. "Done."

"Come on, Elijah," I said, tugging on his shirt. "Let's get out of their way."

One by one, we stood up and started to gather supplies for dishwashing by the creek. I felt for Kai and Brooklyn; I really did. I knew what it was like to get seriously off track. I'd fallen off the tennis trophy–honor roll tightrope in the spring and landed hard on the asphalt streets of suburban Massachusetts without the slightest idea where I belonged next.

But we weren't in Lexington now. And when you fell off track at TrackFinders, you were still in an exhilarating, life-filled alpine wilderness. Who cared which way we turned?

"You know, I'd be fine just hanging out here helping Theo all week," I told Brooklyn and Kai. "In case that helps."

"Good to know," Brooklyn said.

Greyson glanced at me, then back at the counselors. "Ginny's right. We don't need you to plan anything. I'd be down with staying here and finishing my structure. Maybe I could even teach the rest of these guys how to do it."

"I thought you said weaving's just weaving," Elijah told him.

"It's not. It's art."

Kai looked a little more awake.

"We could play pine cone baseball," Vidal volunteered. "Every night, even. Like a whole World Series."

Elijah nodded.

"I can't hike too far anyway," Dash told the counselors. "Maybe Theo could teach me how to make pancakes. I could be, like, the camp cook."

"You'd just eat all the chocolate," Elijah told him.

"Hey, at least I had an idea. What are you going to do?"

Elijah pulled his shoulders all the way up to his ears in a dramatic shrug. "I like doing tech support," he began. "But if there's still no tech, maybe I could just sort of ... hang out?"

"Like a mascot?" Dash teased.

Elijah rolled his eyes. "Like an apprentice. Intern. Student. Mentee."

Kai gave his first real laugh since he'd returned to camp. "What do you think, Brooklyn?"

She didn't jump for joy or tell us we were geniuses, but this was Brooklyn. "Give me a minute to think it all through," she said. And then, sensing she was popping a communal balloon, she added, "But this sounds promising. Or even good. I mean, maybe we can make something like this work."

> ⋗⋖ ⋎ ⋗⋖ ⋎ ⋗⋖ ⋎ ⋗⋖ ⋎ ⋗⋖

We were all pretty high on ourselves. For the rest of the day, we brainstormed plans, menus, and adventures as we played at being camp directors. No one said the word "milestone" once—not even Brooklyn.

The high didn't last, of course. Once we were actually putting ideas into motion, the euphoria broke down fast for all the same reasons camp had been hard before. Days were long and hot, research was tedious, and even with just five teenagers, there was almost always somebody doing something that annoyed the rest of the group. Elijah got two horsefly bites on his cheeks, and the swelling was so bad around his eyes, he looked like an oyster. Theo's assistant returned to work and made it clear he had a low tolerance for amateur hour at the lichen study sites. And Dash and Greyson got into a lot of petty arguments, or so it seemed to me. But for all this, it was better. Better than when Maddox had been with us. And definitely better than not being here at all.

After we'd worn out our welcome at the lichen plots, I convinced Kai to chaperone me back to Pika Peak, where my best tech-support-intern-mentee and I added several hours of pika footage. Elijah promised he'd help me edit it into final form when we got back home. I was glad, in a way, that we'd been chased away from the lichens. I wouldn't have wanted to miss out on the added time in the company of Van Gogh and the other pikas. On one of my last and best afternoons, a couple of babies emerged for the first time since we'd been on the slope. They were half the size of the adults, but already nimble and determined.

We filmed them for an hour, and then Elijah went back to his tent for a siesta and I wandered back to Theo's research site. I found her alone, moving her plot lines.

"Can I help?" I asked.

Fortunately for me, she said yes and seemed to enjoy hearing my day's report about the young pikas. She knew more about them than I'd first realized.

"Those babies have their work cut out for them," she told me. "They have to establish their own territories and stock up a personal supply of food to last them through the winter. All before the first frost."

"Seriously? Wow. And I thought it was pretty good that I just learned how to make a grilled cheese."

"That's why you still need your parents," Theo said pointedly.

"Fair," I told her.

I picked up a pair of Greyson's plot corners and held them while Theo repositioned the other set farther away. When she gave me a nod, I pulled the strings taut and lowered them into place.

"On days like today, I feel like I could sit on a rock watching pikas full-time, every summer," I told Theo—questions swirling, answers eluding. "But I still can't figure out what the point of it is. Knowing what we know."

"You could become a scientist, like me. Please."

"But they'll be gone by then, remember?" I said, reminding her of Mr. Stelling's devastating science lecture.

"We don't really know how long they'll last," Theo said, "despite what your teacher taught you. In fact, I'm pretty sure your solo spot is where I did some sampling a few years ago, and there weren't any pikas there then."

"So maybe the populations are adapting a little? Is that what you mean?"

"That's what I'm *wondering*," she corrected. "I'm not pretending pikas can outrun climate change, Ginny. But with spunky little nuts like that Van Gogh of yours—Hey, why did you call her Van Gogh, anyway?"

"Chunk out of her ear," I said, tugging on one of mine.

"Ha. Anyway, here's the way I see it. You can look at the forecasts and give up the game, or you can roll up your sleeves and get to work. Me, I favor rolling up my sleeves. I have relatives who tell me, 'Don't talk about climate change around me anymore. It's too depressing.' But you know what? I feel better knowing I'm doing something. It sure beats the alternative. And after I've put in an honest day of research or teaching, I think I can actually enjoy the sweet moments of my life more than someone who's loaded up with denial. Or guilt."

Enjoy the sweet moments more? I wasn't sure if I could ever get to such an enlightened place. "But what if everything I love starts to die on my watch?"

Theo sighed. "Have you ever lost someone you love?"

I hesitated, reluctant to share the hurt again. But this was Theo. She deserved an answer. "My grandparents both died from Covid," I told her. "They weren't even that old. They were strong, happy—what my mom called forces of nature."

"I'm so sorry."

"It happened really fast. My mom thinks I'm traumatized by their deaths, and maybe I am. But you know . . ." I swallowed. I'd been thinking about this for so long without ever really putting it into words. "I think I'm more traumatized by all the denial that came first. Especially from my dad. He kept saying, 'No worries, Ginny. This virus won't affect us. No way, no way. We'll be fine.'" I shook my head, my voice quavering. "We were so not fine…"

"Have you ever told him how you feel?"

I shook my head again. "It would be too mean."

She seemed to understand.

"The thing is," I said, "it can *happen*. And if all these changes are going to hit the world like that—fierce and fast—and we just have to sit there and watch things die one by one . . ." I trailed off. I was starting to regret spending so much time with the pikas. "Those beautiful babies," I said, my chest hurting with the sadness and the unfairness of it all. "I don't want them to die. I want the world to be okay. For them."

"I know," Theo said. She gave a slight smile. "And that's probably how your parents feel about you and your sister."

She was probably right.

Theo pressed her lips together, thinking. "I'm just a biologist, Ginny—not a philosopher or, I don't know, a minister. But here's something I know: At some point, every living thing is going to die. Sometimes it's wrong or painful or premature—and losing anything you care about is pretty much the hardest thing a person has to bear. But if we always know death will come—and that we are going to die—then don't you think we should spend as much time as possible tending to the life that's there? Supporting it? Loving it with every cell in our bodies?"

I thought about the scrappy lichens on the rocks beside us and up in the nearby trees. I thought about how Theo kept showing up summer after summer, through the droughts and the wildfires and the mounting signs of unstoppable change. That was some kind of loyalty—to love when it wasn't easy, to love what you knew you could lose.

Or maybe that was just love itself.

"I do," I said, feeling a sadness so immense I knew it would always be inside of me. And then for some reason I started to giggle.

"What is it?" Theo asked, blinking with surprise.

"Sorry. I think I'm just getting punchy. But it sounded . . ." I laughed harder. "'I do.' All of a sudden it felt like I was saying my wedding vows."

Theo smiled. "Different kind of commitment, I suppose. But same basic idea. In sickness and health?"

I nodded, giggles gone, ache and promise remaining.

➤·◄ ❧ ➤·◄ ❧ ➤·◄ ❧ ➤·◄ ❧ ➤·◄

On our last full day of camp, we took a daylong hike up a new mountain, which I decided to call Tubman Peak in Zinzie's honor. Dash still wasn't capable of a strenuous climb, so we arranged to meet him and Theo at her favorite scenic overlook on the way back down. It was a perfect place for a picnic dinner—a broad rocky ledge, like stadium seating, with a wide valley spreading out at our feet. As the sun dropped, the colors settled into richer greens and grays. We couldn't pull ourselves away. Kai was telling stories about fly-fishing, and Elijah was making triple-decker crackers out of rye crisps that exploded when he bit into them, and I had absentmindedly reached forward and started fiddling with Vidal's hair. I made a tiny French braid that started at the temple and wrapped around to the nape of the neck, incorporating as many of the little pieces as possible, all the way to the other side. I was just beginning to add little flowers when Theo put her hand on Kai's arm to silence him, and lifted the other to point out a dark shape moving across the valley below.

We went statue-still.

It was a bear. A large brown bear with great shoulders and a square snout that she swung to the left and to the right as she made her way along the edge of a narrow creek. And then, as if that weren't enough, two small cubs spilled out of the bushes and scrambled up to join her. For all of two minutes, we saw them—a trio, a family, a wonder; a visitation from what felt like another world, though of course we were the guests and they were the locals who had allowed us in for this all-too-brief visit.

We were spellbound for at least another minute after they disappeared into the creek-side bushes, grown hazy in the twilight. Then we erupted into crazed chatter, needing to name what we'd seen and grateful that Theo was there to confirm what we already knew. These were grizzlies, the big ones, the very real deal. After she said it, we went quiet and awestruck again.

"Just think," Elijah said, shaking his head slowly back and forth. "There are kids who will never get to see a thing like that."

"I know, right?" Dash said.

"Well, not unless they spelunk up like all of us," Greyson said wryly.

"I'll ignore that comment," Brooklyn said.

But Kai was beaming, worse than ever.

A few minutes later, Brooklyn put her hands on her knees in the universal symbol of *let's get back on task now, people*, when Vidal suddenly stood up.

"Vidal, you okay?" Kai asked.

But maybe Kai and the others had noticed the braid. And the small flowers that decorated it like a wreath.

"Tonight I'm Vita," she said firmly. She leaned her head down close to mine. "That's what Lola calls me," she said quietly before straightening up to address the rest of the group. "And I want to share my artwork. But over there, where it's safer." She pointed away from the rocky ledge.

"What?" Elijah said, his eyes buggy.

"Dude. Cool it," Greyson said, giving him a jab with his elbow. Luckily, he did.

There are things you can see and describe, and there are things your words will never do justice to—at least not unless you're someone like Zinzie, who's a magician with words. I felt that after seeing the grizzlies. And I felt that as I watched Vita's dance. The movements were blunt and then flowing. Sad and suddenly funny. Strange but then somehow familiar. I recognized the slap of a smashed s'more to the head. The plodding steps of hikers. The smooth pirouettes of a batter, swinging at pine cones. A mosquito, definitely a mosquito. And then, at the very end, the hulking march of the brown bear leading her cubs across the valley. We were mesmerized. I didn't know a body could do that—turn those pieces of hurt and confusion and wonder into a gift, something awkward and brave that I guess you could say was our story.

When Vita was done, we snapped our fingers, clapped, and cheered—like a chorus of spring peepers waking to the new season.

CHAPTER 20

"Tell me everything, everything," Zinzie said. We were curled up close on the hammock in my backyard, far from Vivian's curious ears. "Did you kiss him every night?"

"The privacy was pretty scarce out there, Zinz."

"Oh," she said, disappointed.

"At least till the last night."

She grinned. "Have you texted him since you got home?"

"Since the plane touched the runway."

"I wonder when you'll see him next."

I shrugged. "Hard to say. But I like knowing he's out there. Like the pikas. Can I tell you about the pikas now? Please?"

"Dang, you haven't changed at all," she said, shaking her head.

"There was Van Gogh, with only one good ear. And Elijah Junior, who was the smallest but the cutest."

"You can tell them apart?" Zinzie made a face. "Those little furry rabbit things?"

"Some of them," I told her. "And maybe if I go back..."

"Are you going to go back?"

I thought about Bead Lake on a still morning. The zip of activity on the talus slope. Theo laying out a new study plot around the lichens. It was so hard to believe this life would just keep going, even after I left. But it was so good to believe it, too.

"I hope so," I told her. "Dad says if I work hard this year, they'll let me figure out my own summer next year, within reason."

"He really said 'within reason'?"

"Lawyer talk, Zinzie. Tell me you're not surprised." But sometimes it was actually kind of nice the way Dad was so eager to turn hazy dreams into plans and itineraries.

Zinzie took my hand and we had a long, semi-distracted thumb war, which of course she won in the end. When she looked up, her eyes looked extra big behind the glasses. "It's okay being home, though, right? In boring old Lexington with boring old me?"

"Zinzie. You're the least boring person I know."

I didn't want to admit how strange it had been to reenter my house after all that time in the mountains. The rooms felt both completely familiar but also impossibly small—like the walls were going to close in around me and press me back into the shape I'd been when I'd left. My parents and Vivian trailed after me at first, so eager and expectant that I made an excuse to go upstairs. I drifted to my room, dropped my backpack on the floor, sat on my bed. There was a business card from Theo in my phone case. There was a pebble from Pika Peak in my pocket that I pulled out and rubbed between my thumb and finger. Did astronauts hide moon rocks in their pockets, too?

I was about to make myself go back downstairs when Mom knocked softly on the door, asking to come in.

"What's that?" she asked, noticing the business card.

I told her about Theo and her lichen research. Then I couldn't help mentioning the pikas, and the bears. And then I told her almost everything.

I think I knew why so much was spilling out for a change—because the whole time we sat there, she didn't say anything, really. She just listened. Maybe listening was her real superpower.

"Dad's probably going to start looking up salaries of field biologists now, isn't he?" I asked her when I was done.

"Maybe."

"He always gets ahead of things," I said.

"Don't we all," she said, with a quick lift of the eyebrows.

She had me there. When the world was like it was right now, I couldn't always be looking at the farthest point on the horizon, or I'd miss so much. Right now, my world had pikas in it. And Theo and Elijah and Greyson. And my family. And my very best friend beside me now, crushing me at another thumb war. That was a lot of sweetness.

"You know," I told Zinzie, "I'm thinking high school could actually be okay."

She released my thumb and smiled wide. "Ex-cel-ente."

Front country, backcountry—wherever I was, I could make my own path, switchbacks and all.

Tomorrow I would look up the next meeting of those kids in Cambridge, roll up my sleeves, and get to work.

ACKNOWLEDGMENTS

This novel was written in the corner of a house in the middle of a pandemic, but it had the support of a community stretching across the country with expertise in everything from pika biology to high school tennis to adolescent psychology. With deep appreciation, I want to acknowledge the following for their input and advice: Jamie Kelsey, Anne Knott, Claire St. Antoine Mercurio, Paul Mercurio, Andrea Pipp, Chris Ray, Barbara Rowley, Arthur St. Antoine, Mary Saint-Antoine, Helen Shepherd, and Jason Targoff. A number of fellow writers took time out of their busy schedules to offer feedback at critical junctures: Susan Gray Gose, Jennifer Rapaport, Jim Shepard, and Rachel Sontheimer. Lucy Cleland, my agent at Kneerim & Williams, got me launched with her inimitable combination of intellectual and emotional acuity, then found me an ideal creative partner in my editor at Chronicle Books, Taylor Norman. Taylor's keen sensitivity to young people and their stories was extraordinary, and her unflagging enthusiasm for this book, essential. Added thanks go to Jill Turney for her winsome chapter openers and comic book panels, and to the brilliant Sally Deng for her exquisite rendering of Ginny and the landscape of her soul. Daily inspiration for this project came from many writers and colleagues whose good work gives me hope for the planet—among them, Cheryl Charles, Katie Frohardt, Robin Wall Kimmerer, Jen Kretser, Rich Louv, Rue Mapp, Tiya Miles, Sam Myers, Gary Paul Nabhan, Gary Tabor, Terry Tempest Williams, and Kelsey Wirth—and from the creatures great and small whose lives will always be more extraordinary than we can know. Last but never least, I owe this book's very existence to my immediate family: Addie, who planted the seed; Margot, who tended the sprout; and Robin, who knew just what it would take for it to bloom.